A Secret Nevermore

Book 2 in the Mirri Langley Series

Michelle Massie

CONTENTS

For anyone who has ever had a secret . . . and the little old lady with a
maroon walker.

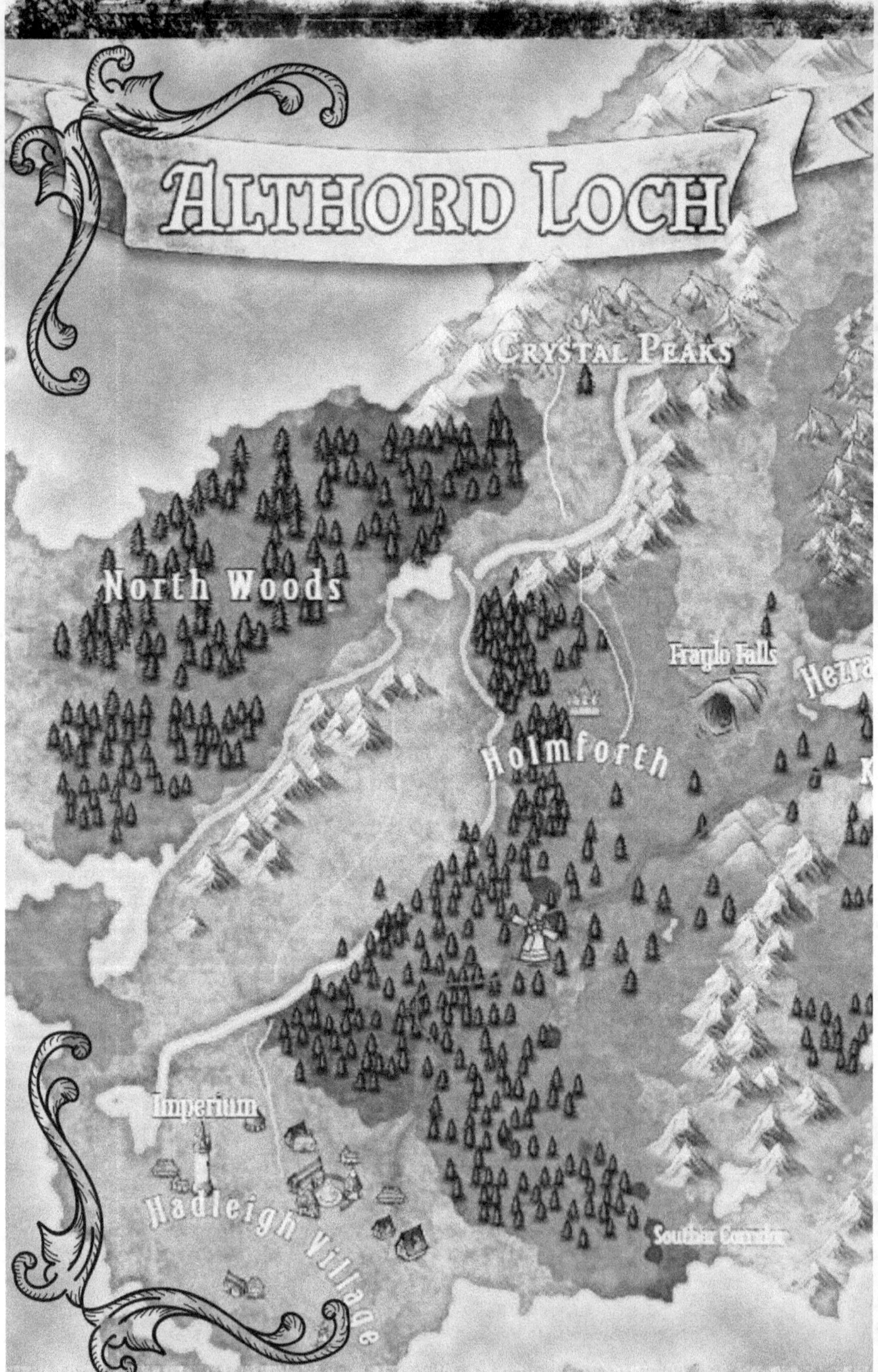

ALTHORD LOCH
CRYSTAL PEAKS
North Woods
Fraylo Falls
Hezra
Holmforth
Imperium
Hadleigh Village
Southar Corridor

Koltarian Kingdom
Waglor Ravane
Fangar Swamp
's Hollow
atea Crossing
The Fiddler

Chapter One

Koltarian Kingdom

As the man with long white hair gave me a tired smile, he ladled a cup of steaming soup into my bowl. With a stab of guilt, I realized that in seven days, I still had not asked his name. I pushed that guilt aside for now. I had more important things to deal with tonight.

The soup tasted more like mushy farl roots in water than actual food. For the last seven days, the old man fed me this soup for breakfast, lunch, and dinner, and I could feel my body waning under the desire for actual food. I smiled up at him, and he patted my shoulder as he turned back to the kitchen.

I put the bowl to my lips and sipped the bland soup politely, wondering if tonight, I could finally complete what I had come here to do. What I had been trying to accomplish. I could only imagine what my accomplice thought out there, watching the temple from the woods. Had he really stayed the whole seven days? There was no way to know. In a building with no windows and one door, my mind was getting a bit . . . shall we say, meebeled after this many days of quiet, dark, and little conversation.

The man found me around the back of the temple days ago, in a grove of ponpon bushes. I staged myself there, for we knew the man in the gray sweater came out every morning before sunrise to water the gold and blue blossoms. My dirty face hid beneath my long, braided white wig, and I wrapped my filthy and torn dresses around a few thorns. I sat and waited for the man to check on his precious flowers.

He had been beside himself with grief that his flowers had caused this young Kolt woman, face covered with tear stains down her cheeks, so much pain. In less than a minute, he had untangled me, led me inside, and made me a cup of tea beside a roaring fire, a soft blanket draped over my shoulders. I sipped my tea and continued to make sure my wig was on straight, and kept up the facade of a poor abandoned girl. I could get the Homlock by sundown, I reasoned. Easy as tamin gurd, my father would have said.

Things did not go exactly as planned. He insisted on fixing me a bed in the study's corner, where he did his work. I sat for hours with books and small trinkets to stare at, pretending to be grateful and comfortable on a pile of blankets and rags. Strange art decorated the walls, pictures that looked as if drawn by children—swirls and blotches of color that made no sense.

I watched the man work, in the same gray sweater every day, studying him, thinking about the Homlock for hours at a time. He would look through books and study objects, all day, every day, writing furiously on parchment in front of him. An umbaldi, I assumed. I had never met one, but I knew that they were the ones to see if you had a question about the past. Or a curse.

Though we discussed the past and Kolt history, I had yet to bring up the Homlock. Seemed odd to come out and ask for it. But tonight. Tonight, I would ask him. I would get out of this temple, rid myself of this wig, and eat decent food.

"Would you care for some more, dear?" he asked, lowering himself into the chair.

I smiled and shook my head. "No, thank you," I said as I patted my mouth with my napkin. "Have you had a busy day? Lots to do?"

He gave a weak laugh and nodded as he took a sip of soup. "Oh, too much. There's so much to do, so much to do. Are you enjoying the book I gave you?"

I nodded eagerly. "Oh, yes, thank you. It is very interesting."

I had thumbed through it, mostly looking for a picture of the Homlock. But I would not be that lucky. Things like Koltarian history, the importance of self-preservation, worshiping the Mother Kolt, what she had gone through before her death, and so on. And on. I spent most evenings staring into the fire while he scribbled away at his parchment. But the book had given me the out I desperately needed.

"Can you tell me more of the Mother Kolt? She is very interesting." I drained the last of my soup and set my bowl down, leaning into the wobbling table. He had fashioned an old end table that held a lantern beside his desk into a small dinner table so that I would have a place to eat my mushy farl roots. Three times a day. The lantern now sat on the floor next to the wall.

"Ah, yes, the Mother Kolt." He nodded, sipping his soup. "She is an important part of our heritage, you see. A worthy Koltarian who gave birth to a child and died tragically. She saved the souls of seven warriors on the battlefield, using the power of the Homlock."

My ears perked up at the mention of the Homlock, but I forced myself to remain silent while he finished.

"Such a beautiful woman, with a heart of meroso. She stood out among a crowd and did not appear as other Kolts did. Had a hard life, with children and others who doubted her true parentage. She persevered, through it all."

"The Homlock?" I asked, cocking my head.

He nodded, taking another sip. "Yes, it was—"

A cracking sound made us both jump. A log rolled out of the fire, splaying ashes out over the wooden floor.

"Goodness, goodness," He stood, reaching for his cane, and shuffled to the fire. Using a metal stick, he shoved the log back into the fire and scraped the ashes back in with his leather boot.

Gritting my teeth, I sat back in my chair. I pinched the bridge of my nose as he poked at the charred logs. So close. I sat with my arms crossed, trying to control my breathing. Finally, he returned to his chair and bowl of soup, our latest conversation forgotten.

"You were saying about the Mother Kolt?" I asked.

"Hmm?" He settled his napkin back in his lap, concentrating on his dinner.

"The Mother Kolt? She saved the seven warriors? How did she do that, exactly?"

"Oh! Oh, yes. You see, she used the Homlock, which holds power we don't quite understand. She saved their souls, lifted their burdens, and revitalized their lives, even through her burden. That is why we worship her today." He picked up his linen napkin and wiped his mouth, thinking the history lesson was over.

"What about the Homlock?" I asked in my most innocent voice. "Did they ever find it?"

"Yes, yes, they did. We keep it in a safe place, a matsala place. It must be protected at all times."

Darn. I needed a bit more than that. "What did it look like?"

He gazed off as if he was seeing it hanging in midair. "A beautiful gold pendant with a ruby stone. Very precious." At that, he stood, grabbing his cane and stacking my bowl on top of his empty one.

I gave it one more try. "And that is what she used to lift these men's burdens?"

He nodded as he made his way into the kitchen. "Yes, dear, that is what it's known for," he called over his shoulder.

Sitting back in my seat, I nodded to myself. He had affirmed what I needed to know. Now all I had to do was wait.

◆

I lay on the pad, watching the small light from underneath the curtain. Every evening, after we sat by the fire and had our mint tea, I would retire to my "bed," my pile of linens arranged on the floor. He would close the curtain into the hall, bidding me pleasant dreams, carrying the small candle that he lit in the evenings. Every night, I lay there until the small light died away, waiting to sneak into the hall, prowl up and down the hallway, and search for any sign of the Homlock.

Tonight, I curled up on the lumpy pile of rags, listening to the scratching of the metal curtain rod. I forced myself to count to ten, then crept to the curtain and pulled back the corner to watch him hobble down the hallway and double-check the large chain on the door. I dropped the curtain before he turned, listening to the shuffling of footsteps toward my curtain. The footsteps stopped near my curtain, and my heart jumped as I noticed the shadow of his footsteps under where my curtain hung.

I held my breath until the shadow moved. Peeking back around the curtain, I waited for him to open the door to his room, where I assumed he stood. His room was the same room where we ate and sat by the fire to the right of my curtain. But he stopped directly across from it, staring at an empty wall, and blew out his candle. He reached up to the candlestick that hung there and turned it sideways.

I raised my eyebrows as I watched him from not two feet away through the slit in the curtain. The candle on the wall remained in the holder, turned sideways when the wall in front of him swung open. He stepped forward, into the room I did not know existed. I waited for the wall to swing back into place, concealing him in the secret room, but it remained open.

Pulling back my curtain, I tiptoed along the wall to the secret door. Craning my neck to see into the dim room, I watched him set down his candlestick holder on a small table and reach for something. I moved over another inch to see what he held.

My eyes widened when I saw what he held. He brought the shining dagger down to his side and stood still. So long, in fact, that I wondered whether the curse had overtaken him. Possibly a trance? I stifled my gasp as the man lifted the knife and sliced his forearm, letting the blood drip into a large white bowl sitting on a small wooden table in front of him.

He stood, his eyes closed, murmuring words I could not hear. I waited, pressing my lips together. What was he waiting for? All the blood . . . I closed my eyes as long as I dared, forcing down the sick feeling in my stomach.

The man reached down and produced a white cloth, pressing it to his arm. After holding it for several seconds, he picked up a band of twine, slowly winding it around the blood-soaked cloth.

That's when I saw it. Hanging high above the bowl he had dripped his blood in, dangling, waiting to be worshiped. The gold chain held a large ruby stone, at least the size of my thumb. Thin golden pieces surrounded the stone, perhaps to hold it in place. The Homlock.

Hanging on a hook sticking out from the wall, the Homlock dangled above the bowl that contained the man's blood. I swallowed, trying to contain my throbbing heart.

I ducked just as the man turned, candlestick in hand, arm wrapped in the bloodied cloth. The man shuffled toward me and his secret entrance. Somehow, he re-lit his candle, and I caught sight of the sweat glistening off his forehead.

I dove back behind my curtain, crawling under my covers, heart pounding. His feet shuffled across the floor, though they seemed much slower tonight, then the slow creak of the wooden door opening.

After hearing the faint click, I crept back to the curtain and pressed myself to the wall, creeping toward the candlestick that hung there. Sweat was forming at my temples. This was it. I would finally have it. In my hands.

Holding my breath, I reached up slowly and wrapped my fingers around the candlestick. I gritted my teeth as I pulled the damp metal toward me, knowing I was now feeling the sweat and pain the old man was experiencing. The wall swung open easily, and I let out the breath I had been holding. I stepped in, glancing through the room, my breath coming in fast gasps. A torch was lit in the corner, and the small table stood under the Homlock. The room seemed large with so few items in it, as if even my light voice would echo. My eyes zeroed in on the pendant that hung from the wall.

In one long stride, I stood in front of it, staring at the gold pendant holding the dark jewel that I had been searching for. The Homlock. The thing that could lift my burden, release me from the gift I never wanted to begin with.

Reaching up, standing on my tiptoes, I made to grab the necklace. I gasped as a pain shot through my body, starting at my fingers and running down through my toes. Gripping the wooden table in front of me, I forced back the tears of pain that radiated through my body and took a deep breath.

I looked down, confused. The Homlock did not want me to touch it. It knew I was here; it needed me to sacrifice something for it. How .. . how did I know this? I looked over my shoulder, feeling like I was not alone in this empty room. *The dagger.* I jumped back as I stared down at the small table. It spoke to me. It—no, ridiculous. Completely ridiculous. Still fresh with blood, it lay there—not speaking, not whispering, not telling me to do something. Straightening my shoulders, I picked it up, ignoring my trembling hand. My stomach turned as I looked down at the bowl in front of me. A reddish haze circled through the water, making soft red circles throughout the bowl.

I gripped the dagger. How much of myself did I cut? How deep? Should I use my arm or my hand? The questions ran through me as goosebumps developed over my flesh. Pushing the thoughts from my mind, I pushed up the sleeve of my dirty dress and sliced my arm before I could change my mind.

The pain went straight to my head. It hit me like a bolt of lightning, like an earthquake forming in my ears. Crying out, I put a hand to my head, dropping the dagger to the floor, feeling the warm liquid ooze down my arm. I heard the soft plunk of blood meeting water and opened my eyes in a daze. The water swirled faster and faster, a tidal wave in this small ceramic bowl, spinning as fast as my muddled brain.

"No!"

I swung around, blood streaming down my forearm, my head still in a daze. The man stood in the doorway, hands to his cheeks, a look of horror on his lined face.

I froze to the spot in front of the bowl, not sure of anything except the sensation of oozing liquid dripping onto my bare toes.

"The Homlock! You—you must not—"

He staggered toward me, a hand on his chest. His face cringed in pain, and he fell to his knees at my feet. "The curse," he coughed. "The curse—" He sputtered something incomprehensible and fell at my feet, his blue eyes staring straight at me.

His voice came out almost mechanically as if someone else was speaking from inside his withering body. "Fire from the sky, life will not sustain. If taken without true hands, one risks the curse to steal away, which they hold most dear." He took a choked, painful breath.

For a split second, I stopped. What did that mean? Which they hold most dear—what could that mean? Shaking my head, I turned back toward my real goal. Reaching up with my bloodied arm, I snatched the Homlock off the hook, throwing it around my neck.

As I turned to run away from the place and never return, the man grabbed my ankle with a death grip I did not know he possessed.

"Where the dagger met the dusk . . ."

I went to turn away, but something held me back, something besides his icy grip on my leg. "What?"

"You must return . . . Where the dagger meets . . . the dusk . . ." And with that, his open eyes went blank and his grip fell limp.

My breath had stopped in my throat. I looked toward the door, then back at the blank stare of the man at my feet. He was . . . gone. I backed away, shaking my head, knowing a dead man was lying in the room with me.

That's when the building started to shake. I fell against the wall, confused, and looking around wildly. The man . . . he was . . . dead. A loud crash sounded over my head, loud enough that I shrieked and put my hands to my ears. The room filled with smoke, a slow swirling smoke moving around me, following my eyes, hands, and turning with my body.

I looked up. The ceiling now held a smoldering hole, as if lightning had struck, leaving only smoke and charred wood remaining. The building shook again, and I screamed, giving one last look at the man on the floor.

And then I ran. Far, far away.

Chapter Two

Branson, Missouri

Mirri yawned, her eyes watering. Mr. Lane was at the front of the room, writing bullet points on the whiteboard, in his mind-boggling lecture on the French Revolution. To keep herself awake, she began doodling up and down the edges of her notebook, lines that twirled and swirled, lines that made no sense. Sitting next to the window was always a bad idea for this class—the warm rays that hit her face could put her to sleep in a second, along with this teacher's monotonous tone.

Gazing around, Mirri noticed she was not the only student in this state of semi-awareness. The guy beside her was actually snoring a bit, his head resting on his hand propped up on the desk. Checking the clock above the teacher's desk, Mirri groaned, realizing she still had to sit through eleven minutes of this weariness. Inwardly, she sighed, and took a drink from her water bottle.

She listed out dinners she could make for the week while twirling her brown hair around her finger. Maybe a meatloaf? Probably a casserole—then her mother would have leftovers to take for dinner.

It occurred to her she hadn't even seen her mother in two days—the amount of sick and premature infants kept the NICU busy these days, what with this new strain of flu virus going around.

Mirri didn't mind eating dinner alone. She always had a book or her computer. Three nights a week she didn't get home until nearly dinnertime anyway, thanks to extra track practices. And so much homework these days. More than enough to keep her busy. She wasn't lonely, exactly, just . . . indifferent. The few times a week Mirri and her mother tried to sit down for dinner was more of a strain on her brain, anyway. Always struggling to hold a conversation. Both of them trying to come up with a topic that would last them over two or three sentences.

Mirri sighed, putting her chin in her hand. She admired her mother—her determination and what she did for a living, but they had about as much in common as a fruit fly and a Munchlin. She had a strange obsession with bird-watching, where Mirri would rather walk through an antique store or read a good book. Since Mirri's father died last year, it seemed the gap between her and her mother had only widened, leaving them both on opposite sides—far, far away, with nothing but obstacles getting in the way, like overtime shifts and extra track practice.

Glancing up at the white clock that hung above the white board, Mirri took another drink from her water bottle. If only she could sit outside, reading a book, basking in the warm sunlight. The fluttering green Loofa at the window could curl up on her shoulder like she remembered, so soft against her face—

Mirri gasped, swallowing a large gulp of water. Coughing violently, she bent over her desk, hacking and sputtering while her glassy-eyed classmates turned in her direction. Mr. Lane stopped writing and turned to see which one of his students was trying to hack up a lung.

Mirri turned and leaned over her knees to rid the water from her windpipe. Gasping, she wiped her mouth and smiled through watery eyes.

"Wrong pipe," she squeaked out.

There were a few snickers, but most of her classmates turned back to their cell phones hidden under their desks. Mr. Lane walked over and handed her a tissue, patted her on the back, and returned to the whiteboard to resume his captivating lecture.

Face burning, Mirri wiped her eyes and mouth, peeking back toward the window. All she saw was that same green bench sitting under the beautiful sky. She leaned back, sure she had seen a Loofa hovering outside the window. Glancing over her shoulder, Mirri checked to make sure no one had their head turned in her direction. Coast clear. She snapped her head back toward the window and leaned to the wall. Where had she gone? She peered through the window, trying to see as much of the outside world as possible. Putting her hand on the dusty windowsill, Mirri leaned in further until her nose touched the dirty glass.

Mirri snatched up the pen sitting on her desk and tapped on the glass, just a touch. She waited. Jinx would hear it. Nothing. She tapped again, louder this time, eager to send the signal that she knew. She waited, almost drooling in excitement onto the fogged-over glass, trying to peer down to the ground, knowing Jinx was out there somewhere—

"Mirri?"

Mirri snapped to attention, her pen clattering to the floor in what seemed like an echoing roar in the quiet classroom. Her teacher was staring at her with a waiting look, and to her horror, the rest of the class followed suit.

She felt the blood rushing to her face so soon after her choking fit. Mirri cleared her throat. "Yeah?" she asked.

"Do you know the answer?" Mr. Lane asked with narrowing eyes.

"Um, no." Mirri forced an apologetic smile, looking down at the doodles on her paper, wishing she could sink into the blue-lined white paper. She longed to look out the window but forced her eyes to remain front and center.

Like a sign from God, the bell rang overhead, freeing Mirri of the humiliation of the last eleven minutes. She grabbed her bag and notebook, not even bothering to throw her backpack over her shoulder. Hurrying out of class, Mirri half-walked and half-ran down the hallway. Taking the side exit instead of the main one, she broke into a run.

Luckily enough, this side of the school only had dumpsters, a few benches, and a long stretch of grass. All the other students would hurry away from their 7:30 a.m. to 3 p.m. prison, eager to continue their cell phone games and texting. Mirri slowed as she reached the line of windows in the building. Her history classroom must be one of these windows.

"Jinx?" Mirri called out in a hushed voice, afraid to draw any attention to her cause. "Jinx?"

"Mirri!" a squeaky voice exclaimed to her right.

Mirri jumped back from the red brick wall of the school. Before Mirri could examine the concrete wall further, a ball of green fluff appeared and wrapped itself around her neck.

"Jinx! How did you—how did you do that?" Mirri said, returning the ferocious hug from her dear friend.

Jinx unwound herself from Mirri's neck. She hovered in front of Mirri, beaming. "My new gift! I have the power of disguise!"

To demonstrate, she moved back in front of the school's red brick wall. She disappeared, though if Mirri squinted her eyes she could see a vague luminescent outline of a Loofa. Yup, there she was: a fluffy, flying creature with six legs and the cutest face Mirri had ever seen.

"That's amazing," Mirri murmured.

Jinx reappeared and folded Mirri in another tight embrace. "I have missed you so much, Mirri!"

Mirri laughed and stroked her velvety fur. "Me too." She hadn't seen her fluffy green friend in almost a year now, since the last time she was in Althord Loch, the magical village where Jinx lived. She pulled Jinx away to look into her eyes. "But what are you doing here? How did you even get here?"

On cue, Mirri turned to look over her shoulder, making sure no one was around to see her talking to a flying green fluff ball with six legs.

"It is very important, Mirri. We must go immediately."

Mirri paused. "Go where?" She couldn't mean . . .

"Back to Althord Loch!"

Mirri stared at her. "What? No way, Jinx, that's crazy! I barely got back last time!"

Jinx grabbed her hand and squeezed it with a soft paw. "Getting you back will not be a problem. We have created another portal." Her eyes got wide, and she spoke in a hushed tone. "The true problem lies ahead."

She stared at her flying friend for a moment. Was this really happening? To go back to Althord? Or was Jinx just being Jinx, who had a flair for the dramatic? Mirri had to admit she missed her magical friends terribly. She shifted her weight underneath her backpack.

"I'm . . . I'm not sure, Jinx."

"But Mirri!" Jinx cried. "You do not understand! It is of utter importance you return! The consequences would be dire! We will get you home, this I know!" She grabbed Mirri's face with her tiny paws. "Please?"

Mirri stared at the field, watching the oak tree in the distance. Leaves swirled around the trunk, creating a mini, colorful swirl. Back to Althord. They needed her. Her friends needed her. Smidge, maybe even Kryptus? Real friends? The thought was terribly tempting.

"Okay." Mirri gripped the straps of her backpack. "Let's do it."

✦

They stopped outside of the hazy glass doors to Evermore Antiques. Well, that made sense. Of course the portal would be in Rose's shop. She was a Druid from Althord Loch, after all.

At first, Mirri was worried about the Loofa being seen, but her new talent at concealing herself made their trip through town simple. No wonder they had sent Jinx. But *why* had they sent her? Jinx would only repeat there was a problem. A serious problem. Mirri was getting nervous, and her nails were chewed to the skin by the time they reached the antique shop.

Taking a deep breath, Mirri entered through the glass doors, the same doors she entered at least a few times a week. Mostly in the mornings, right after Rose opened, so that they could sit and chat without worrying about customers overhearing. Mirri looked around the shop, scanning the area for Rose. If there was a problem in Althord, Rose should know.

Mirri looked toward the register, keeping her eyes peeled for Rose. A teenage girl leaned behind the register and nodded toward them, then went back to her cell phone. Rose had just hired her last week.

Mindy or Mandy or something. By now, Mindy-or-Mandy-something recognized Mirri and paid her little mind.

"Where is Rose?" Mirri said under her breath. "I should tell her what's going on."

"There is no need. She knows of the problem," Jinx whispered back. "Hurry!"

Mirri gave a halfhearted wave to the girl at the counter, who was too busy on her phone to wave back. Trying to act nonchalant, Mirri strolled down the main aisle, following Jinx, glancing over her shoulder. Another portal. Would it be like last time? Mirri vividly remembered the feeling of her bed disappearing out from under her and falling, swirling, reaching for anything—completely losing control. It was terrifying.

Jinx took an automatic right at the back aisle. Mirri sped up, relieved that they appeared to be the only customers. But where was Rose?

Mirri stopped when Jinx turned back to her fluffy green Loofa self. She was hovering in front of an ancient brown television set. Well, it would have been brown at one time. Now, it was so scuffed that the brown only showed in a few places.

Jinx was holding her paw to the screen and fiddling with controls. She gave a small whimper.

Mirri looked over her shoulder again. "This is the portal?"

Jinx reached out to touch the screen of the television, her mouth hanging open. "It . . . was."

Chapter Three

"*W*as? What are you talking about?" Mirri walked closer to the console and looked at where Jinx's tiny paw sat. It looked fine to her.

"It cannot be," Jinx said.

She pressed random buttons that would have changed the channel seventy years ago, but now the television remained a blank cube, dusty and scratched. Her tiny little paws shook as she pounded harder on the faded buttons. "The portal is gone. How . . . how are we to get back?"

"Uh, what exactly is wrong with it?" Mirri said. She was standing in the back corner of Evermore Antiques with a flying, talking Loofa, staring at an ancient television set.

"The lekki. It has disappeared!" Jinx's wings fluttered so fast Mirri could not see them. She hovered in front of the television, her green fluff trembling.

"Lekki?"

"The light. The light that delivers us back and forth." Jinx turned to face Mirri. Her voice rose to a shaky, high-pitched wail. "I have failed! I have failed my assignment!"

"Shhh! Jinx, it's okay!" Mirri pulled her furry friend into her arms and stroked Jinx's trembling back, looking around frantically. This was getting ridiculous. She sat down with Jinx on an antique flowered sofa near the television, dropping her backpack on the floor. Jinx's whole body had gone slack. "Now, tell me about your assignment. Why do they need me in Althord?"

"Kryptus has sent for you specifically. He says you are the only one," Jinx said in a monotonous voice. She laid her head on Mirri's leg. "Soon, it will be too late," she moaned, with her face buried in Mirri's lap.

"Me?" Mirri asked, more confused than ever. Jinx's depressed state was not helping matters. Mirri picked Jinx up and held her so they were nose to nose. "Jinx? Why does Kryptus need me?"

Jinx looked at Mirri and then let her head sag. "It is something I cannot tell you. But it is of utmost importance we return."

"Why can't you just tell me?"

Jinx looked up at her with wide, watery eyes. "I . . . I . . ."

A squeaking noise made them both jump. An elderly woman, pushing a maroon walker covered in bumper stickers, was slowly making her way down the aisle to Mirri's left, studying the selection of antique dolls staged on a table.

Mirri stood hastily, nearly tripping over her backpack. She shoved Jinx behind her and turned, pretending to be fascinated with the antique television set. The scratching sound of wheels against the concrete floor came closer as Mirri tried to search for Jinx without moving her head.

"My dear?"

Mirri closed her eyes briefly, then put on her brightest smile. She was a natural at dealing with old ladies, being a frequent flier of antique stores.

"Yes?" Mirri said, turning to the woman. The woman's walker held a basket, and Mirri noticed a strange painting of a man walking around as a carrot leaning inside it.

"Can you tell me where the restroom is?"

Mirri breathed a silent sigh of relief, still unsure where Jinx was hiding. "Of course. Straight down that way, in the corner." Mirri pointed away from her and Jinx, toward the right side of the store.

"Mirri, isn't it?" The old woman smiled, with lines that pulled at her eyes. She had long silver hair pulled back in a low ponytail, and thick glasses perched on her pointed nose.

"Yes." Mirri nodded with a smile.

The woman chuckled softly, then winced, bringing a hand to her side. "Yes, Rose talks about you all the time, dear. She is quite lucky to have you."

Mirri felt the tugging at her pant leg first. She ignored it, very aware that Jinx was trying to get her attention. "I'm lucky to have her."

"Oh, this dreaded weather," the woman commented, fanning herself with a wrinkled hand. "Some days, I regret even coming outside."

The tugging on Mirri's jeans increased, the smile on Mirri's face frozen as the woman in front of her kept chatting away.

Jinx whispered, "Mirri!" as Mirri swung out her right leg and cleared her throat loudly.

Mirri continued nodding and smiling in all the right parts of the conversation, biting the inside of her cheek as the woman droned on about the weather and her difficult air conditioning system. Jinx had stopped tugging at her pant leg at least, though this did little to ease Mirri's mind. Where had her invisible friend gone?

Out of nowhere, as the woman was describing her son's pool in Florida, the painting resting in her cart toppled out of the basket and slid toward Mirri's feet, coming to a rest on top of her sneakers. Mirri jumped back as the woman frowned at the floor.

The woman scratched her head. "So sorry, dear, I didn't mean to drop that on you. My goodness, how clumsy I've gotten!" She went down slowly to pick up the painting.

"No, no, please, let me get it," Mirri said, bending to grasp the canvas. She picked it up, studying the picture. "That's—uh—interesting, isn't it?"

Mirri held the canvas up for a moment, studying it. A man with a black top hat was walking with a cane, holding a large orange heart-shaped object. But the weird part was the man's body resembled a carrot. With two legs.

The woman beamed. "Yes, I saw it first thing when I walked in. Reminds me of the good old days."

Mirri placed it back in the woman's basket gently. "There you go."

"Thank you, dear. Well, I shall see you next time, hmm?" She grasped Mirri's hand with one of hers and gave her a small squeeze. "Stay well, dear."

Mirri watched the woman limp off, counting the seconds until she was out of hearing range. She looked around nervously, checking for any other prowling customers.

"Mirri!"

She nearly screamed as Jinx whispered in her ear. She put a hand to her chest as Jinx's green glow materialized in front of her, hovering next to Mirri's head.

"Geez, don't do that, Jinx," Mirri hissed.

"I am sorry, Mirri," Jinx said, looking behind her. "But I believe we have another problem."

"Yes, I'm getting that," Mirri said, putting a hand to her head.

"No, no, Mirri. The portal. I think the new portal is going away from us."

"What? What portal? Going where?"

"I think the portal is in that woman's picture, heading toward that bath room she mentioned."

Mirri stared at her. "That painting? You think that painting is the portal? Why?"

"Did you not see it?" Jinx's eyes got wide, and she dropped her voice to an unnatural tone. "That picture contained . . . a lekki."

Mirri rolled her eyes and looked over Jinx's furry head to the end of the building. The elderly woman was still shuffling slowly toward the bathroom, pushing along her squeaky walker.

"Are you sure? Like, completely sure? Because I will not steal some old lady's painting unless you are completely, one hundred percent—"

"I am sure!"

"Fine, whatever." Mirri bent and tossed her backpack over her shoulder, then paused and dropped her bag, stuffing it under the flowered sofa. She strode down after the woman, her heart beating madly. What was she supposed to do? Knock a sweet old lady out and run away with her painting? Slip a new painting in and take the old one?

Mirri gritted her teeth as her mind spun with possibilities. Jinx flew next to her, camouflaged well, whispering loudly in Mirri's ear.

"There! She is stopping! What do we do now?"

Mirri stopped in her tracks, then shoved her hands in her pockets. Pretending to be intrigued by the old-fashioned dresses hanging along the wall, Mirri watched the woman out of the corner of her eye. The woman was reaching around into her wire basket and lifted a large purse onto her shoulder. She pushed the walker against the wall, with the painting still in the basket. Mirri watched her hobble into the bathroom hallway and disappear.

The walker sat unattended next to the bathroom hallway.

"What do we do now?" Mirri said out of the corner of her mouth. She didn't know where Jinx was, but hoped she was close.

"We must retrieve the painting and activate it, I would assume. It must be a static portal."

"Activate it? How would we do that?" Silence. "Jinx?"

"I . . . I am not sure. It would require a very significant object to activate a static portal . . . I am wearing an activation charm." Jinx's voice trembled as she reached around her neck and pulled a small silver ball through her green fluff that Mirri hadn't realized was hanging around her neck. "But I have nothing for you. How am I to get you back to Althord?"

Mirri's mind raced. Oh, God. Suddenly, her brain snapped into action.

"Wait—Jinx!" Mirri dug in the pocket of her jeans.

"What? What do you have?" Jinx's voice came out high and excited.

Mirri produced her key chain. She separated her house key, the key to her mother's Honda, and Mrs. Pinn's house key. She held up the key they used to open the gate to Avi's resting site, only a year ago. "This."

"Your key! The key that led us to Avi! How did you know to bring it?"

Mirri shrugged, holding the key in her palm. "I always have it."

Mirri had received it from her father ten years ago, but had not known it was the only way to open a gate to Avi's grave in Althord Loch—a place where she would be forced to fight through a magical forest, find the Staff of Avi, and battle the evil Panthera.

"So, what do we do now?"

"You must hold the key as we enter the portal," Jinx said. "You go and distract the human. I will prepare the portal, and we will enter together."

Mirri swallowed. "Okay." She hurried toward the women's bathroom, ignoring the butterflies fluttering through her stomach. She entered the hallway and stepped into the bathroom as the toilet flushed in the handicap stall.

Mirri stopped, clutching the key to her chest. Distracting an old woman couldn't be that hard. She looked at herself in the mirror, noticing the terrified expression on her face. Clearing her throat, she forced her shoulders to relax and stepped to the sink, shoving her keys back into her pocket.

The stall door creaked open, and the woman shuffled her way to the sink. Mirri grabbed a paper towel, pretending to dry her hands.

"Why, hello dear," the woman said, smiling and making her way to the sink.

"Hello!" Mirri ran her hand through her hair. "Uh, I meant to ask you before."

"Yes, dear?" the woman asked, running her hands under the water.

Mirri stopped. "Where, uh, did you say your son lived in Florida?"

"Oh, he and his wife live in southern Florida. Right on the beach, too. You have to peel my grandson away from that beach, you do." She shook her head and laughed, reaching for a paper towel.

Mirri strained her ears to hear anything from outside the bathroom. Had Jinx gotten the painting yet? What was she doing with it, anyway? Mirri had forgotten to ask. How do you even enter a magic portal?

"Dear?"

Mirri snapped her eyes back to the woman. "Sorry?" she asked, pasting her fake, overly-cheesy smile on her face.

"Do you know Florida?"

"Oh, well, no, not really. But I've always wanted to. Sounds wonderful." A loud thump occurred outside, causing Mirri's insides to squirm. The woman picked up her purse and turned slowly to leave.

"Wait! Uh, I have one more question. About Florida."

"Of course." She smiled at Mirri, raising her eyebrows. "What is it?"

"When is the best time to visit? See, I would like to, um, plan a trip. When is the best time?"

"Oh! Oh my, let me think." The woman adjusted her glasses and scratched her ear. "I was down in late August, I believe . . . Oh, the weather was plain awful. Humidity, you know." She laughed. "Half the time, I was terrified of a hurricane coming right through. Always been terrified of hurricanes, I have." She reached down into her large purse and dug around. "Let me check my date book. I know I wrote it down somewhere. Write down everything! Who knows how I used to get along without it!"

Mirri kept nodding and smiling, at the same time edging toward the bathroom exit. She was supremely relieved that these bathrooms didn't have doors, just a winding hallway you had to enter from the store. The woman continued to mutter to herself and comb through her belongings. Mirri leaned out of the exit in time to hear the frantic whisper.

"Mirri! Hurry!"

"Would you excuse me for a moment? I . . . left something right outside."

The woman was flipping pages of what Mirri assumed was a date book. "Where are these wretched glasses?" she mumbled as she sifted through her bag.

Mirri took the opportunity and hurried back into the store. The bizarre painting was lying on its back, the carrot-man facing up.

"Hurry! Now!" Jinx whispered.

"But—what do I do?" Mirri whispered back, reaching for her key ring. "I—I—don't know what to do!"

"Jump in!" Jinx shrieked, making Mirri wince.

Mirri felt the tug on her arm. She put a foot out toward the painting, feeling the sweat break out of her neck. "Uh, just—jump?" Silence.

"Jinx? Jinx!" No answer. "Oh, God," Mirri muttered to herself.

She took a deep breath, held the key to her chest, and stepped into the painting.

Chapter Four

Mirri turned, coughing and gasping, trying to pull air into her mouth. For a split second, she thought she was drowning . . . She felt great pain . . . Now, as she gazed around, Mirri realized she was very much alive. Lying face down in a creek.

Shivering furiously, Mirri pushed herself into a sitting position and wrapped her arms around her body. Lush, green forest surrounded them on all sides. The breeze that floated through the air was a vicious attack on Mirri's bare arms. She shifted to her knees, wincing as she dipped her hands into the shallow water to stand.

"J—Jinx?" The shivers reached Mirri's vocal cords.

"Mirri!"

Mirri turned toward the small voice, relief flooding her brain. The green glow was getting bigger and brighter the closer Jinx flew. It took only seconds for Jinx to reach Mirri and wrap herself around her bare neck, Jinx sobbing hysterically.

"Oh, Mirri, I could not find you, I was afraid you had not made it. I didn't know what to do! Oh, what I would have done if I had lost you in the portal! However would I go on if—"

"Jinx! I—I need to get somewhere . . ." Mirri put a shaking hand to her forehead, running a hand through her damp hair. "I feel—weird." She shook her head, re-wrapping her body with her bare arms.

Mirri looked around, her mind feeling so heavy. The sun was rising in the sky, just over the treetops. She recognized this place. This was the creek she and Smidge crossed to get to Esperanze's hut. She was sure of it. In the distance, a tiny ringlet of smoke stretched for the sky. Just over that hill was the crazy Druid's home. They were not far from Hadleigh Village.

Mirri rubbed her arms. "C'mon—let's go."

Ignoring the freeze spreading through her body, they made their way through the dense forest. Much denser than Mirri remembered. She silently thanked herself for deciding to wear jeans that day. Her T-shirt, however, she would have reconsidered had she known an ancient portal would deposit her in an icy creek.

Trembling, Mirri threw a leg over a fallen log. Her hands were having trouble grasping things, and Jinx was doing her best to help Mirri over obstacles. "You—you never told me," Mirri stopped to pull her other leg over the log, "why they needed me here." Her limbs were becoming stiff and hard to work. The dizziness came in waves, and Mirri leaned against a tree, listening to the chattering of her teeth.

"I think it best that Kryptus tell you, Mirri." Jinx came down and wrapped herself around Mirri's neck in a sort of Loofa-scarf.

"But—why?" Mirri breathed, noticing her breath fogging in front of her. What was Jinx not saying? Something was not right. She climbed and hiked faster, forcing her frozen muscles to move. *Hot chocolate. Quilts. Fuzzy slippers.* Warm things. Hot things.

Finally, Mirri could hear the sounds of the residents of Hadleigh Village through the trees and brush, along with bangs and yells. These were friendly sounds. No screams of agony or cries of battle. Mirri was shaking so hard it felt as if her brain was rattling against her skull. This was not a normal headache. At least, like no headache Mirri had ever experienced.

Jinx rubbed Mirri's arms with her long body, stretching out to cover her bare arms. Mirri appreciated the gesture, though it didn't help. She shoved away the last of the trees and tumbled onto the stone road, tears springing to her eyes at the jolt of pain that went through her knees.

"Mirri!" Jinx flew off Mirri's shoulders and grabbed her under the arm to help her human friend to her feet. "We are close, Mirri! You can do it!"

Mirri took a deep breath and forced herself to stand. She began limping down the road, her limping soon turning into a jog. Track practice was paying off. They passed the Mal-root field, or what Mirri thought was the Mal-root field. It was now green, with full plants as tall as she was. Her vision was fogging over. She narrowed her eyes as she jogged along the road, concentrating on the green glow flying in front of her.

Creatures stopped to stare, some with confusion on their face, others with pure joy. Villagers whispered 'The Keeper' and 'She's back!' Had Mirri not been freezing, she would have loved to stop and chat with an oversized Munchlin, or talk to one of the tiny elves wearing suspenders. The strange looks she got must have been from her lack of winter attire. The elves all had on fuzzy sweaters over their overalls, and a Tripod wore a long brown cloak. All were appropriately dressed for such harsh weather. Surely, by now, icicles were hanging from her T-shirt. She must look ridiculous running around this place in the freezing cold with her skinny bare arms, which were now turning a grayish white.

There. Up ahead. The Imperium. Sleek and silver, at least fifty stories high. A beautiful building this time of day and surely more peaceful now that it was under Kryptus's rule.

Breathing was becoming difficult. Here they were, yards from the front entrance, and Mirri was questioning whether she would make it the rest of the way. "Jinx . . . I . . . I don't know if . . ." The rest of Mirri's sentence dissolved on her tongue as she fell to the ground.

"Mirri!" she heard Jinx's voice, though she didn't see her.

Jinx, Mirri thought, wondering why she could not hear her words. Jinx . . .

❖

"Thank you," Mirri said with a smile as the elf handed her a bowl of something warm. She still shivered under her blanket, but sitting in front of the fire was helping some of the feeling return to her limbs. She sipped out of the large bowl and turned her head to cough as the scalding liquid made its way down her throat.

Ouch. They had told her she would need to drink the whole bowl. No one had told her what had happened, but she noticed a few winces as she told them the story of dizziness and foggy vision. Apparently, Jinx and a Humungus named Anwar had brought her into the Imperium after she collapsed. Mirri remembered being wrapped in a blanket and large hands, sitting her up in a chair. Since then, she had been slowly becoming more aware, her mind clearing, remembering where she was.

Hmm. The heat felt nice. Mirri sipped on the scalding hot liquid, letting the steam drift up to her face. Jinx was called from the room, but left only after Mirri insisted she go. She fussed over the blanket, wrapped it tighter around Mirri's neck, and gave her a strangling hug. Jinx assured her she would be back as soon as possible.

"Hello?"

The door opened on the other side of the room, letting in a large beam of light. Mirri turned her head, still wrapped in the scratchy blanket and holding the bowl.

A blonde woman in a green dress walked in and leaned over Mirri, putting a warm hand on her forehead. She shook her head and sat in the other chair near the fire, spreading her dress out in front of her. "Thank goodness you are all right." The woman leaned back in the chair, pushing her golden, curly locks behind her. "Why in the world are you here, Mirri?"

Mirri narrowed her eyes. The woman's bright red lips were in a frown as she sat in the chair next to Mirri. Her long blonde hair fell all around her, almost reaching the floor from her position. Mirri studied the woman, staring at her green eyes. There was something familiar about her, but she was sure she had never seen this woman.

Mirri paused. She did not like starting conversations at a disadvantage. "Well, why are you here?"

"Ah, playing that card, are you?" The stranger nodded. "Yes, I should have known. Just like your father. Never wanted to appear weak." She shook her head, with the ghost of a smile appearing on her lips.

"*Rose?*" Mirri almost dropped her bowl and blanket.

She looked up at Mirri and chuckled, tossing her golden hair behind her head. "Haven't been a Druid in a few years. What do you think?"

The last time she had seen Rose, she had been a slightly overweight sixty-five-year-old woman with eyeglasses and gray hair she kept tied back in a tight bun. Mirri knew Druids aged backward after a certain point, but she had never imagined Rose so . . . stunning.

"I didn't even recognize you . . . How old are you?" Mirri blurted out.

Rose raised her perfectly shaped eyebrows. "Normally, a lady would not answer that truthfully. But I suppose you deserve to know." She gazed into the roaring fire. "In my Druid form, I would be about 200 or so. Hard to keep track after a certain point. Time moves much differently here."

Rose gritted her teeth and yanked at the long green sleeve that ran down to her wrist. "Do you believe this get-up they are having me wear? Elders insisted I look the part of the Druid." She sighed and tugged at the waist of the dress, muttering something about 'the nerve of that Tripod.'

"It's so lovely," Mirri said, reaching out to feel the gold embroidery that ran up the sleeves. "Is this what you used to wear?"

Rose snorted. "Yes, sadly. When I had the hips and frame of a young woman." She crossed her arms in front of her again, tugging at the dress over her chest. Mirri pretended not to notice the cleavage that was displayed on her front, or the blush in Rose's cheeks.

"Eat up," Rose said, nodding at her bowl. "You'll feel much better."

"Right." Mirri took a sip of the cooling liquid, which tasted like sunflowers, or how Mirri imagined a sunflower tasted.

"They told me what happened. Using a static portal can often lead one to the mordum state. Highly uncomfortable, I imagine."

"A static portal?"

Rose nodded. "Yes. That portal had been out of use for many years. I had no idea it was even still in my shop. You're lucky it got you as close to Hadleigh Village as it did."

Mirri gave a laugh. "Yeah, some luck. Felt like my brain was squeezed through a garden hose." Gulping the rest of the soup, Mirri set the bowl down on the floor next to the chair and wiped her mouth with the blanket. "What portal did you use? How did you get here?"

Rose smiled. "Ah, I have much more reliable ways to get here." Her voice dropped an octave, almost as if she was muttering to herself. "And had I known you were coming, I would have brought you myself. Then this would have never happened." She stared at the fire with a slight flair to her nostrils.

Mirri raised her eyebrows. Rose was using her angry voice. Somebody was in trouble if Rose was speaking in that tone.

"Do you, uh, know what happened? To that TV portal Jinx came through? Why did it stop working?"

Rose rubbed her forehead. "I am not sure. Portals in Althord have just come back into use. They were discontinued for so long during the Panthera rule. I guess we still have some more kinks to work out." Rose took a deep breath and stood, pulling Mirri out of her chair. "Well, let's get going. Kryptus has been waiting."

Mirri's heart jumped. As much as it surprised her, she had missed Kryptus. And Rose—she must have missed Kryptus more than anyone.

"You've seen him, Rose?" Mirri asked, her eyes gleaming.

Rose and Kryptus had been in love years ago when they both lived in Althord Loch. While Rose had been in Mirri's world, they could only speak in dreams.

"Was it amazing to see him again? After so long?" Mirri grabbed Rose's hand and waited for the story of running into each other's arms and sharing a passionate kiss.

Rose smiled and put a hand on Mirri's back. "Something like that," she said in a clipped tone.

Mirri frowned. That didn't sound like the love story of a Druid and centaur that had not seen each other in a century. Something was wrong. Rose's eyes did not tell the story of a lovesick woman.

They stepped into the brightly lit hallway. Mirri winced briefly, and then fascination took over. Creatures of all varieties walked the hall, some on two legs, some on four. One white creature flew high above their heads, in a sort of back-and-forth motion, with its nose in a book. Mirri stepped back into the wall as a centaur marched down the hallway, holding his halberd high.

She remembered creeping through the desolate hallways lit with torches and horrifying statues with glowing red eyes. The trip that she and Kryptus had made through the Imperium last year was one Mirri would never forget, and hoped she would never make again.

The Panthera ruled over Althord Loch when Mirri was last here, the tribe who controlled all of Althord Loch. Amara, the leader of the Panthera, forbade magic and had the power to sense when any creature used it. Punishment was reclamation to the Mal-root field—that is, grinding bodies of citizens to dust and using it as fertilizer to grow their crop that fueled their power.

From the looks of it, things had changed under Kryptus's rule.

Mirri hurried along next to Rose. "So why do they need me here? No one will tell me what is going on."

Rose continued to walk on, waving here and there at workers in the Imperium.

"Rose? Why are you here?" Mirri was getting frustrated. Why wouldn't anyone tell her?

"Soon, Mirri," Rose said. "Everything will become clear, I promise. But we must get to Kryptus first."

They stopped when they reached the end of the hallway. Mirri stared at the wall, expecting it to disappear. Doors did not exist in this building; walls instead simply disappeared at an entrance.

Rose turned and stood, a fake smile on her face, and her hands clasped. Before Mirri could ask what they were waiting for, the feeling of being flushed down a toilet overcame her. However this time, it felt like being flushed *up* a toilet. Instead of going down through the floor, they went up. Mirri's hair felt like it was being pulled to the ground, along with her confused stomach. After a few seconds of whirling, the room stopped spinning, along with her stomach.

Luckily, she kept her balance, though her arm shot out to grab Rose. Rose held her for a moment, until Mirri straightened up, her cheeks burning. She was the *Keeper*. She had fought her way out of the Imperium and defeated Amara, yet she couldn't even handle their magical elevators. Mirri tossed her brown hair to one side and forced her shoulders back a bit.

Mirri gazed around the massive halls as they walked. Her feet echoed in the large hall, and all other sounds of daily life quieted. This hallway she recognized. Maybe. It was hard to tell. These halls all looked the same, an orange-ish color on the walls with a red stripe at the top. This time, though, it was well-lit, with no torches or gargoyles. Rose led her down the hallway, free of creepy monster statues.

Rose turned to face the wall to the left. Mirri watched as the barrier in front of them disappeared. She still had no idea how to find these doors. Mirri followed Rose on her heels, sure that the wall would reappear if she waited too long. Mirri looked around the large room, a smile growing on her face, all feelings of embarrassment forgotten.

Kryptus, who stood at the head of a long table holding his trusted halberd, looked up and gave Mirri a smile with his customary nod. Smidge stood to the left of him, hands clasped in front of him. They looked strange standing next to each other—Kryptus, a tall, muscular centaur with a gray horse's body, standing next to a three-foot elf who barely made it past his legs. But Mirri didn't care. Excitement overcame her, and she ran to the centaur and elf.

"Kryptus!" She threw her arms around his middle.

Kryptus patted her back in greeting. "It is good you have come, Mirri." She ignored the bland welcome she received from the large horse-man—it was just his way.

Mirri pulled back from him, beaming, and turned to the elf. "Smidge!" She leaned down to hug the elf, who she had missed more than anyone. She held him in a tight embrace, waiting for the return hug she expected.

Smidge gave her a small pat on the back. "Thank you for coming, Mirri."

Mirri let go of her dear friend when she realized the return hug was not coming. She stood slowly, confused. Smidge wore a tight smile and nodded at Mirri. A nod. That was all. A *nod?* After everything they had been through? She had not seen her friend in almost a year, and she got a Kryptus-like nod.

Mirri stood, clearing her throat. She stepped away from the head of the table, pushing her hair behind her ear. She turned and walked back to stand beside Rose, hoping no one noticed the tears forming at the sides of her eyes. Mirri stood with her head held high, looking straight ahead at the enormous map that took up most of the opposite wall but seeing nothing.

"Now that the Keeper has arrived, we may begin," Kryptus said.

It was just then that Mirri noticed the other creatures seated around the table. In her excitement, she had not even seen Meleara, a Hezra she had met in Hezra's Hollow. How could she miss the enormous crea-ture with antlers spread down her back and a humongous feathered tail? Also seated at the table was a pale green rabbit (well, she assumed he was a rabbit; he didn't have any fur) with crooked glasses and a tuft of white hair out the top of his head, a woman with dark skin and three antlers protruding from her head, and an overly large "man" with large eyes and hair running down his arms and chest. The horns coming out the sides of his head curled down into spirals.

Kryptus nodded at Rose and Mirri, and Rose motioned for Mirri to take a seat at the table. Mirri sat with her arms folded, trying to hold the tears in her eyes. She looked at Kryptus with a scowl.

"Friends, we are here to begin the next stage of rebuilding our society. Punishing the guilty who are deemed responsible for our previous downfall. Only when they are punished can our village truly feel at ease and reassured." Kryptus paused, and Mirri had the distinct impression he was speaking in her direction. He cleared his throat. "First, the most important and most heinous of the crimes. The killing of Avi, our beloved ruler."

Mirri's eyes widened, and she glanced around the room. Was she going to see Lavinia again? The evil woman disguised as a Panthera that took an entire kingdom as slaves? Mirri could still smell the woman's foul breath. She still had nightmares about black snakes creeping toward her face, powerless to stop them. The vile creature who had hung her from a wall and hurt her friends, all the while keeping up the facade of being head of the Panthera. Mirri's hands trembled. She forced them into her lap as she stared straight ahead, determined to appear as professional as the others.

Kryptus began again, as Mirri stared at the wall, afraid to look toward him. "Friends, I present the killer of Avi. Gwenna of Holmforth. Avi's daughter."

Mirri, sitting very straight, turned her head toward Kryptus. Standing next to the centaur, arms bound at the wrists, was a woman with red hair and glasses. She wore blue cotton pants and a matching shirt, dirty and wrinkled. Medical scrubs. The woman had her eyes pointed to the floor, but it didn't matter. Mirri would recognize the woman anywhere.

It was her mother.

Chapter Five

Mirri stepped out of the Imperium, feeling the sunlight hit her cheeks. She wrapped her arms around herself, grateful for the long cloak a centaur had offered her. Mirri stopped, looking around at the various creatures milling around the stone road. Directly in front of the Imperium stood a small building with elves pounding on a half-constructed roof. Another creature stood in front of the opening of the building, spraying the outer wall with something from a hose connected underground.

Next to it, another small structure came to life, with a blue creature on four legs and feathers yelling commands to elves on ladders, using tools that were making loud plopping noises. Despite her mood, Mirri had to smile. Seeing all the residents working together, collectively rebuilding their world, lifted her spirits. *It's a shame none of their magical powers could erect buildings,* Mirri thought lamely.

"Mirri!" Jinx flew in Mirri's face, eyes wide. "What happened? How is your mother? Did you see Smidge?" The Loofa fired questions at Mirri faster than she could answer them.

"Yup, saw everyone." Mirri sat down in a huff. Mirri slumped down on the homemade bench and wrapped the cloak around herself. "Mom's just fine. In prison. For murder, apparently."

Jinx landed near Mirri. She hung her head. "I . . . I'm sorry I did not tell you sooner. I did not know how to!" Her beady eyes were bright with tears. She slid closer to Mirri. "I do not think your mother has done the things they say."

"Why does everyone think she did it? How could they think that?" Mirri's lip trembled. "I don't get it."

Jinx shook her head. "I do not know. I have only heard that Avi sent your mother away as a young girl."

"With . . . Rose? Why?" Mirri frowned. That made no sense. Rose and her mother? Left together? They didn't even know each other, for heaven's sake. Didn't even like each other. Mirri bit her bottom lip, thinking hard. She remembered that day. The day at Rose's shop.

Her mother was supposed to meet her at the antique store one evening. It was Rose's birthday, and Mirri insisted they all go out to Rose's favorite restaurant that night—a small Italian place with garlic bread to die for. They had planned on going to dinner, all three of them. Mirri had unsuccessfully tried many times to get the three of them together, but an overtime shift or other emergency always came up—like Rose needing to visit the next town for some priceless antique.

Mirri had been late, of course; flooding in the girls' locker room meant twelve sweaty girls had to stand around and wait for the boys to finish in *their* locker room. Before Mirri walked through the glass doors, she could hear it. Yelling. At first, she was worried—was someone trying to hurt Rose? Then she realized the voices were both familiar.

Mirri slid in the glass door silently and stood, trying to be invisible. Rose and her mother were fighting—and not just some petty squabble, either. More of a full-on screaming match in each other's faces.

Mirri watched, in shock, as her mother pointed a finger at Rose's chest and yelled, "For once, you need to realize it's not all about you!"

Rose swatted her mother's finger away, seething. "Did you think I had a choice? Ever? Did you ever stop to think that once, I never wanted to go in the *first* place?"

Mirri gasped. A bit too loudly. Both Rose and Mrs. Langley stopped to look toward the doors, breathing hard. Stray hairs stuck to the side of Rose's face flushed face while Mrs. Langley's eyes were glassy, and the fists she held down by her side an unnatural shade of white.

A moment of silence followed that seemed to stretch on for hours. Both women stared at Mirri, glanced at each other, then to the floor. Rose straightened her hair and cleared her throat, and her mother played with the hem of her shirt, pretending it needed to be stretched and laid perfectly across her middle.

Finally, her mother spoke. "I'm so sorry, Mirri. That was, um, very inappropriate of us." She smiled at Mirri with strangely wide eyes.

"What is going on?" Mirri's voice came out a bit more than a squeak.

"We were, uh, having a little discussion. That's all." Mrs. Langley's eyes refused to meet Mirri's, instead studying the pants she wore, looking down and smoothing them out.

Rose stood, still as a statue, hands clasped tightly across her waist. She studied a spot above Mirri's head intently.

Mirri broke the awkward silence. "Oh. Uh, okay." Mirri pushed her dark hair behind her ear. "Can we just go home? I, uh, have a lot of homework anyway." She gripped the strap of her backpack. All Mirri could think of was escaping this horribly awkward situation. But she didn't want to leave her mother and Rose together.

"Yes, let's!" Mrs. Langley said, throwing her bag over her shoulder. As Mirri turned to leave, her mother glared in Rose's direction once more.

Even though it had been over a month ago, it still bothered Mirri—and she worried it was all her fault. In any case, she had not suggested dinner again.

Things were making sense now. Rose and her mother had known each other for all those years . . . They had left Althord Loch together to come to Mirri's world. . . But why? Why did Rose, of all people, leave with her?

Mirri watched the workers in front of them. Elves, a Chesapile, and that big guy might be a Munchlin. All of them working together. It was wonderful to see them working together and laughing. A genuine community where creatures had no fear of reclamation or punishment for using their powers.

"They think my mom has . . . that she . . ." A tear rolled down Mirri's face. "Is my mother really Avi's daughter?"

Jinx looked at her, then back at the ground. "Yes, Mirri. She grew up in Holmforth with her father and older sister. I was not aware of this information until recently," she whispered.

"That means Lavinia is . . . my aunt?" Mirri's eyes grew large, and her insides turned unpleasantly. That horrible woman who had tried to kill her. Who had tortured her for information. Her flesh and blood.

Jinx put a small hand on Mirri's leg. "I'm so sorry, Mirri. For everything."

Mirri gave her a tearful smile and scratched her under the chin. She had missed Jinx so much. Her spirit and her buoyancy. They had been through so much together.

And Smidge. He had said practically nothing to Mirri. No hug or words of encouragement, only a pat on the arm and a nod. What happened to the elf that rescued her from a stampede, announced her status to a disbelieving world, and risked life and death to save this world with her? Her best friend?

"What has happened to our friends, Jinx?" Mirri said. "Smidge and Kryptus . . . They have changed."

Jinx hung her head. "Everything has changed, Mirri. Smidge is the Voktare. I believe he fears Althord does not find him otantik."

"Otantik?"

Jinx paused. "He fears they only see him as an elf. He believes he should be . . . different. More than he is." She sniffed. "Do you understand?"

Mirri nodded. "Yeah. I do."

They sat silently, watching the villagers of Hadleigh Village go about their day. Jinx climbed into her lap and rested her head on Mirri's knee. Things were different now.

◆

"Did you know? The last time I was here?" Mirri stood with her arms crossed, glaring at the centaur she had once considered her friend. The time she and Jinx spent outside, just staring and thinking, had caused her hurt to turn to raw anger. As the Keeper of Althord Loch, she should have been involved. She should have been notified. It was completely unacceptable. When Kryptus had summoned her back to the Imperium that day, she entered with her head held high. She wanted answers, and she was going to get them.

Kryptus stared out the window, holding his halberd. "Yes."

"Why didn't you tell me? And why did everyone tell me Amara killed Avi? And what in the world is a Mah—Mah—whatever that was? A deity?"

Kryptus sighed and leaned on the window ledge. "It was a cover. Very few knew Avi was killed before the last battle."

"But why?" Mirri's frustration was only growing. "And how could you not tell me my mother was from here? That I was Avi's granddaughter? That Lavinia is my mother's *sister*?" Mirri spat the last words as if they tasted bad. "That horrible woman . . . she's my aunt." Mirri turned and ran her hands through her hair. Lavinia was her flesh and blood. It was sickening.

"It was not essential to the plan."

Mirri turned back to Kryptus, mouth hanging open. "The plan? The *plan*? We are talking about my family! Who said anything about a plan?" Her hands were shaking, and she fought the urge to pummel the enormous creature with all her might.

Kryptus faced Mirri, eyes wide and serious. "I know, Mirri." He sighed. "Yes, Lavinia is your mother's older sister. But there is something else." He paused as if arguing with his inner self. "There is something you don't know about the night Gwenna came back."

Mirri froze. "What are you talking about?"

Kryptus stood silent, then turned to grasp Mirri's shoulders. "No one can know this, Mirri. You give me your Va'da." His eyes burned into hers.

"Yes, yes, I do!" Mirri gasped, immediately understanding the meaning behind the word Va'da. "Just tell me!"

Kryptus nodded and looked straight into her eyes. "That night, I—"

A door flew open and Kane entered breathlessly. "Kryptus! It is the prisoner! She has taken ill!"

Mirri's heart jumped. The prisoner? Her mother? Her eyes locked with Kryptus for only a split second, and then he strode to the young centaur that brought the news. "What has happened?"

"It is Gwenna! She will not wake!"

Mirri gasped, throwing her hand over her mouth as Kryptus turned to her. "Come!"

"What's wrong? What's wrong with my mother?" she called from behind them as she dashed down the hall behind the centaurs.

They waited for Mirri at the end of the hall as Mirri hurried to Kryptus's side, gripping his arm as she prepared herself for the toilet lift.

After a long and nauseating ride on the lift, going down several floors, Mirri, Kryptus, and Kane stopped in the middle of a dark, circular room, stone covering the floor and all the walls. Torches bright with fire hung all around her, circling her, enclosing her. Stone hallways branched off every few feet, and as she gazed around, she felt an air of unease: a heavy feeling all around her made her skin crawl.

Shakily, Mirri followed Kryptus down a dark stone hall, her head clearing as she remembered why she was in a stone dungeon to begin with. Mirri fought to see over the multiple centaurs clustered around the iron gate. After squeezing her way between Kryptus and Kane, she stood at the entrance to her mother's jail cell. Her mother lay in a heap on the floor, her blue scrubs vibrant against her bleak surroundings. A toilet sat in the corner, near a thin mattress on a wire frame. Two centaurs stood over her mother, speaking in low voices. Mirri drew in a sharp breath as one of the centaurs turned. Theodisis.

"Why is the prisoner on the floor?" Kryptus glowered. "Get her on the bunk. Now." His stare locked on Theodisis, and Theodisis's eyes narrowed back.

The centaurs lifted Mirri's mother onto the bunk, and Mirri dashed to her side. "Mom? Mom?" Mirri shook her mother's frail shoulders gently. "Please, Mom, please wake up!" Her voice became shrill.

Mrs. Langley's head lolled limply to the side, her red hair falling over her pale face.

Kryptus put a hand to Mirri's shoulder. "She draws air. She is still with us." He turned to Theodisis. "What happened?"

The young centaur stepped forward. "I delivered her meal, Kryptus. She appeared well."

"And then?" Kryptus glared at Theodisis. "You were on watch, no?"

Theodisis looked bored. "I heard a crash and entered her cell and found her like this. I ordered Kane to retrieve you."

Mirri was still lying over her mother, cradling her face in her hands. "Please, Mom, just wake up," she whispered, tears streaming down her hot cheeks.

Kryptus shoved Theodisis away and put a hand over Gwenna's closed eyes. He stood straight. "She is in a deep state of nal taru. Put there by deceit. We must take her to Esperanze immediately."

He turned to Theodisis. "Inform the centaurs there has been a poisoning. Discard all meals. You will search for the saboteur. Check on the well-being of all prisoners at once."

He turned to Kane, the young centaur. "We shall take Gwenna to Esperanze. Bring her."

Kane nodded, then stepped forward to pick up Mirri's mother. Mirri was still clinging to her mother's still body. "It's all right," Kane whispered. "I will be very gentle with her."

She watched Kane put an arm under her mother's neck and one under her bent knees. He picked her up easily, cradling her head against his chest.

"Come," Kryptus ordered.

He led the way out of Mirri's mother's cell, and together they stepped to the center of the dungeon. With one hand, Mirri grasped her mother's hand, intertwining their fingers. With her other arm, Mirri held tight to Kryptus as the lift sucked them upward and deposited them at the front entrance to the Imperium. This time, Mirri remained standing, her feet planted wide out to the sides.

Smidge was waiting, pacing back and forth in front of the exit, and hurried to Kryptus's side. "Shall I begin the investigation, Kryptus?"

"No. Theodisis has started the investigation. You stay here and wait for my return." Kryptus and Kane marched out the front door, Kane cradling Gwenna in his arms.

Smidge opened his mouth to reply but then pressed his lips together and let his shoulders droop.

Kryptus paused, then called over his shoulder. "You will work with Rosemeade. Begin preparations for trial."

Smidge looked up and nodded eagerly. "Yes, Kryptus," he said, raising his chin, then strode down the hallway of the Imperium.

Mirri hurried after Kryptus and Kane, remembering how difficult it was to keep up with a centaur on a mission. Mirri jogged to keep up with the large, four-legged centaurs, glad that she was still wearing the cloak. The wind had picked up, waving trees back and forth and whirling leaves across the path.

"Mirri!" Jinx flew up next to her, keeping even with her jog. "What has happened?"

"My mom, we have to get her to Esperanze!"

Jinx nodded and flew to the centaurs, hovering above Kane's head.

Kryptus turned into the forest, holding branches and trees aside for Kane. Jinx attempted to help as Kryptus batted her out of the way. Kane fought his large body through, covering Gwenna's face and body as best he could from the sharp branches that stuck out from all angles.

They made the trek into the forest toward the Druid's home, Kryptus leading the way, occasionally stopping to help Kane cover Gwenna, or hold aside branches, stepping on vines to allow Kane to cross, and occasionally putting a hand to Gwenna's face.

While Mirri ran after them, doing her best to keep up with galloping centaurs, it occurred to her that Kryptus was showing a great deal of concern for her mother. Did he treat all prisoners like this? Mirri could not imagine him being this worried about Lavinia. He knew her mother from long ago. He must have. Had they been close? Closer than she first thought? Hopping over the brook, she followed them up the hill, then down to the stone walkway, the centaurs stepping over the rickety little fence that surrounded Esperanze's home.

Kryptus marched to the base of the enormous tree and pounded on the door. Green moss and vines still clung to the tree, framing small and crooked windows that were placed at odd angles all over the bark.

"Esperanze! It is Kryptus!" Without waiting for an answer, he pushed the door open and held it for Kane, who had to bend at the waist to fit his enormous body and Mirri's mother through.

Jinx stopped and waited for Mirri, hovering in the air. Mirri jogged after them, holding her side.

As Mirri tripped over the front door ledge, crashes and the shattering of glass sounded in the next room. Breaking through the braided curtain, Mirri hurried to her mother's side on the tall table that had once served as Esperanze's experiment station. Glass vials, ceramic bowls, and strange-looking plants littered the floor all around the table, as if someone had brushed everything off the table in haste.

Esperanze stood on a stool next to the table, leaning over Mirri's mother, pushing back the unconscious woman's nostrils. Her shawl fell around Gwenna's body, Esperanze's long red hair laying all over the sleeping woman. She muttered things like, "Very odd," and "A strong curse." Esperanze climbed on the table next to her mother and leaned the side of her head against Gwenna's stomach. "Hmm, very strange indeed . . ."

Esperanze turned and threw a leg over Gwenna's still body, so she was straddling the lifeless woman. Using her fingers, the druid began walking her hand up and down her mother's arms, again putting her ear to Gwenna's stomach.

Mirri clenched her teeth and fought the urge to smack herself in the face. She did not have the patience for Esperanze's stunts right now.

Esperanze straightened and vaulted to the floor, colliding with Kane, and knocking herself to the floor, landing in a pile of blue, steaming liquid. Kane bent to help the woman up, and she stood, smoothing her long skirt, brushing at the spreading stain on her skirt.

"I will help Gwenna," she announced, her shoulders back and her face serious. Her voice lowered. "Though her condition is grim. Her mind needs to process the condition. Once her mind has fulfilled the darkness's quest, she will be able to see through the fog."

Kryptus nodded, as if this made complete sense.

Mirri stood to the side, bewildered. What was she talking about? "But is she going to be okay?"

Esperanze stepped to her, her eyes growing wide. She grasped Mirri's face with both hands. "The fog which we cannot see through is both light and dark. She must see through the dark. The journey will be long. But Esperanze will guide her. Esperanze has been through this fog," she murmured. "It will be a Pangum Baran!" her voice rose to a dramatic roar, making Mirri jump away. She rubbed her face where the woman had bruised her and looked toward Kryptus, gritting her teeth.

"Thank you, Mother Esperanze," Kryptus bowed his head. He looked at Kane. "Remain here."

"Come," Kryptus murmured to Mirri, stepping through the curtain.

With one last look at her mother lying on the table and Esperanze dancing around, speaking in what sounded like pure rubbish, Mirri slowly exited through the curtain.

Mirri and Kryptus stepped outside the hut. "I am not leaving her," Mirri said. "That crazy woman in there—"

"Her methods are pure, Mirri. You must trust in her." Kryptus looked toward the forest, back toward the trail to the village. "The Loofa will remain here with your mother. You and Kane will go back to the village."

"What? Leave her here? Absolutely, never, no way—"

"We have little time, Mirri," Kryptus interrupted her. He spoke in a low voice. "You are here to prove Gwenna's innocence. You must find out what happened that night."

Chapter Six

Mirri gasped, and she immediately felt Rose's hand on her knee. Her mother stood next to Kryptus, eyes down, red hair falling around her face, looking like a guilty criminal. Her blue scrubs looked as if they had been sitting in a trashcan for a week, and the dark circles under her eyes stood out against her pale face.

Murder? Her mother? Wait—how was her mother here? *Why* was her mother here?

Mirri stood abruptly, the chair making a loud screeching noise as she pushed it backward. "Mom?" Mirri stared at her mother. "What is going on? What are you doing here?" Mirri wanted to run to her mother, but Rose's firm hand gripped her elbow.

"Rose? What is going on?" Mirri turned to Rose, who immediately looked down at the table, her long blonde curls falling over her shoulders. "Why didn't you tell me? Why didn't *anyone* tell me?" Mirri shook her head, refusing to believe the scene that was playing out in front of her. "I—I don't understand what is happening." Mirri's voice was shaking, and her breath was coming in gasps. She gaped at her mother, the one Kryptus called Gwenna.

"Mom?" Her mother refused to meet her eyes. "Kryptus?" Mirri's voice quivered. "What is happening?"

"Why don't you let me state the facts?" Kryptus said, though his voice didn't have his usual bite to it. This time, it almost sounded sympathetic. How you would speak to a young child. Very un-Kryptus.

Mirri looked around at the calm expressions of the other creatures seated around the table. Just sitting there, acknowledging what their leader was saying. Calling her mother a murderer . . . Calling her Gwenna.

Rose tugged on her arm and Mirri sunk down in her seat next to Rose, her eyes never leaving her mother's face. How could they think her mother was capable of murder?

Mirri looked at Kryptus. *Please help me*, she begged him silently.

Kryptus pursed his lips and stared back at Mirri. *I will try.*

Mirri stared into his deep brown eyes a second longer. Slowly, she nodded. Kryptus had heard her.

Smidge stood next to Kryptus, the sweat glistening on his small brow. He was staring straight ahead, shoulders back, with his tablet held tightly against his chest, refusing to look Mirri's way.

Mirri folded her arms over her chest. She sat stone-faced, staring at the wall, trying to make sense of the scene playing out before her.

Kryptus cleared his throat. "On the night of Avi's death, a witness placed Gwenna returning to the home of her father, Avi. She left soon afterward, running into the woods. She left through a portal that night, the same portal her father had sent her through one year before, with Rosemeade," he nodded in Rose's direction, "to protect her from the Panthera." He looked around the room, avoiding Mirri's hardened stare. "They found Avi afterward. Someone had strangled him with a length of beads and stolen the Mahara Deity from above his mantle."

Silence. Mirri was trying to keep her breathing normal. She concentrated on her chest, rising and falling. Rose sat next to her, gripping her hand under the table.

Kryptus picked something up off the table in front of him. A length of beads. He turned to Mirri's mother. "Are these your beads?"

Mrs. Langley nodded without looking up.

Kryptus dropped the beads down to the table. "The judgment will stand. Gwenna of Holmforth shall be sent to the prison barge of Feyank, to be transported to the brilo mines in Koducu." Kryptus paused. "Indefinitely."

"What?" Mirri exploded from her seat. "That's it?" She slapped her hands on the table in front of her and stood, knocking her chair back to the floor. "That is how you decide if my mother is guilty? By a stupid length of beads?" She was yelling but did not care.

Mirri ran to her mother and grabbed her hands. "Mom, tell them! Tell them you didn't do it! Please!" Mirri had tears streaming down her face but did not care. "Tell them!"

Mrs. Langley looked up at Mirri with her wet green eyes and pursed lips. "I'm so sorry, Mirri," she whispered. Mrs. Langley grasped Mirri's hands tightly, with her hands still bound at the wrists. "This is how it has to be."

Mirri stepped back, shaking her head. "No, no, that is not how it is! You didn't do this; you couldn't have! Why are you taking the fall for this?"

Mirri looked around at the villagers seated at the table. They had no qualms about her mother's guilt and would put her in the mines for all eternity, all by a stupid string of beads. They directed looks of sympathy at Mirri, but no one stepped in to put a stop to this ridiculous trial.

"I'm sorry, Mirri," Kryptus said from beside Mirri. "But the evidence proves . . ."

"No!" Mirri yelled with such force that Kryptus looked taken aback. She picked up the necklace and held it for all to see. "All it proves was someone used these beads to kill him! That's it!"

Mirri turned to the creatures seated around the table. "Did anyone of you" —she pointed at the villagers seated around the table, still holding the beads— "see my mother kill this man? Huh? Did a single person watch my mother strangle him? *Did you*? All you know is *someone* used her beads to kill him!" By now, she was screaming fiercely, and scaring herself. But she had no choice. If her mother wouldn't help herself, then by God, she would.

All those seated at the table shook their heads.

"Then your 'evidence' is circumstantial!" Mirri slammed her hands down on the table again, breathing hard.

She was pulling legal terms from her latest cop show, and boy, was she glad she had watched three episodes in a row last night. She stood, panting, staring at the creatures seated around her. Mirri took a deep breath. *Think. Think.* A moment of silence stretched on. Straightening up, she turned to Kryptus.

In her most controlled voice, she began again. "Where I come from, people are given a chance to defend themselves. We call this a trial." Mirri looked at Rose, praying she would help this time. "Right?"

Rose nodded, finally looking up. "Yes."

Meleara, the Hezra, spoke up. "But why such a trial? Your mother has confessed to the crime, has she not?"

"No!" Mirri yelled again, then bit her tongue. "She said, 'this was how it had to be.' She never said she murdered Avi." Mirri looked around the table. "Am I right?"

The large man with horns spoke in a gruff tone. "Why don't we just ask her?"

All heads swung toward Mrs. Langley. Mirri spoke first, hoping it would help her mother reach her senses. "Mom?" Mirri said, grasping her icy hands. "Did you kill him?" she asked. Mirri would never admit it, but she was terrified at that moment. What would her mother say?

Mrs. Langley looked up again and stared into Mirri's eyes.

"Mom?" Mirri gritted her teeth and squeezed her mother's hands. "Did you use these beads to strangle your father?" Mirri tried, tried with every inch of her soul, to beg her mother to say something. *Please, mom. Tell them you didn't. I can't lose you, too.* She squeezed her mother's hands until she could feel the beating of her heart in her own palms.

Mrs. Langley's lips parted, as if trying to say something to her daughter, but failed. She shook her head, tears running down her face. "No," she sobbed. "But I am to blame." She fell against Mirri, shaking. "It's my fault, Mirri." Mrs. Langley cried onto Mirri's shoulder. "I'm so sorry."

Mirri wrapped her arms around her mother's frail body, practically crushing her ribs. "It's okay, Mom. I'll figure this out."

Silence filled the room, except for the sniffles and occasional sobs from Mirri and her mother. After several minutes, Mirri stepped away, wiping at her face. She turned, feeling braver and more confident than she had since she walked through that portal.

"We need to hold a trial. To find the actual killer of Avi." Mirri stood with her arms over her chest. "My mother just said she did not strangle him." She looked at Kryptus. "It is the only way."

"But she also said she is to blame. Doesn't that make her guilty of this crime?" The hairy man pointed out.

"That is purely speculative," Mirri spat out, hoping she was using the word correctly. "Don't you want to find the actual killer of Avi?"

"Mirri, please explain this trial," Kryptus asked, putting a large hand on her shoulder.

Mirri took a deep breath, patting her mother on the back as she sobbed into her shoulder. "We hold a trial when a person is accused of a crime. A group of people called a jury are presented with facts and decide if a person is innocent or guilty. The accused is allowed to speak, and questions are asked to find out if the person is guilty of the crime."

Mirri stared around the room. The creatures were looking at one another, Kore with an expression of confusion on his face.

"It is the only way to find out who really put those beads around his neck! Don't you want to know who killed Avi? It is the only way!" Mirri feared she was losing this argument. In this world, apparently, all you needed was someone to blame. It didn't matter who actually did it.

Mirri looked around desperately, pressing her lips together, gripping her mother. The others were looking at one another, as if the idea of finding the actual killer had never occurred to them.

Kryptus broke the silence. "Perhaps Gwenna should have the chance for trial. It would be fruitful to find the actual murderer if Gwenna did not commit this act."

He raised his eyebrows at Rose. She looked up at him, as if sensing this, and gave a nod, with her lips pursed.

The large hairy man spoke again. "And what if Gwenna is not being truthful?" He looked at Mirri. Clearly, this man had no sympathy for her current predicament.

No one spoke, but all looked at Mirri. She took a deep breath. "If the trial proves Gwenna . . . was to blame, then she will be punished. Just the same as if we prove someone else did it. The trial will bring the murderer to justice." Mirri nodded at the man firmly, hoping her little speech sounded convincing.

Kryptus spoke out. "I believe Mirri's idea has merit. It would be a fair and ethical way to prove someone's guilt or innocence."

Mirri's heart jumped, and she nodded. "Yes, yes, that is the whole point of a trial. To prove it."

"All right. We shall lay out our opinions now." Kryptus nodded toward the Hezra. "Meleara? Do you concur?"

Meleara nodded, her enormous antlers swaying toward the table. "I concur."

Kryptus glanced toward the woman with antlers and large ears. "Uma? Do the Tripods have any reservations?"

"The Tripods concur."

"Pattick?"

The green rabbit with the glasses nodded. "Gwenna should have a chance to prove her innocence," he said in a raspy voice.

"Kore? Your opinion?"

The large man hesitated.

Mirri glanced nervously at Kryptus. What would happen if this creature did not agree?

"I will concur," Kore said with a frown, shifting in his seat.

Kryptus nodded. "Smidge?"

Smidge looked up at Kryptus.

Kryptus gave a small sigh and tried again. "Humdinger? Your opinion?"

Smidge's chin tilted up. "I concur."

Humdinger? Smidge was now going by his full name? But Mirri didn't have long to ponder this.

"It appears we are in agreement. Gwenna will take part in this trial, where her innocence has a chance to be proven."

Mirri let out a sigh of relief. She turned to her mother and pulled her into a hug once more. Why wouldn't her mother even raise her head?

"I would assume we will need time to prepare for this trial. Rose-meade? Would you join me in preparation?" Kryptus asked.

"Yes, Kryptus," Rose said to the wall in front of her. The iciness in her voice made Mirri wince.

"Kane! Dante!" Kryptus barked.

Mirri's head swung to the door. Two young male centaurs marched in, both with dark hair that sat on their shoulders and marched to either side of Mirri's mother to stand at attention.

"Take Gwenna back to holding."

They both nodded and led Mirri's mother toward the door. For a moment, Mirri held tight to her mother's hand, refusing to let go. Mrs. Langley looked up at Mirri with a tearful smile, and Mirri nodded, letting a tear slip down her cheek. Her mother's head hung back toward the floor as they led her away, like some sort of criminal. Like a murderer.

"Kane!" Kryptus called before they could exit the room. "I need an update from Theodisis."

The young centaur nodded. Mirri caught his eye before he could look away. He held her gaze for a moment, then looked away quickly, but not before Mirri noticed the pink in his cheeks.

"This meeting is complete," Kryptus announced.

The occupants of the chairs stood, some more slowly than others. The green rabbit's long ears dragged along the ground as he hobbled from the room with his cane, adjusting his glasses. Meleara was not even sitting in a chair but on the floor, Mirri realized, as she stood gracefully, bowed at Kryptus, and took her leave. As the hairy man with horns walked past her, Mirri had to tilt her head back to look up at him. He glanced at Mirri as he left, and Mirri was sure she noticed a sneer. She made a mental note to avoid him at all costs.

Theodisis appeared at the door and stepped aside for the creatures to exit the room. Mirri narrowed her eyes at the centaur in the doorway. He glared right back. She hadn't seen Theodisis in over a year, but her feelings for him hadn't changed. But she didn't have time for petty insults at the moment.

Mirri stood, her arms crossed tightly across her chest to keep her body from shaking. She gripped the sleeve of her T-shirt to hold the fresh tears in her eyes before she turned to face the Kryptus. The centaur, who had just blind-sided her, dragged her mother before her in invisible handcuffs. The centaur who had lied to her. Her friend.

Mirri took a deep breath and spun to face Kryptus. "What is going on here?" Mirri demanded. "My mother never would have done this! I know it! Why couldn't you have just asked me? Before announcing to the world that she was a murderer? All you had to do was ask! Why couldn't you have told me before—before—" Mirri stopped, pressing her lips together, her body convulsing. She had no words that could express the hurt, the betrayal she was feeling at the moment. Mirri's arms dropped to her sides. "Why couldn't you just tell me?" she whispered.

Kryptus looked at Mirri, and then at least had the decency to look down at the floor. "Mirri." He took her shoulders in his hands. "Things happened much faster than I anticipated."

Theodisis cleared his throat loudly from the door of the room, clearly annoyed that Mirri and Kryptus were having a discussion they did not invite him to.

"We will discuss this later. I have other duties now." Kryptus nodded and stepped past Mirri toward Theodisis, their heads bent, speaking in quiet tones, Kryptus's halberd positioned next to him.

Mirri stood, her shoulders sagging at the insulting brush-off she had just received from her friend. More tears formed in her eyes as she angrily swatted them away—how could anyone possibly hurt her more at the moment?

Smidge appeared in front of her. "Do not worry, Mirri. We will do trial for your mother. If she is innocent, she will be sent home." The elf patted her on the arm and walked out of the room.

Mirri stood alone in the empty room, staring after her friends, or who she had *thought* were her friends. What had happened here?

Chapter Seven

M irri stared at him. "Me? How? That was a hundred years ago!"

"You have no choice. You must go to Holmforth, to Avi's home. Where he was killed." He put a hand on Mirri's cloaked shoulder. "Kane will assist you." He looked away. "You must find the real culprit if we are to convince the elders of her innocence. It is the only way to clear her name."

"But . . . I don't know how," Mirri stammered, running a hand through her hair.

"Kane!" Kryptus called. The young centaur appeared immediately.

"Take Mirri to Pattick. Get her to Holmforth. You are to assist her in finding the truth." He held the centaur's gaze. "Do you understand why I ask this of you?"

Kane nodded. "Yes, Kryptus."

"Go now! Your Loofa friend shall remain here and inform me of your mother."

Kane grabbed Mirri's hand, surprising her. "Come!"

With one last desperate look at Kryptus, she let Kane tug her away and lead her up the hill.

❖

"Where . . . Where are we going?" Mirri panted. She had always considered herself in good shape, thanks to track practice and her fairly long legs, but she was having a difficult time keeping up.

"Would you like to ride on my back?" Kane asked, noticing Mirri's troubles.

Mirri stopped, her ragged breaths coming out in a fog. Truthfully, she would love a ride. But it seemed a bit . . . well, weird. "Uh, thanks, but I should probably walk. I don't know how to ride a horse." She looked down at the ground as she felt her face turn red.

"No, I insist! It would be an honor, miss! We shall make the journey much faster."

Mirri considered it as she trembled underneath her T-shirt and rubbed her frozen hands together. The cloak provided little in terms of warmth. "Okay, sure."

He kneeled, putting one of his dark horse's knees to the ground, to allow Mirri to climb on his brown back. She threw a leg over while holding the hand he offered and settled on his back, pulling the cloak tightly around her.

"Let's go!" Kane said, taking off at a gallop.

Mirri, losing balance at the surprising speed, reached out and around Kane's well-toned stomach. Suddenly bashful, she tried to pull her hand back but realized she would not remain on his back without holding on to him.

Pushing her embarrassment aside, she clung to his waist and put her head into his back to block the stinging wind. One hand held the cloak, though now it was flapping wildly in the wind behind her. As Kane galloped through the forest, Mirri squeezed her eyes shut, replaying Kryptus's words in her mind. You must find the real culprit. He also believed in her mother's innocence. She would solve the mystery of Avi's death, take her mother away, and never let her return. It was the only option.

By the time Kane slowed, Mirri's teeth were chattering, and she had lost the feeling in her hands.

"We are nearing Pattick's hut." He kneeled again, and Mirri tried to swing her frozen limbs back off but tumbled to the ground.

"Miss!" Kane picked her up under the arms gently and stood her on the ground, keeping his arms under hers for an extra moment.

Mirri smiled up at him and felt a warmth spreading through her cheeks. He wrapped the cloak back around her shoulders and rubbed her upper arms.

"You continue to tremble. I worry the cold is dangerous for you."

"It doesn't seem to bother you," Mirri said. She remembered how warm his muscular back had felt while she rode on his back. She cleared her throat quickly and looked down.

Kane shook his head as they continued up the worn path. "The changing weather does not affect centaurs. Though when I was young, my mother insisted I wear a cover whenever I went outdoors." He gave a small laugh.

"Where is your mother?" It had not occurred to Mirri that she had never seen a female centaur. Come to think of it, she had seen very few females in Hadleigh Village.

"She and the other females teach the children in the North Woods. That is where the young learn. The females teach and raise the children, preparing them for what lies ahead. I returned to Hadleigh Village just this year to begin my merale with Kryptus."

"What is a merale?" Mirri asked breathlessly, taking Kane's hand as he helped her up a steep hill.

"My . . . future. What I will do with my life." He turned to look at her with his brow furrowed. "Does that make sense?"

"Yes." Mirri smiled.

Kane pulled her up the rest of the hill. "What about you? What do you want to do in life?"

Mirri shrugged. "I'm not sure anymore. I had wanted to be an archaeologist."

"What does this arch-ar—what does one of these do?"

Mirri smiled. "An archaeologist. Studies the past. Remains of culture. I love antiques."

She gazed off, remembering how excited her father had been when Mirri announced her goal one Sunday afternoon when she was about ten years old. She could still remember the smile on his face.

Mirri turned back to face Kane. She realized he was still holding her hand. Abruptly pulling her hand from his, she looked away, once again feeling the heat in her cheeks, even in this freezing cold.

"Uh, where are we going?" Mirri walked ahead of him, feeling both foolish and rude. She hoped she hadn't hurt his feelings. But she needed to concentrate. There was so much at stake.

"Pattick's hut. He specializes in portals." Kane moved ahead of Mirri, stepping out of the forest and onto the road. He held the tree back so Mirri could exit.

"This way." He pointed down the dirt path away from the village.

They had only gone a short distance down the path when he pointed to a grassy hill. "That is his hut."

Mirri looked where he pointed. "Where?"

"His home is well concealed. Follow me."

They winded around on the dirt path, and Mirri stopped short. A door. Up ahead, a round, brown door, complete with a tiny window in the center was visible, but just barely. His door led right *into* the hill.

Impressed, Mirri followed Kane to Pattick's home. Looking around, she stepped up the stone steps and followed the trail to his front door.

Kane knocked politely on the door, towering over the entrance. Mirri looked up at the tall centaur, wondering how he was supposed to fit in Pattick's hut.

The door creaked open. "Ah, Kane, is there news?" The same hairless green rabbit stepped out, dragging his ears behind him, his wooden spectacles perched on top of his head.

"May we come in ?" Kane asked.

"Yes, yes, of course, forgive me!" He laughed a throaty laugh and opened the door wide for them.

Kane gestured for Mirri to enter first, and she stepped into the dim hut. She stood to the side with her hands clasped in front of her, squinting through the darkness, while Kane leaned down and wedged himself through the small door.

A click and light filled the room as Pattick stepped away from the lantern hanging on a large stick. The lantern sent light in every direction, in all different colors, illuminating the dark room, as Mirri looked around with wide eyes. An enormous bookshelf lined one wall, reaching all the way to the slanted ceiling. The shelf must have contained hundreds of books, various trinkets, and small statues.

The wall on the opposite side held various flat stones sticking straight out, making perfect shelves for more fascinating and intricate objects Mirri could not identify. Up above, bits of earth and roots stretched down toward them, like humongous drips of grass and frozen mud.

A cluttered desk sat in one corner, filled with papers, more antiques, and a round object on a pedestal. Tools sat in the center of the desk, as if Mirri and Kane had interrupted Pattick working on a project.

Mirri wandered over the dirt floor, covered in leaves and random bits of earth, and gazed around in wonderment. Carvings of intriguing creatures stood in corners, and an amazing trunk on wheels sat next to the bookshelf. A basket filled with stone pots sat next to the desk. Bits and pieces of objects, treasures, and anything Mirri could dream of lay scattered all around this tiny room.

"Mirri?" Kane interrupted Mirri's state of amazement.

"Sorry?" She laughed. "I just can't believe these things . . . Where did you find all of this?" she asked.

Pattick laughed and hobbled over to her. "These are my life's treasures. What do you think?" He looked around the hut, a smile on his face.

"I think . . . I could spend days in this room. Your things, they are *amazing*," Mirri breathed. Sitting on the desk was a small wooden box, delicately carved with the most beautiful symbol on top. Mirri ran her finger along the carving, unable to comprehend the time it had taken to make such an intricate design.

"Yes, my father and I had quite the knack for treasure hunting," he said, resting both hands on the cane in front of him.

Mirri was examining the stone trunk next to the shelf when a tiny reflection of light bounced off the shelf between two dirty books. Mirri's brow furrowed as she reached for the light, moving the books apart and pulling out a small stone. It was as smooth as silk, bright white, and in the shape one might call a star . . . A lopsided star. Mirri turned the stone, gasping as the color of the stone changed. It was now a pleasant green with a hint of yellows. She tilted it again, toward the light, and let it change again, to a bright purple mixed with blue.

"Wow. What's this?" She held the stone up to Pattick, who stood behind the crowded desk, digging through a drawer.

Pattick called to Mirri from across the room. "Find another treasure?"

Mirri held the stone up for him to see.

He glanced in her direction with his glasses still perched on his head. "Why don't you keep it, dear? Think of it as a makra charm. Good energy." He nodded to her as he dropped the tools into a bucket next to his desk, making a loud racket.

"Oh, no, I couldn't." Mirri set it back on the shelf.

"No, please, I insist. Nothing would make me prouder than knowing the Keeper was holding one of my treasures."

Mirri smiled and pocketed the oddly shaped stone, thinking she could use every bit of good luck possible.

Kane cleared his throat. "As I was saying?"

Pattick turned back to him. "Correct! We must focus! Ah, I get so distracted in this old age," he chuckled, shaking his green head.

"Sorry," Mirri said to Kane. "Let's focus."

"A portal! You say you need a portal?" Pattick pulled his wooden spectacles down to his eyes, and he turned back toward his desk. "Let's see, Holmforth, Holmforth . . ." he muttered to himself, flipping through pages of a crusty-looking notebook. "No, not that one." He shoved the notebook aside and picked up another. He began thumbing through the pages slowly, running his finger down each page.

Mirri gazed around the room, wishing her father could see this place. He would have loved these carved works of art, especially after he had tried to take up wood carving. Hadn't gotten very far with it, and he and Mirri often joked and laughed at his wooden works of art more than they admired them.

She picked up a pair of spectacles missing one lens. The carving work here was impressive—the arms of the glasses that fit around

Pattick's ears were carved to look like tree bark. They were exquisite. If only her father could see them, Mirri thought sadly to herself.

"Haven't been to Holmforth in quite a while!" Pattick announced. "Going to check below!"

Grabbing his cane, he made his way slowly toward the corner of the room. Mirri watched as his long ears rustled the leaves and dirt that lay all over the floor, creating a little dust cloud behind him as he walked.

"Help an old rabbit out, will you, Kane?"

Kane nodded and stepped to Pattick, moving at an extremely odd angle, keeping his upper body stooped over to avoid the earth that seeped in from the ceiling, but he hadn't complained once.

"Right there, son. Yes, grab that right there. Now pull!"

A creak, a puff of dirt, and a section of dirt floor lifted.

Pattick pulled a dusty cloth from a shelf and began coughing into it. "My, my, haven't been down here in a while. Might take me a minute or two to get back up, all right?" he said, nodding to Mirri.

Probably take longer than a minute, Mirri thought.

"Why don't you let me go down?" She wasn't sure this guy could get down there in his condition. Or worse, he wouldn't be able to get back *up*.

Pattick scratched the tuft of white hair on top of his head. "Yes, I suppose a young body would be a better idea."

Mirri peered down in to the hole. "Uh, what—what do you need?" It didn't look too deep, more like an over-sized wormhole that ran below his hut. Mirri swallowed. It was quite dark in there.

"There should be a trunk, dear. Not too far down." He reached up to a shelf and pulled down a strange curved object with a ring on top, blowing off a thick layer of dust. "Use this, dear." He sat the object on Mirri's shoulder, and it lit up instantly, adhering itself to the curvature of her upper arm.

Mirri raised her eyebrows. "Wow. What do you call this thing?"

"A Snackree light device. Had it for years," he added, adjusting the device. "There."

Mirri gave a small smile and peered down at the dark hole. She swallowed. Don't be silly, she admonished herself. You have been in much worse places. She took a deep breath and lowered herself into the hole until only her waist was above ground. Giving Kane one last glance, she forced a smile and ducked into the tunnel.

CHAPTER EIGHT

Down on her hands and knees, Mirri crawled through the tiny hole, feeling her back rubbing against the dirt and roots above her. She coughed, pulling her shirt up over her nose. The foul stench of animal remains filled the hole, and Mirri's stomach did a cartwheel as she thought about what dead creature might be down here with her.

She crawled slowly, wishing she had thought to take the cloak off. It kept tugging at her neck as Mirri slowly made her way further into the tunnel. The unmistakable sound of wood splitting filled the tunnel, and Mirri winced, hoping she had not destroyed some priceless relic Pattick had collected. She moved aside roots hanging in her way as she went and tried to keep her eyes peeled for other objects littering the ground.

Mirri's mind began to fill with images of being stuck down here, a prisoner in a tunnel barely big enough to hold her own body . . . spiders, rats, or worse . . . crawling all over her paralyzed body. Taking a deep breath, she forced the thoughts out of her mind. She ignored her racing heart and concentrated on keeping her breathing even.

She yelped as her hand cracked through something hard, stabbing at her palm. Leaning at an awkward angle, Mirri turned her shoulder to angle the small beam of light to the ground. She examined the curves of what looked like half of a cream-colored mask.

She held a piece of the mask, guilt gripping her insides, when the Snacktree (or whatever it was called) device flickered. Mirri fiddled with the light, wishing she knew how it worked. To be plunged into complete darkness, under the earth among rodents and insects, sounded horrifying. The light flickered again, and Mirri's breath caught in her throat as the light disappeared, swallowing her whole. She felt her pulse quicken and the sweat form at her neckline. She shut her eyes and crawled quickly, no longer caring if she broke some forgotten antique, and collided with something large, causing her heart to jump.

Feeling the wood, she recognized the shape of a trunk. Breathing a sigh of relief, Mirri found a handle and tugged. It seemed heavy but doable. Mirri clenched her teeth, knowing there was no way she could turn around in here. So instead, she crawled backward, inch by inch, then reached forward and tugged the trunk handle toward her. After only a few minutes, the pain in her back had risen to her neck, the trunk continued to get caught on low-hanging roots, and sweat began dripping into her eyes.

Mirri silently swore at the cloak, cursing herself for not taking it off sooner. It stuck under the trunk, tugging her neck backward, attempting to strangle her. She had to get out of this hole. Now. She began crawling faster, ready to tear her cloak off her neck, until finally, she bumped into the wall behind her.

Mirri clambered out of the hole, taking Kane's outstretched hand. He pulled her up in one fluid motion, and Mirri fell into him, taking heaving breaths. She stood there a moment, hoping he didn't see the tears running down her cheeks. Kane kept his arms around her, and she let herself relax into his bare chest, trying to calm her fluttering heart.

Mirri stepped back, wrapping her arms around herself. "Thanks," she whispered, pushing her hair behind her ears. He picked up her cloak, which had fallen on the floor, and wrapped it around her neck.

Kane reached down into the hole and pulled the trunk out easily. It fell with a *thud* onto the dirt floor, splaying matted leaves and twigs up off the stamped ground. Mirri stepped around the dome-top trunk, admiring the antique. She ran her hand along the top, feeling the smoothness of the aged wood. The trunk was carved out of a kind of cherry wood—even dirty, Mirri could see the richness of the red-brown color. The small lock looked flimsy and fake—it may be interesting, but it wouldn't keep anyone out.

"I think we've got it!" Pattick announced and flipped open the trunk. Years' worth of dust wafted into the air as Mirri stepped back, waving her hand.

Pattick pulled out a large, heavy-looking book and flipped it open. He flipped through the stained and crunchy pages madly, and Mirri cringed as a page ripped in half. Several colored tabs stuck out of pages on the top, bottom, and side of the pages.

"Here we are," he said, running his green finger down a page.

Mirri turned to peer in the trunk. Several enormous books, a thick stick with holes down the side, and little dulled trinkets she longed to reach out and examine sat covered in dust. Imagine what she could find in this dusty, magical trunk.

Mirri reached toward the trunk just before Pattick slammed the lid shut. "Sorry about that, dear. Did I hurt you?" Pattick asked with his nose in the book.

Mirri shrugged, vowing to keep her hands to herself from now on.

Pattick leaned on his cane, struggling to stand. "All right, you two, step to the napran!"

Mirri gave Kane a curious glance.

He smiled. "This way." He stepped to the center of the room, and Mirri followed.

Pattick limped to his desk and heaved the heavy book down on top, wide open. He leaned over and pulled out a small suitcase, setting it on the desk heavily. He stopped to take a breath.

"My," Pattick said, wiping his forehead. "Sorry, you two, we're going to have to do this the old-fashioned way."

Pattick opened the latch on the suitcase, setting the lid upright, and Mirri craned her neck to see the interior. Her eyes widened as she watched Pattick fiddle with the various knobs, dials, and what looked like a compass. He flipped a gold lever, and numbers appeared on a small screen. Maybe they were numbers. They were like no numbers Mirri had ever seen. Possibly letters?

Pattick disappeared under the desk, then popped up, holding a small gold piece on a long chain. It was an odd shape, sort of like a small golden spiral. He inserted the gold necklace into the suitcase and fiddled with a control while studying the book in front of him. He turned a dial to the left, just a touch, and looked up with a smile.

"All right, I think we've done it!" he announced, clapping his hands together. He turned the necklace from its position in the suitcase and pulled it out. "Here you go!" Pattick tossed the chain across the room toward Kane's outstretched hand.

Kane put the strange necklace over his head as Mirri reached out and grabbed his arm. She swallowed nervously, having no idea what to expect from the ancient suitcase.

"Ready now, you two? You know how it goes, Kane. Let me know when you are ready to return."

Pattick hopped up on the desk and opened another cabinet. From there, he pulled two large, green and red wires out and connected them to either side of the suitcase, the other ends staying stuck in the cabinet.

Pattick pressed one last button and called out, "Good luck!"

A spark, a bang, and the hut around Mirri disappeared.

❖

Mirri got up slowly, reaching for Kane's outstretched hand. She stood, pulling her cloak tightly around her, shivering. What she would give for her skiing jacket.

They appeared on a dusty path surrounded by abandoned huts, huts that, at one time, Mirri could tell, had been warm and inviting. She gazed around, taking in the rotting wood, caved-in roofs, and musty smell.

"This is Holmforth? Kind of spooky, huh?" she asked through chattering teeth. The sun was setting, making a chilly day even colder.

"Yes. This is where my family is from. Avi lived here, too." He glanced at her. "Your grandfather, right?"

Mirri gave a nervous laugh. "Uh, yeah, I guess. Still sounds pretty strange, though." She wiped her running nose with the back of her hand. "It's so quiet. "

They began walking down the dirt road that ran between the homes. Mirri studied each house as they passed, taking in the wooden porches and archways. This all seemed so familiar.

"Wait a minute—I've been here," Mirri muttered, gazing around.

There—the row of bleached pickets that leaned up against that house. Mirri remembered thinking she and her friends could hide under it. The house across the way—Mirri recognized the hole in the window of the second floor. It made a perfect circle—like someone had thrown a golf ball through.

"This is where my mother grew up?" Mirri asked in amazement.

Kane nodded. "Yes. I believe Avi's hut is in the center of town." He pointed down the road. "The centaur's huts are further down. My uncle told me stories of how they built this town. Let me show you Avi's home. Your mother's."

Mirri followed behind, holding the cloak at her neck. "So, your uncle is from here, too?"

"Yes. Theodisis and my father built the house themselves."

Mirri stopped. "Theodisis is your uncle?"

"Yes," Kane said shortly.

"Oh." Mirri wasn't sure what to say. She couldn't very well tell Kane his uncle had to come to Graynard's hut, screaming for her arrest, ordering the other centaurs to destroy an elf's hut. He was an arrogant, self-centered jerk whom Mirri despised. She couldn't tell Kane that, either.

Kane sighed as they walked through the empty, quiet village. "He is not the best of uncles."

"Well, at least yours wasn't an evil tyrant that took an entire village as her slaves."

"Yes, you are right." He smiled. "Maybe I feel better about my family now."

He pointed to the left. "I believe this is Avi's home."

Mirri's heart beat faster. She stopped in front of the quaint, grayed-out house and stared. Sun-bleached boards stuck out in various angles about the house, as if someone had tried to pry their way into Avi's living room. An arched window sat next to the door, cracked and peeling white paint covering the frame. A lone tree, gnarled and brown, waved in the breeze next to the porch with the missing railing.

Mirri imagined a clean, white paint covering the house and a full, green tree with blooms to sit under. Children laughing, their father sitting on a rocking chair on the porch. Maybe spreading a blanket in the front yard to have a picnic. Her mother had spent her childhood here, grown up within these walls. It all seemed too unreal.

Mirri took a hesitant step forward. She stepped up onto the porch, looking down as the wood creaked under her feet. She could imagine her mother here, entering her house at curfew time. Maybe sneaking in occasionally? Sitting on the railing laughing? Grasping the front doorknob, Mirri paused, then pushed the door open to get her first look into her mother's childhood.

Mirri peered in the dimly lit room, still gripping the doorknob. The only light came from the setting sun, barely shining through the dirty windows. Decay and mustiness surrounded Mirri and flowed out around her, seeping out into the village. She took a deep breath, ignoring the smell, and stepped through the doorway.

Stillness. Mirri stood in the room and gazed around. The hearth that stood around the fireplace bore ancient, wide cracks, and held inches of soot and dust. A large vase sat on the hearth, cobwebs holding it steady to the wooden fireplace below. Two chairs sat around the fireplace with cushions sewn out of yarn. One cushion had a gaping hole in the center, most likely the meal of a rodent or animal.

A small rug woven in a circular fashion lay on the floor between the chairs. At one time, it would have been beautiful—it must have included every color of the rainbow. Now stains and muck overcame its beauty, with strands of yarn trailing out the sides and more holes to match the cushions.

To her left was a simple square wooden table with four chairs seated around it. In the middle of the table sat a lone glass jar, too dirty for Mirri to see what was inside. A bookshelf sat behind the table, rows and rows of books covered in a fine layer of dust and dirt. Mirri normally would have longed to examine them, but at the moment, she was lost in time.

She jumped as the floor creaked behind her. Kane had entered the room behind her, the aged wooden floor moaning in protest.

Mirri stepped forward, moving toward a narrow hall, barely daring to breathe. She passed a door on her left that came up to knee height. Leaning over to grasp the handle, Mirri turned the knob. It stayed where it was, hidden away from her prying eyes.

Mirri frowned, wondering what could hide in the small door, then continued toward the door that stood wide open. She stopped in the doorway, gazing around at the small bedroom, imagining her mother lying on one of the small beds in either corner. Both had a quilt lying neatly across the bed, with a pillow resting at one end. Mirri squinted her eyes, trying to discern which bed was her mother's. One quilt was yellow and red, the other yellow and blue. Blue was her mother's favorite color.

A large dresser stood in the corner, holding up a large mirror, cracks running down through the glass at various angles. A lone picture frame stood in the dresser's corner. Mirri carefully picked up a wooden frame, bringing the cobwebs and dirt with her. Using a corner of the cloak, Mirri wiped away the dust to see a handsome man with graying hair standing behind two girls, seated in different chairs. One had frizzy hair sitting on her shoulders, the other dark hair that ran down her back.

It was her mother's family. Her sister and father. Avi and Lavinia. Mirri stood, dumbfounded, staring at the picture of her mother as a young woman standing next to her sister. Had they gotten along? Or did they fight all the time? Was Lavinia horrible to her sister, as horrible as she had been when Mirri met her?

Mirri touched the glass, reluctant to set down the picture. She bit her lip, wishing she had a bag to stow it in. But she sat the picture back down in the clean spot it had left on the dresser. Mirri gazed around at the room her mother must have shared with Lavinia.

The floor let out another loud creak, a sign that Kane had entered behind her. "I believe I know where they found Avi," he said in a hushed voice.

"Right," Mirri murmured, looking around her mother's childhood bedroom, reluctant to leave. It had never occurred to her how little she knew of her mother's childhood. Mirri longed to stay, to lie under the quilt her mother once slept under, or peek in the dresser to look at a piece of clothing her mother might have worn. Mirri could feel her here, in this very room. It's funny. She felt closer to her mother in this dusty and empty place than she had ever felt in her life.

Kane put a hand on her back, leading her out of the room. It's possible he understood, maybe even sensed Mirri's reluctance to leave. She let Kane steer her away from her mother's presence when his right hoof stepped directly through the wooden floor. Mirri yelped in surprise, putting a hand on her chest. He swayed back and forth, trying to keep his balance with one foot down underneath the house and three feet in. With some struggling, he and Mirri finally removed the board behind the hole, Kane removing his wedged hoof from the hole.

They stepped into the hall carefully, now knowing that the wooden floor did not appreciate the weight of a half-horse half-man. Kane ducked under the next doorframe, Mirri pausing in the hall. Could this be his room? The man, the legend that she fought for, risked her life, and read his innermost thoughts? Mirri crept in the door, holding her breath.

A large bed sat under a window with a stained white curtain hanging over it. A picture of a woman was sitting on a dresser in another wooden frame. Mirri stopped to stare at the woman in the picture with her long dark hair flowing around her shoulders, and a small smile on her soft face. Was this her grandmother?

She jumped when Kane spoke into the stillness. "It is said that they found Avi lying next to his bed, with the beads around his neck." He was staring down at the empty floor next to the bed.

The murder location. She felt a small chill run through her body. Someone had taken their last breath right here where she stood. They stood there, staring at the dust covering the ground, Mirri trying to picture the moments that led up to Avi's death. Did he struggle? Was it a fight until the end? But nothing came to her mind. No feelings of closeness, no foreshadowing of the future. No instinct, telling her who had done the horrible deed while she stood in the exact place where he died. Just . . . nothing.

The room was just an empty room. Nothing was amiss, nothing wrong with the surroundings. Not surprising, considering this happened over one hundred years ago.

Mirri suddenly felt foolish. What had they expected? Bloody footprints? The murderer's hair and fingerprints lying all over the place? She chewed on her bottom lip, trying not to show her disappointment, then turned to walk away. A crunch under her foot made her stop in her tracks, too scared to breathe.

"What was that?" Mirri whispered, looking up at Kane. His eyes had gone wide, perhaps as excited as she was at the thought of finding a clue.

She slowly raised her foot and held it in the air, holding the footboard of the bed. Gently, she reached down and swiped at the bottom of her sneaker. Little crumbs of something came off in her hand.

Carefully, Mirri stepped aside and squatted down. "I think it's glass. But just a little of it."

"What does that mean?" Kane asked, bending down to look.

Mirri paused. "I don't know. I guess it could mean nothing. Something glass broke right here." She lifted the corner of the quilt. Crouching down further, she peered under the bed. More dust, and perhaps a few more glass shards.

She stood and peeked out the curtain to the window behind Avi's bed. It was still intact with no cracks. Nothing seemed out of place or suspicious. Mirri sighed. "Let's keep looking."

After investigating the only other room in the house, the bathroom, Mirri and Kane returned to the living area. "This is pointless," Mirri grumbled. "Like we were really going to find anything."

"I agree. Let's look around the village while we're here," Kane said.

As they exited the silent house, Mirri stopped to scan the room one last time. There must be something, she thought to herself. Anything. Her eyes landed on the wall above the fireplace. Something had hung there. The wall had a cleaner look to it, less dust, right there above the mantle.

Quickly, she stepped to the fireplace and stood on her tiptoes. The coloring of the wall was brighter here. In the shape of . . . a circle, maybe. She studied the wall above the fireplace, determined to find some clue, some hint that others had missed. Her eyes fell to the floor, examining the rotting floorboards around her. Some streaks in the dust, but not a single footprint besides her own.

"It looks like something hung here," Mirri said.

Kane joined her in front of the mantle. "This is where the Mahara Deity hung. It was stolen the night Avi was killed."

"The Mahara Deity," Mirri muttered. "I assume it's important?"

"Well, yes. It is a symbol of life and death for my people. It always hangs in the leader's home. They left the deity hanging even after the town was evacuated."

"Evacuated?"

"Yes. Avi was killed after they evacuated Holmforth. He came back here to summon Gwenna." He paused, still looking at the empty place on the wall. "Or so I am told."

Mirri nodded, chewing on her bottom lip. So Gwenna came back to Holmforth after they evacuated the town. So, who were these witnesses that placed her mother at the scene? She made a mental note to address this point, nodding to herself.

It was something, she thought. Right? But was it? She shook her head, gritting her teeth. Kryptus wanted her to come here to find the truth. She hung her head as they exited the house. Right now, the truth seemed so far out of her reach.

Chapter Nine

With every step through the town, Mirri became more and more discouraged. She was not some ace detective with cunning skills, merely a teenager who occasionally went on a Law and Order binge-watching marathon. Why did Kryptus think she could solve a murder that happened 109 years ago? How could anyone?

They reached the end of the dirt path and the last run-down hut. A field of golden grass lay ahead of them, stretching out toward a forest. She had failed Kryptus. She could not prove it was not her mother who killed Avi. Mirri wearily suggested it was time to go back, then stopped.

"Did you hear that?"

Kane stopped and looked around. "No. What?"

Mirri strained her ears. "A humming noise. You don't hear that?" She turned and walked toward the field, her interest piqued. Something interesting, finally.

She turned toward the end of the road, walking past the last abandoned hut and into the field with overgrown grass. She stopped and listened, desperate to hear the noise again.

"Yes, I hear it!" Kane said. "Hurry!" He galloped off, leaving Mirri to run after him. They made their way through the dense field, pushing their way through the thick yellow grass to the base of a hill. The humming intensified, stretching toward the forest. Kane bounded up the hill, barely containing his glee, but Mirri stopped short.

Could something evil be lurking up there, something dark with cruel intentions? It didn't matter, she reminded herself. They had to investigate every possibility. Ignoring the shiver that ran down her back, Mirri climbed the grassy hill and stopped next to Kane. She stared while breathing heavily, her eyes widening at the sight in front of them.

"What are they?" she whispered.

"I believe they are insects. I have never seen them before."

"They're so cute," Mirri murmured, staring at the yellow, ribbon-like bugs. Their golden tails stretched down into a delicate curl, with strange green antennae stretching far above their heads. They hovered over a small patch of green a few feet in front of them. Slowly, the insects turned to stare at Mirri, forming a tight circle, and held their position, staring. The insects were studying them.

Surprising even herself, Mirri stepped toward the field of mystery bugs. As she stepped between them, they leaned and nuzzled against her as if trying to remember her scent, to imprint it into their minds. She reached out and stroked the body of the mysterious yellow insect, running her fingers over the velvet-soft skin. It seemed to sigh in pleasure, its wings fluttering furiously as if it enjoyed Mirri's touch. Smaller curls protruded off the body, up the ribbon as Mirri stroked them.

Mirri looked back at Kane in surprise. He still stood on the edge of the field, looking uneasy.

"It's okay," Mirri called. "I think . . . I think they are nice." She held her hand up to the bug. "Watch!"

"Mirri, I don't think you should—"

The bug leaned into her hand, almost as if it was sniffing her. She giggled. "Really, Kane, it's no big—"

Mirri gasped as the bug wrapped itself around Mirri's hand. Tight. Mirri's heart jumped, and she immediately tugged at her arm with her other hand. She yelped as another leaned over and took her upper arm in its clenches.

"Hey!" Mirri cried out. She struggled against the insects. All over bugs were stretching out, reaching for her, winding their thin ribbon-like bodies around her extremities in a painful grasp. The small, thin insects had a powerful grip and wound their thin bodies up and down Mirri's arms.

"Mirri!" Kane yelled.

"Help me!" she gasped, yanking at the bugs.

Kane galloped in, beating and pulling at the yellow bodies and wings along with Mirri. But they stretched further and further, like a bizarre piece of chewing gum, refusing to release Mirri from their grip.

The field began to spin in front of Mirri. Bright colors danced in front of her eyes, making beautiful shapes and rainbows. She could hear Kane's booming voice in the background, somewhere far away. Exhaustion washed over Mirri, so sudden and strong that she let herself fall into the field, away from Kane, away from bugs, away from everything.

"Mirri, wake up!" she could hear Kane's booming voice, somewhere far away, but didn't care. She would only close her eyes for a minute.

Mirri took in a sharp breath and opened her eyes. She stared at the sunset over the trees, enjoying the vibrant colors that stretched through the trees. Mirri yawned and turned, dipping her hand in the cool creek running next to her. Water flowed gently over rocks, making a deliciously relaxing noise. She smiled and let the cold water run over her hands, basking in the tranquility of this quiet place.

Wait a minute. Mirri's eyes snapped open, and she sat up in one motion. *Trees. Forest. A creek.* Mirri's eyes traveled over her surroundings. No, no, this was not where she was supposed to be in the world.

"Kane?" she whispered.

She took a small step forward, then another, and noticed how her feet didn't make any sounds as they moved over dead leaves and brush. She stopped and looked around. Where was she?

And then she was there A young woman, probably eighteen or nineteen, running barefoot through the forest, a white gown billowing around her in the wind. A long, beaded necklace bounced against her chest as she ran. Her red hair was down to the middle of her back, her eyes wide with excitement.

Mirri moved to follow the young woman but was having a difficult time telling her legs to move. She fell toward the ground, slower than a falling body should, but instead of feeling the harsh earth, it felt more like she landed on a soft pillow. Mirri rolled over on her back and stared at the sky. It was so beautiful, the setting sun over the clouds. She could just lie here forever, she decided. The stream next to her made a lovely trickling sound. Closing her eyes, Mirri smiled and listened to the relaxing sounds of nature all around her.

"Mirri!"

Her name. In the distance. But she was so tired . . . Galloping. Kane? Had he found her? She could hear something large running toward her. Mirri turned, still lying on the ground, and watched the centaur and young woman with the red hair running, but this time running toward her. He was familiar, this centaur, with his brown hair and his dark eyes . . . But he looked so young.

The centaur turned and motioned with his hand. "Hurry!" he demanded. The young woman was gasping as she ran; fresh tear tracks ran past her chin. She carried something in her hands. Something small, like a tennis ball wrapped in a cloth.

"Wait! I'm coming!" she gasped as the centaur galloped off.

The girl stumbled and fell, grabbing at her long nightgown. Her necklace was gone. She pushed herself to her feet and ran straight for Mirri. Mirri held up her hand and waved it at the running girl.

The girl ran for Mirri head-on and breezed straight through her.

Mirri gasped as the woman's body connected with her own. It was the strangest sensation—like she could feel her pain, like she could feel the girl's beating heart next to her own. She had been crying. Mirri touched her own cheek, not sure if they were her tears or the girl's.

Confused, Mirri hurried after them, trying to keep the sounds of the centaur's hooves in her ears.

"Kryptus, please! Slow down!" the young woman called.

Mirri ran toward the voice, desperate to hear more. Hopping over a puddle, Mirri ran, skidding to a halt when she heard the quiet whimpering. Ducking under a low-hanging branch, she stopped short, not at first seeing the large centaur body directly in front of her.

"It is because of her, is it not? Rose? That awful woman?"

The centaur took the young girl's chin in his hand. "You are very young, and in time will find true love. I am not this love." He kissed her on the forehead. "Goodbye, child."

"No! Kryptus! She is a fraud and a witch! You are too good for her!" She held tight to his hand, unwilling to let him leave.

"Enough. You must accept the truth. Rose is my one true love, and always will be."

"No!" she screamed.

Mirri gasped as the light soared from the young girl's hand. A light so bright, so powerful, yet she felt no need to cover her eyes. Kryptus and the girl were thrown backward from the bright green light—the girl landing roughly on the forest floor, and Kryptus being thrown into a thick tree, leaves falling all around him.

"Kryptus," the girl moaned, sitting up slowly and holding her hand to her head. She stood shakily, her head turning in all directions.

Mirri continued to watch from her place under the tree, vaguely aware of her heart hammering against her chest. What had she just witnessed?

Kryptus stood, slamming his halberd into the ground to gain his footing. He looked to the ground and moaned, putting his head in his hands.

On the ground in front of him lay a glittering sea of green sparkles. The white cloth lay helplessly amid the green gems, a bland object lying among the glowing ground.

Kryptus turned toward the girl with a look of pure disbelief. "What have you done?" he screamed.

"Mirri!"

Mirri's eyes popped open, and she let out a strangled gasp. Her hands immediately went to her cheeks, feeling her face, her eyes.

Kane kneeled above her, his face twisted in fear, his hands on her shoulders.

"Mirri! Say something!"

"Kane, I'm okay," she managed to choke out. She grabbed at his muscular forearms and sat up. They were in the field, the yellow grass and tumbleweeds surrounding them. She was lying on the ground, her cloak wrapped tightly around her body. Mirri turned her head in the direction of the running girl. Where had she gone?

The sun shone down brightly, and birds chirped in the distance. "What happened? I was—I was not here, and the girl was running," Mirri said. She looked directly at Kane. "Where is the girl? Did you see her?"

"What girl?" The look in Kane's eyes was confusion mixed with terror. "The insects. Do you remember the insects?"

Mirri stopped and stared into his eyes. Insects? Why on earth would he be thinking of bugs at a time like this? The girl . . . the centaur . . .

Wait—the bugs. Yellow and glowing. She could remember how they felt on her skin. Squeezing her. Mirri looked down at her hands. "What did they do to me?" she whispered.

"They attacked you. I tried pulling them, I tried pulling you. I picked you up and ran, and suddenly, they just let go." Kane picked Mirri up off the ground. He put both hands on her shoulders. "I just ran, ran here as far as I could get before I put you down. You weren't moving or speaking. I was afraid you were lost to me."

Mirri turned slowly, taking in her surroundings. It was daylight. There was no stream next to her. She put a hand to her forehead. "It was a girl and a centaur running for something. But it was the forest, I—I was next to a stream." She looked up at the centaur. "What just happened to me? How did I see her?"

"Who?" Kane demanded. "Who was it?"

"It was . . . my mother."

◆

They trudged through the forest in silent defeat.

The comdahl, Kane had called it, was gone. The device Pattick had given them to portal home. Kane had no idea when he lost it but assumed it was ripped off his neck when he was battling the glowing insects. They did not know how to get to the village, nor any idea which direction to go in. No espy, like Mirri had used last year in Althord, and no map to guide them.

Mirri hiked in silence next to Kane, her mind reeling. She needed to think. Kane insisted she needed rest after her encounter with the insects, that she could still experience side effects. When Mirri refused to sit and rest, he suggested she ride on his back. Mirri had repeatedly told the centaur she was fine and did not need a bodyguard.

They had argued about which direction to take, and Mirri made her claim that she had been in this forest not even a year ago and knew her way around better. Kane insisted on following the path, and Mirri flat-out refused, saying it was faster to cut through the forest. They had not followed a path the last time she had made it through the woods. Finally, they reached an agreement and began trudging through the forest to the south, Mirri walking next to the centaur.

Mirri couldn't stop replaying the images in her head. The girl in the white nightgown, the length of beads around her neck. And what had she been carrying when she came back? *Without the beads,* Mirri thought grimly. The centaur—his gray horse's body and his short brown hair. Kryptus had been in her memory. Kryptus and her mother . . . running away from something . . . without the beads. Why was Kryptus with her mother? And what had her mother done? Some kind of power? Mirri couldn't stop hearing Kryptus's voice in her head. The anger, the blame—Mirri had never known Kryptus to lose control like that. The glittering gems scattered over the forest floor . . . Could those have been the Cristalli? Another Cristalli?

She had seen a memory. A piece of the past. That Mirri and Kane both agreed on. The bugs had given her some memory. It was the only thing that made sense. But it didn't make sense. Why had she seen that memory?

And her mother. Had Esperanze cured her? Was she in danger, sitting in the crazy woman's hut with only Jinx for protection? Mirri couldn't fight the feeling that something important was happening right now to her mother, and she was not there to protect her.

Night was threatening to take over, and Mirri's stomach growled in protest. She sighed and looked around. "There's no way we'll be able to make it through the forest at night. We should probably find somewhere to rest until the sun comes back up."

Kane stopped beside her and sighed as well. "I agree. The forest is much too dense in this area."

They found a small clearing, and Kane insisted he would stay awake and keep watch. Mirri argued this as well, saying nothing was hunting them this time. "Just go to sleep already, all right?" she snapped at him.

His insistence on being her protector and treating her like a fragile flower was getting on her nerves. She had already made it through this forest once and had done it with an elf and Loofa. Protection, she did not require. All she required was a way to get back to her mother.

They sat in the clearing, facing away from each other. The tension that filled the area was overbearing, and soon, Mirri began to feel a bit of guilt seeping in. There were worse traits than being protective, she decided. He had saved her. And he *was* a centaur. This is what they did.

Mirri turned to lean against a log so she could see Kane's face. He sat, stonily staring off into the distance.

Leaning her head back, she decided to break the ice. "What was it like growing up with Theodisis as an uncle?"

Kane shrugged but said nothing. Mirri bit her lip. "Is your father in the village? Is he one of the guards?"

"My father died in the battles. Theo is his brother."

Mirri paused. So many fathers. Gone. "I'm sorry."

Kane turned slightly so he was almost facing Mirri. "My mother expected Uncle Theo to step in and act as my father, as is our tradition. But he did not care about tradition." Kane crossed his arms. "He expected me to worship him at every cost. But he is not a centaur *worthy* of worship."

Mirri cringed, worried that she had only made Kane angrier. She wished she had kept her mouth shut.

"What of your family?" he asked, looking at her for the first time since they had sat down.

"It's just me and my mom. My father passed away last year."

"I am sorry as well."

Their conversation stalled again. Mirri put a fingernail in her mouth and chewed. "Do you think she's all right?" she whispered into the silence.

"Yes. Kryptus is a strong leader. He will protect her."

Mirri nodded and pulled her legs up to her chest. How she hoped he was right. She squeezed her eyes shut tight and let a tear leak out.

"I'm scared for her, Kane."

He leaned over and put an arm around her. "We shall reach your mother, Mirri. I promise."

Mirri nodded and leaned her head into his chest. She closed her eyes and breathed in his musky centaur scent.

She would hold him to that promise.

Chapter Ten

Mirri looked around, surprised. Holmforth. Maybe. She was alone on the dirt road, the houses still. The sun was just peaking up over the roof in front of her. But all the houses stood intact: straight whiteboards built up behind steady porches, with no holes in the roofs or cracked windows. She jumped as a centaur marched toward the house she stood in front of and pounded on the door.

The door opened a crack. The red-haired girl peered out, and the sigh she gave was audible. Gwenna.

Mirri stared at Gwenna. Was this another memory? A dream? Deciding she did not care, Mirri hurried toward the house eagerly. Stepping up to the first step on the porch next to the centaur, she watched in fascination.

Gwenna opened the door, a frown already imprinted on her face. "What is it?" she asked.

"I need to speak to your father. He asked me to meet him."

Without waiting for an invitation, he pushed the door back and stepped through the doorway, holding his halberd in his right hand. He pushed Gwenna back into the room, ignoring the icy stare she gave him.

Mirri stared at the centaur holding the halberd. Blonde hair, brown horse's body. It was Theodisis.

"He is not here. So you may leave now." Gwenna put a hand on her hip and stood at the open door. She made a gesture with one arm, one that plainly meant 'get out of here now.'

Theodisis smirked. "It is a meeting which he called. So I believe I will stay. It must be terribly important." He leaned back against a wall and stared at her, his arms crossed. "I will force myself to remain in the same room with you for a while longer."

Mirri stepped into the room quickly and stood in the corner, plastered against a wall. Her eyes swung between her mother and Theodisis, eager to see this little tirade play out.

Gwenna glared at the centaur. "He was called to the forest. A Maylark's life is in danger. He will not be back for some time. I'm afraid your little *meeting* will have to wait." She reached to the table and grabbed her satchel, throwing the long strap over her shoulder. "Goodbye. I must see to the Maylark now." She called over her shoulder as she stepped onto the porch.

"I shall accompany you." Theodisis strode to the front door and stepped onto the porch as it creaked under his immense weight.

"No, you shall not," Gwenna said through gritted teeth. "Father summoned me, not one of his arrogant, pompous guards."

She turned and strode down the steps, flipping her red hair behind her.

Theodisis laughed and followed behind her, using his halberd as a walking stick.

Mirri hurried after, pausing to decide whether she should close the door behind her. But what did it matter? She jogged to catch up with them, eager to hear their conversation. Was there a reason her mother hated Theodisis as she did?

"No, it would be silly of me to ignore a request of my ruler. I shall protect you in the forest and assure that Avi needs no assistance," Theodisis said.

Gwenna rolled her eyes up in her head. "Yes, I'm sure you would ever protect me from danger, Theo."

Mirri followed, a frown on her face. Theodisis insisted on walking beside Gwenna, making her walk off the side of the path, forcing her to steer around bushes and thorny shrubs. Mirri watched Gwenna trip and put her hand down on the trail. Her satchel became stuck in the bush she had stepped over, and Gwenna stopped to unwind it from the thorns.

Mirri glared at the back of the centaur's head as she followed. How dare he be so rude to her mother, the daughter of Avi, for crying out loud?

"You know, for a guard," Gwenna grunted as she yanked on the satchel, "you're not—very—helpful." She finally freed the purse and ended up falling on her rear end on the dirt path.

Theodisis laughed, clearly enjoying Gwenna struggling. Mirri watched him stand there and lean against his halberd. She shook her head. This guy was worse than she had once thought.

"Poor Gwenna. So helpless." He extended a hand toward her, an over-exaggerated gesture. "May I assist?"

She glared at him from her place on the ground and stood, ignoring the hand he extended. "If only Father could see you now. Or Kryptus, for that matter." She looked at him with eyebrows raised. "He would enjoy your little show, would he not?" She looked up at him, a smirk playing on her lips.

The tone of her voice led Mirri to believe Kryptus would not enjoy this, and clearly, Gwenna was trying to provoke him.

Theodisis's eyes narrowed, and he moved toward Gwenna, leaning so that he was breathing in her face. "Listen here, human. You may think you are special with your ill-conceived *gift*." He spat the word 'gift' at her with repugnance. "If you were not the daughter of my ruler, I would not tolerate your insolence."

Gwenna put her hand to her chest in mock fright. "Oh my, how frightened I am, *Theo*. Your bravery and quick wit are so intimidating. Let us not—"

A thundering boom sounded overhead, causing Gwenna to stop and jerk her head up toward the sky. Theodisis followed suit, immediately raising his halberd to a defensive position.

Mirri jumped and looked up at the blue sky, with the sun rising in the east. But that was it. What was happening?

"Take cover," Theodisis directed Gwenna.

"No, I can handle this. You take cover," Gwenna replied, spreading her arms out in front of her.

Theodisis grabbed her arm roughly. "Go, now! There is no time for argument!"

Gwenna pulled her arm away from him roughly. "I do not need your protection, Theodisis!" She glared at him. "Get away while you still can!" And everything faded away. The sounds, the look on Gwenna's face. . . . Gone.

Mirri's eyes popped open with a strangled gasp. She sat up quickly, looking around frantically. It was still dark, though she could see the sun's rays peeking through the trees. Kane sat leaning against a large tree, snoring softly. Shivering, she pulled her cloak tighter around her, shocked at how cold her bare arms were.

She put a hand to her head. Gwenna. And Theodisis. They were together, and something bad was approaching. Remember, she told herself. You have to remember. She squeezed her eyes shut and tried to focus on what she had just seen in front of her. They were arguing about something . . . Gwenna was trying to get away from him?

Mirri rubbed her forehead, trying to relax and let the images play out in her brain. But it was so hazy, like a dream . . . Wait—was it a dream? Is it possible that her brain conjured up these images and this little story on its own? Mirri closed her eyes, seeing a young Theodisis with his halberd. Gwenna with her satchel. It was blue. Yes, and she had fallen . . . No, there was no way that dream just slipped into her subconscious. She knew what had happened that morning in Holmforth.

Mirri stood and squeezed her hands into fists. It was so frustrating. Why was she seeing these things? Were they meant to help her? Or confuse her? She needed to get back to Gwenna. Now.

Mirri stopped and shook her head. Her mother. Yes. Not Gwenna. Elizabeth Langley of 247 Emerson Drive. Planet Earth, Mirri reminded herself.

She marched over to Kane and shook his shoulder softly. "Kane. Come on, let's get going."

He snorted and jumped awake. He rubbed his face and yawned. "All right." He stretched and stood. "Let us continue."

Mirri bit her lip. "I think I should ride on your back. Could we make it faster that way?"

Kane looked at her in surprise. "Yes, I believe so. Please," he added, kneeling down so Mirri could climb on his back.

Mirri put aside her awkward feelings of riding on Kane's toned body and climbed on awkwardly. She grabbed at his waist. "Let's go. We need to get to my mother. Now."

❖

"We're *what*?" Mirri yelled, sliding off Kane's body. "What?"

Kane let his shoulders drop. "I said that I believe we are lost."

Mirri had already jumped off his back, losing her cloak in the process. She tugged it free and wrapped it around herself. It was darkening, and getting colder.

"No, you said you knew where we were going! You're telling me we have been going the wrong way this *entire* time?"

Mirri was so furious she was shaking. She had been so preoccupied with her latest vision, or whatever it was, that she had been riding on his back in a bit of a fog, paying no mind to the direction Kane took. Kane had assured her he knew this part of the woods, and the vast grove of fruit trees they cut through was due east of Hadleigh Village. With the dense tree cover, neither of them realized they had been moving north.

Mirri looked out over the cliff they stood at, studying the completely unfamiliar territory. She put a hand to her forehead to block the sun, searching the landscape for any sign of something familiar. Trees, and more trees. Mountains in the distance. She could hear water but couldn't see where it was coming from. Mirri paced in front of the cliff, running her hand through her hair. She bit her bottom lip so hard she tasted blood. Her mother needed her, and she was miles away from her. Lost, far from her, in the depths of the forest.

"I can't believe this. What are we going to do? We lost a whole day!"

"I'm so sorry, Mirri, my mind was on other things. I don't know what to say." His voice trailed off as he looked down, his shoulders sagging.

Mirri looked back to the forest where they had just emerged, then out at the cliff. She sat down, shoulders slumped, throwing her legs over the ledge. "What do we do now?"

Kane stood next to her, looking out across the cliff. "I'm sorry, Mirri. I don't know what to say."

Mirri shifted where she sat. "I should have been paying more attention. I guess," she said. "Sorry. It wasn't all your fault."

A loud, swooping noise overhead made Mirri jump to her feet. Looking up at the sky, enormous green creatures flew above them, circling over the spot where she and Kane stood. They were immense, strange-looking animals with long necks. Mirri began waving her arms frantically, her cloak and hair dancing out into the wind the animals' wings produced.

"What are they?" Mirri called.

"Maylarks," Kane shouted back.

Mirri stood watching them land, wanting to whoop with excitement.

There were six of them, and as they neared the land, two skinny legs popped out of the bottom of each shell. They at first looked like humongous turtles with wings, but the more Mirri stared, she thought they also resembled a swan. Long white, feathered necks with beaks, a turtle shell, and each had four large wings. Their wings folded back into their shell as they stood, and they approached Mirri eagerly, bowing their long necks as they stopped in front of her.

"Keeper. We have been searching all of Althord Loch for you."

Relief flooded Mirri's tired and worn body. She knew Kryptus would do something. "Thank you so much for finding us. How is my mother?"

The Maylark that had spoken first looked at her and shook his small head. "No, I do not know that. But Kryptus sent us to find you."

"How did you find us?"

"Your scent, Keeper." The Maylark turned his long neck and took something from the creature behind him with his mouth. He dropped a bundle of fabric, wrapped by a cord at Mirri's feet.

Mirri looked at it, then back at the Maylark. "What is it?"

"The blanket they wrapped you in the first day you were here."

"Oh." Mirri gave a small laugh. "I'm glad that happened then, I guess." Maybe there *was* always a reason.

"It was rather difficult to locate you this far from Hadleigh Village. We apologize for the delay."

Mirri shook her head. "No, no, it's all right, thank you! Can you get me to my mother? And Kryptus?" she asked.

"Indeed," the enormous bird replied. "Here." He placed a glass marble with gold flecks in Mirri's hand. Mirri looked at the Maylark. "Is this . . .?"

"A byway. You must go now."

Kane nodded and stepped forward. "We appreciate your assistance. I shall take the Keeper from here."

He put his hands around the portal on top of Mirri's. Mirri closed her eyes, readying her stomach for what came next.

The swirl, the yanking of her limbs, and the nauseating sensation lasted only half a second as they landed on the hard ground in a mess of human and centaur.

"Kane! Mirri! I've been so worried!" came the raspy voice.

Mirri tried to still her spinning vision. Kane picked her up and set her on her feet as she looked around. The bookshelves, trinkets, and piles of antiques. Pattick's hut.

The old green rabbit was there, leaning on his cane, glasses sitting crooked on his face. "What happened? We have been waiting!"

Mirri shook her head. "Long story," she muttered, working to disentangle her cloak from around her. "What's going on? What has happened with my mother?"

Pattick looked hesitant, then spoke. "You should go to Kryptus now. We have a problem."

"What?" Mirri demanded. "What is happening with my mother?"

"I'm so sorry, Keeper." Pattick looked at her through huge brown eyes. His ears hung low, plastered to the sides of his shiny head. "Your mother is gone."

Chapter Eleven

Mirri rode atop of Kane's back, forgetting to feel awkward as she gripped him tightly around the waist. Kane galloped toward the Imperium, though Mirri insisted on going to Esperanze's first. Kane made the logical point that if she wasn't there anyway, why bother?

Kane skidded to a halt at the front of the Imperium, and Mirri jumped off before he could kneel, landing with her hands on the ground. Entering the Imperium, she turned to the left, running for the loud voices and commotion, the invisible door already open and waiting.

Centaurs lined the wall, Kryptus positioned in front of them, holding his own halberd. Theodisis stood off to the side, leaning against the wall with his arms crossed, his face set in a stony glare.

"The previous search is rescinded. It will be continued at a later time. You have your orders. The Maylarks will be standing by to relay any new information. Dismissed!" Kryptus barked.

The centaurs, all carrying halberds, filed out of the room, leaving only Theodisis and Kryptus in the room.

"You have your orders, Theodisis," Kryptus said. "*Dismissed*," he repeated, glaring at Theodisis.

"And what of the search for my weapon?" Theodisis demanded.

"I'm afraid this takes precedence over your weapon. You will continue without a weapon." Kryptus turned to the wall, where the map of Althord Loch hung, and began making markings and drawing lines with his fingers.

"This is blasphemy! A centaur without a weapon! I demand to continue the search for my weapon alongside the search—"

"You will demand no such thing," Kryptus said to the map. "Maybe you will learn to take better watch over your weapon. Now, go. You are leader over the Southwest Corridor. One more argument from you, and I shall make Kane your leader."

Theodisis bristled at the low blow Kryptus had given him. His eyes burned, and his hands balled into fists behind Kryptus's back. Slowly, he turned and stalked out of the room, avoiding eye contact with Mirri and Kane.

Kryptus turned to face them, the relief on his face clear. "Mirri. I am relieved to see you. There has been a development."

"My mom?" Mirri asked.

Kryptus shook his head. "I'm afraid she is missing at the moment. A centaur was standing guard, and somehow, they disappeared. The Loofa as well."

"What? Jinx is gone?"

"And Mother Esperanze. We have already begun the search. I have all my guards on it, as well as the Maylarks. We will find your mother, Mirri." Kryptus squeezed her shoulder. "I will find your mother. You will remain here, where you are safe."

"No, I will come and help. I could stay with Kane—"

"No," Kryptus said, cutting her off mid-speech. "Mirri, I fear there is foul play going on here. You are in danger. There has been talk of sending you back home, but I knew you would not consent to leaving. Please, stay here. I will keep you apprised of any updates."

"But—"

"No, Mirri. No."

Mirri opened her mouth to argue once more. *Please, Mirri. I need you to remain here,* she heard him plead in her mind. She slowly nodded, trying to match the look in his eyes.

Find her, she thought back. Kryptus nodded and removed his hands from her shoulders. He had heard her.

"Kane. You are to join the team in the Southeast Corridor." Kane nodded and gave Mirri's hand a light squeeze. Mirri gave him a smile, then a nod. Kane turned and followed Kryptus out of the room.

"Kryptus?" Mirri called out before Kryptus could exit the building. "Who was the centaur on guard when she disappeared?"

Kryptus hesitated. "Theodisis."

With that, he gave another curt nod and turned, leaving to join the search.

❖

Mirri paced back and forth in front of the large map hanging on the wall. At first, she studied the markings Kryptus had made on the map. It stretched the entire wall, with red lines and circles decorating the length. She glanced away, for the very thought of her mother lost anywhere in this massive area made her queasy. How could her mother survive in the outdoors with nothing? What would she do for food? For warmth? Mirri made a fist while banging it on the flat of her palm, pacing in front of the map. Then she walked back. And then again. There must be something she could be doing. Anything. She ripped the cloak from around her neck, throwing it on the ground, frustration clawing at her insides. Kryptus insisted she stay safe. Had he forgotten what she accomplished? Who she had defeated?

"Mirri?" came a small voice.

Mirri gasped and turned, hoping for some news about her mother.

Smidge stood in the doorway, a timid look on his face. He wore a clean blue shirt tucked into a pair of green pants, with pockets that ran all up and down the sides. No overalls. No hat.

He smiled at her. "May we speak?"

Mirri gave him a harsh look and crossed her arms. "Why? Going to ignore me again? *Humdinger*?" She couldn't resist giving him a jab. The anger still burned, the hurt still fresh with how he had treated her the first day. The first time she had seen him in a year.

He stepped into the room and stood near the table. "I am so sorry about your mother, Mirri," he said, his hands held down in front of him.

"Are you sorry for anything else?"

Smidge looked at her and opened his mouth but stopped.

Mirri glared at him. "What? Can't even act normal around me? Still have to be the tough, fancy Voktare?"

Smidge looked at her in surprise.

"Personally, I liked Smidge better," Mirri huffed. She turned away from him and continued her monotonous pacing.

"You are angry with me."

"Yup."

"I am so sorry, Mirri. I did not mean . . . I was trying to . . ." He trailed off.

"To what?"

He sighed and looked at his hands. "It is not easy, trying to impress Kryptus. It is difficult to be the Voktare. Sometimes I think I am not a well-suited elf for the job."

Mirri shook her head. "Smidge, look at what you accomplished! Look at everything you have done! Why are you trying to impress anyone?"

Smidge contemplated this for a moment. "I do not know," he shrugged. "Sometimes I feel we were incorrect. The prophecy chose incorrectly. Why would an elf be the Voktare?"

"But why not?" Mirri asked, exasperated. "You have already proven yourself. We all were there. You have powers and strength no one else in Althord Loch has. You defeated Amara and saved us all!" She threw her hands in the air and plopped down in a chair. She looked at Smidge with his hands in his pockets and sighed. "Why are you pretending to be something you aren't?"

Smidge looked down at his hands. "I do not know."

"Well, maybe it's time you started helping me find my mother."

Smidge looked up at her with wide eyes. "What do you mean?"

Mirri leaned forward. "In Holmforth, Kane and I ran into a . . . uh, problem. A bunch of bugs. They were—nice, at first." Mirri paused, wondering how her next sentence might sound. "They did something to me," she blurted out. "They gave me visions, memories. And they mean something, Smidge, I know they do, but I don't know what they mean, and they come at random times—"

"Mirri! Calm yourself!" He grabbed her arms. "Now tell me about these insects."

She took a deep breath. "They were yellow and long. Like a ribbon that curled at the end. They—were nice."

Smidge raised an eyebrow. "Nice?"

"Well, at first. It's like . . . they knew me, you know? When I walked through the field of them, they—"

"You walked through the field of them? Why?" Smidge demanded.

Mirri stopped. "I don't know," she confessed. "They started sniffing at me, petting me, and the next thing I know, they had wrapped themselves all around me! Like they were trying to suck out my brain or something."

Smidge gripped her arm. "We must alert Kryptus. These insects sound dangerous. They must be destroyed." Smidge headed for the door, eager to bring such important news to his leader.

Mirri jumped from her chair and grabbed his arm. "No! Please, Smidge, I need him to find my mom. We'll tell him after, okay?"

What she didn't tell Smidge was that she was afraid Kryptus would not believe her. Would lock her up somewhere or send her to Esperanze. Her mother was out there, somewhere, alone, and Mirri had to find her.

Smidge didn't look convinced but nodded. "After."

Mirri pulled Smidge back to the other side of the table. "Now you can help me find out what they mean."

Smidge nodded slowly. "All right. You said they gave you visions?"

"I'm trying to remember. It's almost like—"

Mirri blinked. She looked around. Smidge was no longer standing in front of her. She was standing in the shadows of a large, empty room. The walls were light-colored and tall, as tall as she imagined a castle would be. Was she actually in a castle? For a moment, she wanted to yell something, to see if her voice would echo. Arched windows lined the wall to her left, up as high as Mirri could see. White columns stood throughout the room, various chunks missing from the concrete pillars.

Glancing around, Mirri's brow furrowed. She had never seen this place, that much she knew. Sun shone through a beautiful mosaic window: the mix of blues, reds, and greens reflected near Mirri's feet, the colors doing a bit of a dance on the shining floor. Looking up,

Mirri saw a gaping hole in the tall ceiling, the sun shining through, vines and greenery hanging down. The immense building appeared to be abandoned, like so many other places Mirri had been.

Mirri walked slowly toward the center of the room, waiting. Waiting for the memory to appear. She stopped as she came to a staircase covered in moss and roots. Mirri's mouth fell open when she saw the pool of water just down the stairs, a sparkling crystal blue. Waves of the pool lapped gently against the staircase, telling Mirri this was not a pool of water but something larger.

A canoe came into view in the distance. Mirri squinted, seeing the water stretching on. This was not a castle she stood in . . . Some sort of structure built around the river, she guessed. Or did a river flow into the castle?

The canoe came closer. Dark, curling hair fell over the young woman's shoulders as she stepped out of the canoe near the base of the stairs. The woman held something wrapped in a blanket.

"Chloris, my love."

A soft voice came from behind Mirri, making her jump aside. A man stood, not more than a foot from Mirri, with blue eyes shining. His long white hair hung in a braid all the way to his legs. Mirri stared at the man and gasped as he walked through her to meet the woman. That same feeling, as if she felt his excitement, his pounding heart beating next to her own. Mirri shivered, turning to concentrate on the scene before her.

Though his hair was white, he was anything but old. Quite handsome, actually, with a tanned face. Or perhaps his face looked dark compared to his hair. His chin came to a fine point, and Mirri could see his muscular form underneath his white sleeveless robe.

"Cormac!" the woman cried, running up the stairs toward the man, still carrying the bundle in her arms.

The woman collapsed in his muscular arms as he kissed her forehead. "My dear," he murmured into her dark hair. "Is this it?" He nodded toward the bundle in her arms.

The woman let out a wide smile, her bright eyes shining. "It is, my love. You have a child."

"A child?" he breathed. "May I see?"

As she handed the bundled-up baby to the man, she whispered, "It is your smile."

His blue eyes widened as he looked down at the bundle in his arms. "My child. You will be a perfect sacrifice to my king."

The woman gasped. "Sacrifice? Cormac, our child—"

"Will be a genuine gift to my kingdom. Only with a heart as pure as this can my kingdom flourish." He looked at the woman, who was shaking her head madly, her dark curls bouncing.

"No!" she yelled, grabbing for the child.

Cormac laughed and pushed her away easily. She fell to the ground, shaking. "You lied to me, Cormac! You lied!"

"And you were among the easiest to swindle, my Chloris. Never fear. Your child will not be forgotten. This blood will wash over all of those still loyal to my king."

Mirri resisted the urge to throw her hands over her eyes and plug her ears. *Get up*, she wanted to scream. *Save the baby*!

The woman lay on the floor, weeping. "May I say goodbye to my child?" she whispered.

Cormac hesitated, then looked at the child. "Yes, I suppose you played your role well, my Chloris." He pulled her up roughly with one arm, the other still cradling the child. "Say goodbye to your baby, my Chloris."

The woman stood slowly and leaned to kiss her child in the man's arms. In a flash, she grabbed the child and turned to flee. Cormac reached out and grabbed a chunk of her dark hair as she turned. The woman gasped. "Cormac . . . What are you doing?"

Cormac pulled Chloris by her hair to his body, wrapping one arm around her throat. He gripped her tightly while she held the infant to her with her free arm, the other arm tugging at Cormac's elbow that snaked around her throat.

"Cormac! Please!" the woman cried, tugging helplessly at his arm.

Mirri watched in horror as Cormac pulled a knife from a sheath at his side. Chloris struggled, kicking and biting, but Cormac's muscular body made her attempts fruitless. The knife. Mirri wanted to scream, wanted to warn Chloris he had the knife, but the words froze in her throat. Cormac raised the weapon behind Chloris's slight frame and drove it into her chest, above her breast, blood spurting over the child.

Mirri put a hand to her mouth, unable to move, unable to function. This man killed a woman.

Mirri couldn't peel her eyes away as Chloris's struggling body went slack and the fight in her eyes faded. She slumped to the ground, sliding down her murderer's body, Cormac easily grabbing the infant before she hit the ground. She landed in a pool of blood, first on her rear, then backward as Cormac stepped away, holding the bundle and holstering his blade.

He walked away, leaving Chloris lying in a pool of blood with a vacant expression on her lovely, pale face. A gold pendant fell behind her neck, hitting the ground with a soft clink.

Mirri stared, watching the blood spread over Chloris's dark gown, slowly darkening her chest. Mirri covered her face with her hands, nausea spreading through her body like wildfire. She turned and ran from the woman lying on the floor, wishing she had never witnessed such a horrible act. Smidge! She tried to scream. Smidge! She fell to the floor and waited for the heartache and nausea to pass.

Chapter Twelve

Smidge stared at Mirri in a state of pure shock.

After Mirri awoke from the latest vision, Smidge ran to get her a cool cloth to put on her head. Since then, he gripped her hand, listening to Mirri tell him of the latest memory.

"It was strange, Mirri. You just sat there. I kept calling your name." Smidge put his hand on top of his first, still resting on Mirri's. "I was afraid for you."

Mirri lifted her cheek from the wooden table. She put her face in her hands. "It was horrible," she whispered. "I—I just wanted it to be over."

Smidge nodded sympathetically and rubbed her back.

"You never heard of a bug that did this?"

Smidge shook his head. "No, but there are many magical creatures throughout the forest."

"What about the man in the memory? He didn't sound familiar?" Mirri had to learn who this man was. He had murdered a woman. It's possible Mirri was the only person that could identify this man.

Smidge shook his head. "No . . . I have never heard of a man with white hair by that name." Smidge looked deep in thought. "But I have an idea."

"What? What is it?"

"We could visit Arlo. He lives here in town. After Kryptus returns, we shall find his shop."

"Who is Arlo? Why him?"

"He is an umbaldi. Researcher of the past. And quite bright for a young Leet."

Mirri jumped from her chair. "Let's go. Now."

Smidge looked apprehensive. He shook his head nervously. "Mirri, I promised Kryptus you would remain in the Imperium." He moved in front of her, as if a three-foot elf could really block her path. He grabbed her hand in his. "Let me show you around the Imperium. I have made preparations for the trial—"

"No," Mirri said, yanking her hand away from Smidge. She kneeled down to be at eye level with him. "Smidge, if this was your father, and he was lost, I would do everything in my power to help you find him. Wouldn't you do that for me?"

Smidge gulped, and his eyes looked back and forth. "Um . . . If we could just wait a while longer . . ."

Mirri stood. "I know you don't want to get in trouble. You stay here, and if Kryptus gets back, tell him I snuck out." She reached for her cloak lying on the table. "Just tell me how to find this Leet guy."

"No!" Smidge pounded his hand into his fist.

Mirri raised her eyebrows. Was he going to stop her?

"You are correct, Mirri. You would do anything to help me find my father if you could. Look at all you have done for me already." He took her hand. "We will go to Arlo's together. I will take you there myself."

"Thanks, Smidge! C'mon!" Mirri headed for the door. Smidge grabbed her arm once again.

"No, Mirri, there is a centaur outside the door. He is your guard. We must first evade him to get out of the Imperium."

Mirri rolled her eyes. "My guard? What do I need a guard for?"

Smidge shrugged. "It would seem that Kryptus thought you may try to escape."

They looked at each other and laughed. Laughed so hard Smidge's chubby cheeks turned red. It felt nice to laugh with her friend again. She had not realized how much she missed him—his loyalty and determination. Though small, Smidge stood out from every creature in Althord Loch. She just wished he believed it.

After a moment, Mirri wiped the tears of laughter from her eyes. "Okay, so how do we get out of here?"

"Take my hands," Smidge instructed her.

Mirri stepped forward and grabbed Smidge's tiny hands. He smiled and closed his eyes.

She felt the whoosh of air swirl around her and felt her stomach drop as they appeared on the stone road.

Mirri looked around, her head still spinning. "Wow. You're really getting better at blossoming, aren't you?"

Smidge smiled and shrugged modestly. "I use it every day now. It makes getting back and forth to the Imperium much easier." He turned and headed down the road. Smidge pointed down the road. "That is his home there."

As they walked, something occurred to Mirri. "Hey, what was all the fuss about Theodisis? What happened to his weapon?" Saying his name aloud reminded Mirri of Theodisis taunting her mother in a memory. She grimaced when she thought of him laughing as Gwenna tripped and fell to the ground.

Smidge shook his head as he walked next to Mirri. "It is of great concern. His weapon has been stolen. A centaur's weapon being taken is the greatest thievery. Search parties have been searching for days."

"For a weapon? For *his* weapon? Make him find it himself," she grumbled. "Why would everyone get so worked up over a halberd?"

Smidge looked up at her curiously. "Do you not have thievery in your world?"

"Well, yeah, but a search party for a weapon? What's the big deal?"

"A halberd is a very dangerous weapon if it falls into the wrong hands. It is the first time in my life a centaur has lost one."

Mirri shook her head. Whatever. But secretly, a little piece of her danced in glee at the thought of Theodisis losing his weapon. He deserved it. Quite the embarrassment, she assumed.

Smidge stopped in front of a small hut with wooden light posts on either side of the front door, burning brightly, even though it was broad daylight. Two circular windows decorated the front of Arlo's hut, but didn't look like any windows Mirri had seen before. Were they windows? Instead of glass, they contained several pieces of colored wood put together to fill the frame.

Smidge knocked at the door. It opened just a crack.

"Smidge? That you?" a high-pitched voice said through the door.

"Hello, Arlo. I have brought someone who needs to talk to you."

"Of course, of course! Please, watch your step!" came the voice.

Smidge stepped in and grabbed Mirri's hand. They stepped onto a landing and proceeded down several stairs to get to the floor.

Mirri followed Smidge, peeking around as she climbed down the stairs. The ceiling was high, and shelves covered the walls, filled with books. More books than Mirri imagined one being could own. This place might have more books than the library at school, for all she knew.

Once they stood on the dirt floor, Mirri looked up. The ceilings must have been at least thirty feet up, with rows and rows of book spines. Mirri looked around with wide eyes.

"You must be the famous Mirri," Arlo said.

Mirri peeled her eyes off the walls and turned toward the voice. Her eyes widened as he smiled up at her, but she quickly recovered. "That's me."

He didn't look like Mirri expected. A blue creature with arms, legs, and a head. That was about it. And he was naked. Granted, his body didn't seem to well, *be*, very much. Like a human, but without one defining feature. Kind of like a blank slate. No curves. Like a stick of blue chewing gum with extremities and a head attached.

"So!" He clapped his hands together, though they did not make a sound. "Smidge tells me you want to know about a species in another kingdom?"

Mirri had been studying the room. "Oh! Yes. A man with long white hair." She bit her lip. "His name was Cor—Com . . . I don't remember his name, I guess." She explained his white robe and belt.

Arlo tapped his blue finger against his chin. "Hmm. Long white hair, hmm?"

Mirri nodded. "Yes. He wanted to use" —Mirri swallowed— "a baby for a sacrifice to his king."

"A sacrifice? Sounds like Koltaria. They are the only empire I know that would use a human sacrifice."

The Leet turned without warning and hopped up the wall to her left. Mirri watched, fascinated, as he scrambled from ledge to ledge, finally pulling out a book and leaning back to turn a few pages. In mid-air. He flipped through the book, fifteen feet in the air, his blank blue feet sticking to a bookshelf.

"No, not that one," he muttered to himself, returning the book to its place. He glanced around with his arms crossed, feet still stuck to the shelf.

Mirri gasped as leaped from the shelf across the room to the opposite wall. He climbed up a few shelves and pulled out another book.

"How does he do that?" Mirri whispered to Smidge.

"Oh, Leets are jumpers," Smidge said. "They can also disappear. Arlo is the only Leet I know of in these parts."

And apparently, they can stick to walls, Mirri thought to herself. After all she had seen in this village, a new life form could still amaze her.

"This is it!" he announced as he jumped off the wall and landed at their feet soundlessly.

He carried an enormous book—it looked more like a gigantic encyclopedia to Mirri. She doubted Smidge could even lift it. He heaved the book onto a small table with a *thunk* and flipped it open. Dust flew everywhere as he turned the pages carefully.

"Here." He pointed with a straight blue finger (no fingernails, Mirri noticed) and turned the book to face Mirri. "Is this the man you saw?"

Mirri studied the drawing before her. A man with a long braid, holding a long, curved knife at his side, decorated with jewels. Mirri gulped as her finger traced over the knife the man held. It looked strangely similar to the knife she had seen the man use on Chloris. He could have been wearing a white robe, Mirri supposed, but the armor he wore covered much of his body. He looked the part of a warrior. She chewed on her fingernail.

"Yes. That's him," Mirri decided, partly out of her desire to find out who he was. "Who is he?"

"The Kingdom of Koltaria," Arlo answered. "The Kolts' Empire fell years ago, before my time. Strong, fierce warriors."

Smidge finally piped up, standing on a chair to get a view of the picture over their shoulders. "A Kolt? We have cut all ties with Koltaria, correct? I have never seen one."

Arlo shrugged. "It is said it was a curse that brought the kingdom to a pile of ash. An ancient relic of some sort. Something to do with the Mother Kolt, I believe."

"Who is the Mother Kolt?" Mirri asked

Arlo flipped the pages. "Some sort of religious figure, I believe. They worshiped her. I remember reading that she was much different than regular Kolts. Saved several of their warriors, I think."

"What about Koltaria? Is there still an empire?" Smidge pressed.

"Yes, but I believe they keep to themselves. I would assume Kryptus knows their leader."

Mirri chewed on her bottom lip. What did this man and mystery woman have to do with anything? The frustration was rising in her chest again, that feeling that made her want to throw something. She wished she had never seen that memory, and the woman lying in a puddle of blood had stained her brain forever. And she was no closer to finding her mother or solving the mystery.

"Okay, never mind about him, anyway. What about these bugs that attacked me?"

Arlo's eyes widened. "Bugs attacked you?"

"Yes. That's when I started having random memories filled with random people. I just have no idea what any of them mean!" Mirri yelled. She ran a hand through her hair and took a deep breath.

Arlo glanced toward Smidge, who patted Arlo on the hand. "She is just very confused, Arlo."

"Sorry. I just don't know what to do anymore." She dropped into a chair and put her head in her hands.

"Describe this insect," Arlo said. "I need to know more about it."

Mirri forced herself to concentrate. She shifted in her seat. "Well, they were . . . beautiful. Kind of yellowish. They had a long, thin body that curled up into a twirly thing and clear wings. Weird eyes that glowed. And they" —Mirri cleared her throat— "called to me."

She looked down, studying her sneakers. She didn't realize how odd it sounded until she actually said it. But they had called her. Not by name. They had just—*called to* her.

"They called you. Strange," Arlo muttered, flipping through pages in the book. He slammed the book shut, another cloud of dust appearing in his face. He scratched his head. "Very strange indeed."

"You've never heard of bugs that can do this? Give people memories?"

Arlo looked thoughtful. "Well, no insects, no. But it may be some sort of baraka. Possibly these insects were meant to find you."

"What is a baraka?"

"A baraka is a type of . . . well, message, of sorts. I have only read stories of these happening." Arlo looked deep in thought.

Mirri looked back and forth at them both. "So why do you think this is a baraka?"

"Legend says that the baraka is a gift from the gods. Here, I have it here!" Arlo jumped to the wall in front of the table, landing in front of a shelf of brightly colored, thin book spines.

"This is it!" Arlo leaped to the ground, landing in the same spot he had just left. He opened the book eagerly and turned it for Mirri and Smidge to see. "Abraxas was to be King of the New Land but did not feel justified in becoming royalty. He was depressed and lonely but did not want to burden the people of the New Land with his pain. So he set off on a quest, following the stars. It is said that the stars led him to a fiery pit, but the flames called to him. Trusting in himself, he threw himself into the flames and came out the other side completely unscathed. Said the flames had taught him everything he needed to be

King of the New Land. He went back, proud and strong, and became the greatest king ever to live."

Arlo and Smidge looked up at her expectantly.

Mirri scratched her head, trying her best not to look bewildered. "Uh, okay, but how does that prove this is a baraka?"

Smidge frowned, then turned back to Arlo.

Arlo looked thoughtful. "Well, I don't suppose it proves anything, exactly." He flipped through more pages, looking deep in thought.

"If this is a baraka, how long will I have these memories? Forever?"

"Well, with Abraxas, they gave him the gift until it taught him what he needed to know. I would assume the memories would come only when you needed them. To fulfill some sort of quest."

Smidge stepped in between Mirri and Arlo. "We need to return to the Imperium. If Kryptus finds out we—"

A clang and a loud thump sounded above them. "Mirri!"

Mirri jumped and nearly fell off her stool. Kryptus stood high on the landing, a look of irritation written on his face.

Smidge stood up straight and ran up the stairs to the centaur's side. "Kryptus! It is my fault—I'm sorry—we were investigating! Mirri is having visions, it was important we get more information, I apologize!" his voice was wavering.

"There is no time for that," Kryptus answered. "There has been a development."

Mirri ran up the stairs to Kryptus eagerly. "My mother? Have you found her?"

"No. But we have found the Loofa. Come now." He paused. "I believe your mother is running, Mirri."

Chapter Thirteen

"What? No, no, no! She would never do that!" Mirri said, stamping her foot. She knew she sounded like a toddler having a fit, but did not care. "Kryptus, you *know* her. You know her!"

"I do not know what to believe, Mirri. Come. You must see the Loofa. You can hear what she has to say."

Mirri looked at Smidge. Jinx? What did Jinx have to say about her mother?

She ran toward the stairs, but Smidge grabbed her hand. "No, Mirri, I will take us there. Hold my hands."

Smidge grabbed her hands, and before she realized it, she was standing outside the Imperium. Smidge and Mirri turned and hurried through the large doors together. They stopped when they heard the commotion coming from the end of the hallway.

"I need to see the Voktare!" Jinx shrieked. "The Keeper! I am here to assist the Keeper and the Voktare!"

"Jinx!" Mirri yelled. She didn't know how to find the magical door, so instead began pounding on the wall with her fists.

The wall to her left disappeared, and Jinx flew straight into Mirri's arms. "Mirri!" she sobbed, stuffing her fluffy body into Mirri's chest. "I was so afraid," she whispered to Mirri, her little body shaking.

"What is going on?" Smidge demanded of the centaur that stepped into the hallway.

The large half-horse-half-man looked rather bored.

"We were told to keep the Loofa in the room."

"They were holding me captive!" Jinx wailed.

"Jinx, calm down," Mirri whispered. "It's okay," she soothed, patting her quivering body.

Rose stepped into the hallway, her long blonde hair mussed, an annoyed look on her face. "You would think I had come at her with an axe," she said, glaring at Jinx. "Heavens."

Mirri sighed and carried Jinx back into the room, and handed the still-shaking Loofa to Smidge.

Mirri turned to Rose. "She's just a bit high-strung."

Mirri took a step back. She wasn't sure if she wanted to know what happened in this room before she arrived.

"Okay," Mirri announced once everyone had been seated around the table. She sat Jinx on the table in front of her. "Start from the beginning, Jinx."

Jinx sniffed and began her story. She explained how Esperanze had made Gwenna a tonic, and then they had watched over her for hours. Esperanze had ordered Jinx to rub a salve on Gwenna's feet and hands, and just as she had finished, Gwenna awoke. Then she fell back asleep. They watched over her for a day and a half until Gwenna awoke again.

Esperanze made her tea and smelt, (elves favorite food) while Jinx went out to pick berries. When she returned with the berries, Gwenna offered her a tonic that she said would perk her right up. And that is the last thing she remembered.

"I awoke here, in this room. The other Druid was poking me with a wooden stick." Jinx pointed at Rose.

Rose rolled her eyes back in her head. "I was trying to wake her, as Kryptus instructed me."

"But where did they find you?" Mirri asked.

"They found her in the Southern Corridor, nearly two kilorails from Esperanze's hut."

Mirri spun around as Kryptus spoke from behind her, his booming voice filling the room. "She was wrapped in a blanket and hidden under a pile of leaves." Kryptus marched to the head of the table and turned to face the group. "It appears someone went to great lengths to conceal the Loofa."

"But why?" Mirri asked. "Why go to all the trouble to drug and hide Jinx unless you . . ."

"Unless you were guilty." Smidge's small voice came from beside Mirri.

Silence fell around the room.

Mirri shook her head, unable to think of an argument. " No, no, there has to be an explanation. She would not—there's just no way." Mirri stood up and looked at Kryptus. She turned to look at Rose and Smidge, who had the same look of doubt on their faces.

"Have you forgotten someone poisoned my mother? Someone tried to *kill* her? And what about Esperanze?"

Kryptus had a grim look on his face. Mirri sighed and put her head in her hands.

Smidge nudged her from his seat and gave her a pointed look. She nodded back, understanding his meaning.

She swallowed. There was no easy way to start this conversation, so she blurted out, "I have been having memories. My mother's memories. Kind of."

Mirri felt her cheeks redden, aware of the raised eyebrows she was getting from both Rose and Kryptus. There was no simple way to tell them, so she began from the beginning, describing the insects in Holmforth. "They attacked me. I—I all the sudden was somewhere else, in the forest. I saw Gwenna. And you," she said, nodding to Kryptus.

"What happened in this memory?" Kryptus asked.

"At first, Gwenna was running through the forest toward something. In her nightgown. Then she came back after a few minutes . . . with you." Mirri snuck a peak at Kryptus, wondering if he remembered what had happened next, Gwenna confessing her true undying love for him.

Rose cleared her throat. "Then what happened?"

Mirri glanced at Rose. The Druid's eyes had narrowed, as if she had an inkling of what went on with Gwenna and her one true love.

"They . . . uh, just kind of argued at the portal." She kept her eyes facing down, reluctant to repeat what her mother had said to Kryptus. "Then some kind of bright light." She looked at Kryptus. "What was the light?"

Kryptus glanced at Rose. He shook his head. "That is not important at the moment, Mirri. It is more important that we find your mother," he announced after a brief pause.

"But what if it is?"

"It is not," Kryptus repeated coolly.

"But—"

"Why did you not inform me of these memories earlier?"

Mirri glared at him. "Would it have made you work faster? Try harder to find my mother?"

It was a jab, and she hoped Kryptus remembered. A year ago, he had said almost the exact same thing when he had left out key details of an important mission. Things he thought she didn't need to know.

Mirri felt an overwhelming sense of satisfaction as Kryptus's eyes lowered and looked away. *Ha! How does it feel, you arrogant chump?* she thought, crossing her arms in front of her.

Her amusement faded when Kryptus's eyes snapped back to hers. He gave her an icy stare, one that made Mirri squirm in her seat. She had forgotten he had the ability to read her thoughts. She would have to watch that.

The room turned quiet. Mirri sat chewing on her lip, avoiding Kryptus's hard stare, and running her hand through Jinx's fur.

"So, what do we do now? How do we find my mom?" Mirri picked Jinx up from her lap and set her on the table. "Jinx? Do you know anything that can help?"

Jinx's eyes were bright. She nodded. "I may have heard something," she said. "But maybe not," she added, looking down at the table.

"What did you hear?" Mirri pressed her. "Even if you think it sounds crazy, Jinx, we need to know."

Jinx nodded and looked over Mirri's shoulder. She sat up on her back haunches, in furry-caterpillar mode, and spoke clearly. "I heard Gwenna speak of a place of great importance, a place where . . . the dusk met the dagger."

Mirri looked at Jinx blankly. "What?" Mirri looked around at the others. "What does that mean?"

Jinx looked at Mirri solemnly. "I do not know."

"When did you hear this?" Kryptus asked.

"I am not sure. I was so tired, so very tired. It was dark, but Gwenna must have been near. I sense she was arguing with someone." Jinx looked deep in thought. Her little brow furrowed, making her green fluff glow on her body. "I cannot remember! Forgive me, Kryptus! I should remember! So sorry," she wept, falling into Mirri's chest.

"No, Jinx, it's not your fault! It's okay, really!" Mirri said, hugging Jinx tight. "It's not your fault," she murmured into her fur, glancing up at Kryptus.

Kryptus's eyes went to the ceiling as Jinx sobbed into Mirri's T-shirt. He sighed. "She is correct, Jinx. You have done nothing wrong. Thank you for the information."

Jinx sniffed and looked up at Mirri with a small smile. She nodded, her dark eyes still shining with tears.

"Where the dusk met the dagger," Mirri muttered. "I don't get it."

Mirri looked around the room, hoping someone could explain it to her. The only sound in the room was the clacking and smacking of Smidge's fingernails in his mouth. Rose's eyes were far away, thinking, her jaw set firmly while Kryptus stared at his halberd, his mouth set into a firm line.

"Kryptus!" Commotion behind Mirri broke the silence as everyone turned toward the entrance. Two centaurs, one dark-skinned and one light, burst through the door, each carrying a halberd, breathing hard.

Kryptus immediately resumed his posture as tough centaur leader. "What have you found?"

"We have found Mother Esperanze," the dark-skinned centaur replied breathlessly. The two centaurs glanced at each other.

"And?" Kryptus pressed. "Where did you find her?"

They looked at each other again. The dark-skinned centaur stepped forward. "She was, uh, in one of the elf's huts." He cleared his throat. "Rearranging his fromp drawer."

Mirri looked back at Kryptus. He closed his eyes and put a hand to his forehead. What were fromps? In an elf's home?

Kryptus spoke quietly. "Are you telling me she has been in Hadleigh Village this entire time?"

The two centaurs looked at each other. They spoke in unison, "Yes."

Silence fell around the room. Mirri could swear she could hear her own heart beating as Kryptus stepped forward and stood in front of his two guards.

Their backs immediately straightened, and Mirri could see the sweat forming on their brows. Kryptus stood, looking at each in turn. The seconds stretched into minutes. The centaurs stared straight ahead, their knuckles turning white while gripping their weapons.

Finally, Kryptus spoke, "Who was in charge of the main path today, Willec?" He addressed the dark-skinned centaur.

"I was, sir." Willec stared over Kryptus's shoulder.

"And why, Willec, do you think I put you in charge of the main road today?"

"To patrol the area today, Kryptus. To find and retain the prisoner." He spoke in a clear voice, holding his halberd tightly, though it had a slight tremble to it.

Kryptus leaned forward until he was nose-to-nose with Willec. "Did you fulfill your duty?"

Mirri scarcely dared to breathe. The tension in the room felt heavy, pressing down on Mirri's chest. Smidge gripped her hand, Mirri wincing as his nails dug into her skin.

"No, Kryptus." Willec swallowed.

"Bring her to me." Kryptus stared at the centaur a moment longer. Then he turned and stalked to the head of the table, slamming his halberd down next to him.

Mirri, Smidge and Jinx all jumped at the sudden thump of Kryptus's weapon, Jinx letting out a little squeak. Mirri didn't dare look in his direction for fear of what the centaur may hear her thinking.

Willec looked visibly shaken but straightened up immediately. He nodded and opened his mouth to speak but stopped when Kryptus glared at him. Instead, Willec nodded, and he and the other centaur hurried from the room.

No one spoke. Mirri had never seen Kryptus berate one of his troops. They all sat, too scared to speak. Mirri snuck a peak at Smidge, whose eyes were still wide in fear.

Mirri heard her before she saw her. The high-pitched laugh, her cackling voice. Mirri sighed as the entrance appeared behind her.

"Kryptus, dear!" Esperanze appeared in the room next to Willec and ran straight up to Kryptus. "Give Esperanze a peck, darling!"

Kryptus stood in a stubborn silence while Esperanze grabbed the sides of his face and pulled him to her bright lips. It seemed she had forgotten the fact that he had been in her hut two days ago.

"My, it has been too long! What are we celebrating, dear?" She flipped her red hair over her shoulders and faced the others, one of her hands toying with the pendant that hung around her neck.

Kryptus crossed his arms. "Esperanze, this is not a celebration."

The Druid turned to him with wide eyes, as if he had just asked her an important question. "Dear?" She nodded at Kryptus.

Kryptus sighed. "Esperanze, can you tell me what you were doing in Flimgor's hut?"

Esperanze threw her head back and cackled. "Well, dear, why didn't you just ask?" Her tone turned serious. "It is the twelfth day of the new moon, Kryptus. One must go through the fromps and milbundles at this time." She smiled serenely at him. "I'm sure you have done the same?"

"Yes, of course, Mother Esperanze," he said in a mocking tone. "Who instructed you to go to Flimgor's hut?"

"Why, Gwenna did, of course!" She looked at him in pure exasperation. "She is the lead on the fromp organization system. Very important this time of year."

Kryptus stood with his eyes closed for a moment. "And where is Gwenna?"

"Ah, she is traveling, you see. Needs to check on the other villages fromp situations. Said she needed to get a bit of a jump on things!" Esperanze beamed. Her eyes stopped when she reached the Druid with long, blonde hair sitting next to Mirri.

"Why, Rosemeade, is that you?" she exclaimed, putting a hand to her chest.

Rose spoke to the table in front of her. "Yes, Esperanze."

"Why, dear, it has been too long! Give Esperanze a peck!" Esperanze strode to Rose, trying to wrench her out of her chair, when Rose put a hand out to stop her.

"No, that will be all right, Esperanze, thank you," she said stiffly.

Esperanze took only a brief second to compose herself. "I see. Been away too long, I suppose! Let's all toast with a drink, shall we?"

"Actually, Esperanze, my guard here has been summoned to take you on a tour of the Imperium. Will you join him?" Kryptus looked pointedly at Willec, whose shoulders visibly sagged.

Esperanze looked around in delight.

"It would be my pleasure, Mother Esperanze," Willec said, forcing a smile.

Esperanze bounced over to the centaur and locked her arm in his. "Now, dear, you have to tell me who does your hair! Why, one of my tonics would put the bounce back in it for good!" Her cackle echoed all the way down the hall.

Kryptus turned to Mirri. "It would seem Gwenna sent Esperanze away."

Mirri sat, looking down at her hands. Her eyes were welling with tears, but she refused to let them slide down her face. She didn't know what to say. She had run out of arguments. What was her mother doing? Could it be possible she had . . . she had . . . No. Mirri shook her head furiously to herself. She refused to let herself think that. Putting her face in her hands, she massaged her temples, willing herself to think. Her mother had a reason, a plan. She had left Esperanze's for a reason. Mirri just had to figure out what that was.

Chapter Fourteen

M irri couldn't hide her surprise when Kryptus informed Smidge he would be in charge of the centaurs. Smidge's mouth formed an 'O' at this news, and, for a moment, seemed unable to move or speak. He composed himself in a hurry and took over command of the search for Gwenna. Mirri couldn't help but wonder what Theodisis was going to think of this.

Jinx stayed behind as well, resting on Smidge's shoulder. Maybe to give him the emotional boost he would need as leader of the entire guard. Mirri would have been more concerned for Smidge, but at the moment she had bigger problems.

Kryptus and Mirri were on their way to Arlo's. Kryptus announced he would like to speak to Arlo himself.

Mirri took the opportunity to ask Kryptus about the Koltarian named Cormac. He looked at her in surprise.

"How do you know of this name?"

"I had a memory of him." Mirri shrugged, not eager to relay the details of this memory. The blood of the woman was still fresh on her mind—the pain in her voice, that blank look in her eyes. Mirri gave a shudder, hoping Kryptus hadn't noticed.

"Yes, I know of Cormac. But he disappeared long ago. He was rumored to be the next in line for the throne in Koltaria."

"Rumored?"

Kryptus nodded. "Yes. In Koltaria, the king decides who the next ruler will be. Usually by a series of tests of the king's choosing."

"Do you know anything about, um, sacrifices they might make?" She avoided his eyes, hoping she didn't have to tell him who the Kolt meant to sacrifice. To his credit, he didn't question her further.

"Yes, I knew of sacrifices. They were a brutal race. In the end, it was their own pride that lead to their self-destruction. They are a weak army now."

"I thought it was a curse?"

Kryptus looked at her thoughtfully. "Some have alluded to that. But I don't believe a single curse could bring down an entire kingdom."

Mirri nodded, thinking hard as they turned the corner and the grassy hill came into view.

As they approached Arlo's hut, Mirri slowed, noticing the door laying wide open on the ground. Kryptus noticed as well, and his speed increased.

"Stay here!" Kryptus barked at her.

Mirri paused, deciding whether to listen to his instructions. She crept over to the door and peered down, seeing nothing but more stairs. She took a hesitant step down. Then another. It was dark, but Mirri could just make out the shape of Kryptus with his hand on Arlo's shoulder.

Kryptus fumbled around on the wall, and the room filled with light. Mirri gasped. Books lay all over the floor, pulled from the dozens of shelves lining the walls.

"Are you all right?" Mirri asked, hurrying to his side.

"Yes, yes, I'm fine," he answered, looking around the room. Books littered the floors, pages torn, and colorful spines torn from their book covers.

"What happened?" Mirri asked, looking around the cluttered room.

Arlo shoved a heap off his desk and dug through a drawer. "I came back from the market to this. The lights off, my books . . . my books . . ." His voice trailed off, and he dropped onto his desk chair.

"You're sure you're okay?"

"Hmm?" He had been eyeing his empty bookshelves. "Oh, yes, I'm fine." He sighed. "I'm not sure why someone would do something like this."

Kryptus kneeled on the floor, examining the wreckage. "When did this happen?"

Arlo sat in a chair. "I left for the market after speaking to you and Humdinger," he said, nodding at Mirri. He leaned on the desk wearily. "Who would do something like this?"

"More importantly, what did you have that was worth breaking into your hut?" Kryptus eyed the room. "Is anything of value missing?"

Arlo gave a scoff. "Anything I have of value was written in these books." He shrugged. "Why would a creature destroy my hut for a book?"

"They were looking for information," Mirri said. Kryptus and Arlo turned to look at her. "Well? Isn't that the same reason we came here?"

"What information?" Arlo asked.

"We seek a place where the dusk met the dagger," Kryptus explained matter-of-factly.

Arlo tapped his chin. "My, that is odd." His voice drifted off as he stood and climbed over the torn and disheveled books to reach a shelf. "That is odd indeed. I believe I have heard of this place." He looked at the books all over the floor and sighed. "I guess we should start looking."

Kryptus immediately bent to the floor near the shelf, going through the piles of books, and after a moment, Mirri and Arlo joined him. Mirri sifted through the remains and various pages, not entirely sure what she was even looking for. Dusk? A dagger? She had seen a dagger—in the memory of Chloris. But Mirri remembered the sunlight shining in the hole in the tall ceiling. Not dusk. Not dusk at all. Sighing, she leaned down, picked up a book and started thumbing through the pages.

After a few minutes, Mirri sat on the floor against the walls. This was hopeless. There had to be hundreds of books in this room. And she had yet to find a book with any sketches or drawings. Unless she wanted to sit and read these books page by page, she had no idea how this was going to help them.

"Hey, Arlo? Why was it odd?"

"What is odd?" he asked, flipping pages of a thick text madly.

"Earlier. You said it was odd. That we were looking for this place. How come?"

Arlo stood, looking around the room. He ran a hand over his blue head. "It was nothing. I was asked of this location only yesterday."

Mirri and Kryptus's eyes met. Someone else had known this place?

"Who asked you about this place?" Kryptus asked.

Arlo looked from Mirri to Kryptus. "It was one of your guards," he said, nodding to Kryptus. "Theodisis."

Chapter Fifteen

"Theodisis?" Mirri said. "Why would he . . ." Mirri's mind wandered to the memory she had in the forest. Her mother and Theodisis, their sour relationship, and then something had happened. Something bad.

"It was him!" Mirri gasped. "Theodisis kidnapped my mother!"

Kryptus snapped his eyes to Mirri, the look in his eyes silencing Mirri at once.

"What? Your mother? He kidnapped her?" Arlo asked, his blue forehead wrinkling.

"No need to worry yourself, Arlo," Kryptus said calmly, putting a hand on his blue shoulder. "Why don't I send over a couple of villagers to help you clean up, hmm?"

Arlo looked at Kryptus with wide eyes. "Oh, don't trouble yourself, Kryptus. I'll handle this."

"Don't be foolish, Arlo, this would take days to clean up. I'll send you some help, eh?"

Arlo nodded, his eyes still wide and fearful. "Thank you."

"We need to be getting back. Could you keep looking for any information on this place as you go?"

"Of course, of course."

"Thank you, Arlo. Inform me at once." Kryptus straightened up and gave Mirri a pointed look. "Shall we?"

Mirri nodded, her mind spinning. She hurried out of the messy hut and stepped outside, Kryptus following. Dusk was approaching, and creatures had filled the road ahead of her.

Mirri hurried to join the flow of creatures when Kryptus grabbed her arm firmly. "No one outside of the Imperium walls needs to know of this. I will not have you frightening the villagers," he whispered in a menacing tone.

Mirri pulled her arm away from him roughly. "*Fine*. Now, where is Theodisis?" she demanded.

"I do not know. We must get to Command at once. Come."

But Kryptus faded away. Mirri stood in a field in the bright sunlight.

"Argh! I do not have time for this!" she yelled to no one in particular. This was getting ridiculous. She had to get back to Kryptus. Theodisis had her mother. He had to.

Mirri stood still and closed her eyes. She thought of Kryptus and where they had just been standing. *Concentrate*, she told herself.

Her mind began to flutter. She could feel the cold air of Hadleigh Village. She was going back.

A second later, just as she was slipping away from the field, her eyes snapped open. Back to the field. A loud boom had filled her ears, then a crack. She turned toward the sound. Trees stood behind her, and a single line of smoke was rising in the distance.

Without thinking, Mirri turned and ran toward the smoke. It had to be something important if she was here. Why else would she be here?

A female voice rang out. "This is pointless! Look what just happened!"

Mirri slowed and stopped when she reached the line of trees. She stood behind a large pine and peeked around.

A small elf with a green hat stood in the clearing with a girl. The girl had red hair tied up into a messy bun and was wearing a long, colorful skirt with a white blouse. She had her hands on her hips and was glaring at the elf.

"It is not pointless," the elf said. "Training has only just begun. It will not come easily."

The girl kicked at something on the ground. "I'm tired of this. Why do I even need to train?"

"You have a gift. You must harness it. I will teach you," the elf replied.

"I do not want this gift. Give it to my sister," she replied, walking over to a fallen log and dropping onto it, chin in her hand.

"One does not know why we are blessed with certain things. But we must accept them," the elf said as he sat next to her.

"Some gift," she grumbled.

Mirri watched the two talking. A gift? That must be her mother. Who was the elf? She wished she could take a picture and show it to Smidge. Mirri stepped closer to the two talking. The elf had dark hair and kind, green eyes. If she didn't know any better . . . that was Smidge's father.

Smidge. Kryptus. She had to get back. Forcing herself to turn from the clearing where the girl and elf stood, Mirri closed her eyes again. She breathed deeply. Think of Kryptus. The Imperium. Get back to Kryptus. As before, she began to feel the prickles of cold on her arms, then her neck. Things became hazy and dark as the surrounding forest slowly vanished, like a rippling pool of water in front of her.

Gasping, Mirri sat straight up. Smidge and Jinx jumped back. Mirri put a hand to her head.

"What—what happened?" she asked.

"You had another memory," Smidge said, rushing back to her side.

Mirri looked around. She was lying on a homemade bed, which was actually a pile of blankets on the floor. The room was dim, with a table on the wall across the room.

Mirri tried to stand but fell back against the floor. "Geez," she muttered. The room was still spinning.

Jinx appeared in front of her, worry written across her fluffy ears pinned back against her head. "Mirri? What is it you are feeling?"

"I'm—fine. Really," she added. "I just need a minute." She leaned back against the wall and closed her eyes. What had happened? She had been in the forest, watching her mother and an elf . . . A gift. They were speaking of a gift. And then . . . She couldn't remember.

Her mother. Theodisis. She had to get to her mother. "Help me," she whispered to the pair in front of her. Struggling to stand, Mirri leaned on her friends.

"I have to get to Kryptus," Mirri said.

Smidge and Jinx helped her to her feet. They led Mirri slowly to the wall, which faded away as soon as they reached it.

Out in the hallway, it was dark. "Go inform Rosemeade," Smidge said to Jinx. "I will take Mirri to Command."

The usual nauseating ride on the lift did not help Mirri's pounding head, but she pushed the pain aside and stepped to the archway at the end of the hallway. She waited with Smidge at her side, but nothing happened.

"What—" she started, but Smidge shook his head.

"It's all right. This entrance can only be opened from the inside."

Sure enough, after only a moment, the door vanished from view, and a centaur she did not recognize nodded at her and stood aside.

Kryptus stood at the center of the room, in front of a large table, his halberd leaning beside him. He had his chin in one hand, studying the table in front of him. Mirri hurried to his side and stopped, gaping at what sat in front of her.

The enormous table held a map. But it was a three-dimensional map, holding mini mountains, and little running streams. The trees waved in an invisible breeze. A tiny flock of animals flew over the miniature mountain range near where her hand rested on the table. She had seen a map like this only a year ago.

"Is this . . . Graynard's map?" Mirri asked in a hushed voice, speaking of the grumpy elf she had met last year. The elf that had given his life to help her escape. It was still a pain in her heart to speak his name. He may have been short-tempered and impatient, but he had a soft side, a side Mirri guessed didn't come out often. In the short time she spent with the elf, she had grown fond of him.

Kryptus answered her without looking up from the table. "This is a much more dachiled. Graynard had a far simpler one," he murmured.

Mirri watched the tiny flock of animals flying over a cup-sized lake as Smidge stepped beside her. "Do you require anything else, Kryptus?"

"No, that will be all. Continue with the current plan," Kryptus said, still staring at the table. Smidge nodded and took his leave.

Mirri pulled her eyes away from the table. What current plan?

Before she could ask, Kryptus addressed the centaur standing at the door. "The Southern Corridor has been thoroughly searched. We shall move north into the mountains. Inform the Maylarks."

The centaur nodded and exited the room.

"What's going on? Did you find Theodisis?" Mirri asked.

Kryptus shook his head. "No." He put his finger to the tiny mountain tops, avoiding her eyes.

"Well?" Mirri asked. "What's the plan? And what about Theodis-is?"

"For now, the plan has not changed. We must find Gwenna." Still, he stared at the map.

Mirri couldn't believe her ears. "Are you *kidding* me? What about Theodisis? He kidnapped my mother, and you are doing nothing about it?" she yelled. "Could you look at me instead of that stupid table?" She could feel her cheeks burning in anger. She hated this nonchalant side of Kryptus when he acted as if the biggest emergency was nothing more than a daily task.

He slowly lowered his hand and looked at her. "It has not been decided that Theodisis kidnapped your mother. There are other things to consider."

"Like what?" Mirri spat. Her hands were shaking with rage.

"It has been . . . suggested that something else may be going on. Perhaps it was not Gwenna who was kidnapped."

"What are you talking about?" Mirri wanted to throw his halberd against the wall. "Who else did he kidnap? What about my mother?" This made no sense. How long had she been in that memory? How could she have let this happen?

Kryptus sighed and put his hands on the table. "The elders have brought forth the possibility that your mother is the one who . . ." Kryptus looked at Mirri and took his halberd in his hand. "That she is the one who kidnapped Theodisis."

Mirri stared at him, disbelieving what he had just said. Then she laughed, despite everything. "You're kidding me, right? You think my mother kidnapped a centaur?" She laughed again. "Please tell me you're joking."

Kryptus shook his head slowly and lowered his eyes. "It is no joke, Mirri. I'm sorry."

"No, no, this is ridiculous. Has everyone forgotten this is Theodisis we're talking about? How would my mother overcome him?"

"The same way she overcame the Loofa. It is suggested she gave him a tonic. She is proving quite resourceful."

"And then what?" Mirri spat. "Just threw him over her shoulder and trotted off? A *centaur*?"

Kryptus said nothing. He stared over the map in front of them.

Slowly, he said. "Without a weapon, it is possible a tonic made him persuasive. It is possible he is following Gwenna because she is ordering him to."

Mirri threw her hands up. "Wait a minute, wait—what about my mother? She was *poisoned*. Theodisis was there. What if he was the one to poison her? He was on watch when she disappeared, remember?"

When Kryptus still said nothing, Mirri threw her arms down in frustration and turned away. She stomped around the room with her arms crossed. She didn't understand why everyone was so quick to blame her mother, a simple woman with no magical powers. Tears filled her eyes. Kryptus was supposed to be helping her. It seemed he had made up his mind.

"It is not true, Mirri," he spoke from behind her. "My mind has not been made up."

Dang. This mind-reading ability was thoroughly annoying.

She spun to face him. "Then tell me why," she choked, "everyone is so quick to believe my mother is guilty of all of this."

He closed his eyes and put a hand to his forehead. "There is something you don't know, Mirri."

"What? Please, tell me, Kryptus," she begged. She walked to him and took his hand. "You promised to help me," she whispered. "Please." The tears began to fall, tears she could not control anymore.

Kryptus nodded and pursed his lips. "It is time for you to know." He turned away and walked toward the opposite wall. "You know your mother is suspected of killing Avi. But you do not know the full story." He stared at the wall in front of him and spoke over his shoulder. "It was not the first time." He turned and looked at her.

Mirri stared at him, her arms crossed tightly in front of her. "Not the first time for what?"

"She tried to kill before."

Chapter Sixteen

Kryptus was leaning against the table, looking down at the small mountains and trees that made up the three-dimensional table-map. His face was set in a hard stare.

Mirri sat in a chair across from him, only because he said she needed to be sitting. Her mind was a flurry of activity: images of her mother in blue scrubs being led away by centaurs, then seeing her running from Holmforth in a white nightgown through the forest. Without the beads. The beads that had strangled Avi. Then Gwenna with Theodisis. The look of pure hatred on her face.

"Your mother was young," Kryptus said. "It was no secret that your mother and Lavinia did not get along. She was disobedient to her father and had a wild side."

Mirri sat, shocked. This did not sound like her mother at all. Her mother, a wild child? Disobeying her father? She pressed her lips together tightly, willing Kryptus to go on.

"Lavinia was the quiet one. Stayed out of the way. Never spoke. The exact opposite of her younger sister."

Mirri held her breath. Why was Kryptus telling her about Lavinia?

"There was a brawl. In the town square. Between your mother and Lavinia." Kryptus finally raised his head to look at Mirri. "Your mother tried to strangle her."

"What?" Mirri gasped. She felt dizzy.

"I pulled Gwenna off Lavinia before it was too late. But the damage had already been done. Everyone in town had seen your mother wrap her hands around her sister's neck." He shook his head. "I'm sorry, Mirri."

Mirri sat back in her chair and tried to make sense of what Kryptus had just told her. According to him, her mother was some out-of-control maniac who liked to strangle people.

Mirri swallowed. "That's why everyone thinks . . . she did it?"

Kryptus nodded.

Mirri wrapped her arms around herself. Maybe to shield her body from anymore mental blows. She had to ask him. She didn't want to, but she needed to know.

"Do you think she did it?"

Kryptus sighed and crossed his arms over his chest as well. "I have known your mother for a long time, Mirri. I consider her a friend. And I could never believe a murderer could raise such a wonderful young woman."

Mirri gave him a tearful smile. Compliments like that were rare, coming from Kryptus. Maybe that's why they meant so much.

Mirri wiped her face. "What . . . what was their fight about? Lavinia and my mom?" Though she didn't want to know, she needed to. It was the only way. If her mother had tried to kill her sister, there had to be a good reason.

"I'm not sure. It was late in the evening, and people were pulled out of their houses to come and witness the screams. I pulled Gwenna away, kicking and screaming, and then nobody saw or heard from her again. Your father sent her through the portal that night with Rose."

"Why Rose?"

"Rose was a dear friend, his scribe. She had known Gwenna since birth. I suppose your father knew Rose would keep her safe."

Mirri stood. She began pacing the room. "Something isn't right here. My mother is not the kind of person who would do this. She had no reason to kill Avi that night. Wait." Mirri stopped. "You were there! In the forest! You took her back to the portal!"

Kryptus shook his head. "I only encountered her leaving your father's hut, not entering."

"You . . . You were the witness that placed her at the scene?"

Kryptus remained silent.

Mirri's heart sank. Kryptus had put her mother at the scene, had put it in everyone's mind that Gwenna killed her father.

"We need to find out what she and Lavinia were fighting about. The only person who knows for sure is my mom."

"There is another person."

Mirri turned on her heels to stare at him. "Who?"

"Lavinia."

❖

Mirri's heart pounded as loud as Kryptus's banging on the wall. Mirri stood, chewing on her bottom lip, waiting for the wall in front of her to disappear. Instead, a large door creaked open, and a centaur nodded to Kryptus.

Mirri blinked. She had not realized the Imperium used actual doors. She stepped in behind Kryptus and the guard slammed the door shut behind her. The guard waited patiently for Mirri to follow

Kryptus down the dimly lit hall. Mirri looked down the corridor warily. These halls, she remembered.

Torches hung in the air on either side of them, eerily lighting their way to Lavinia's prison cell. Horrible statues sat poised the entire length of the hallway, their red eyes gleaming at Mirri as she passed. Mirri stayed close to Kryptus as they walked. She remembered these statues all too well.

They housed Lavinia in a separate prison, Kryptus explained. He had insisted on it when he had first taken over as leader. She had her own dungeon, and guards standing over her all day and night.

The silence hanging in the air seemed almost unnatural. Even the usually loud hooves of centaurs did not make a sound. Mirri could feel her skin crawling, as if millions of insects were using her body as a nest. She peeked over her shoulder. The walls were listening. They were watching.

She jumped as the guard behind her bumped her with his halberd. He cleared his throat as a way of an apology, and Mirri nodded back, her hand over her heart. She inched closer to Kryptus, practically walking on his hooves. The sweat was inching its way down her forehead now, burning her eyes. Mirri's head swiveled back and forth as they walked, staring at the walls as they inched closer, then closer. She had to get out of here.

Finally, Kryptus stopped. The hall had gotten progressively darker as they walked, raising Mirri's heartbeat to an unnatural level. Her breath was coming in shallow and fast, and her whole body was shaking. By now, she had her hand on Kryptus's horse's back, gripping at his fur coat.

Kryptus stood a moment and fiddled with something, and the wall slid open. Mirri practically pushed him out into the dank room. Kryptus turned to look at her, standing with her arms wrapped around herself, shaking, looking around wildly, tears of sweat dripping down her face. The centaur behind her gripped her elbow as she started to fall toward the ground.

Kryptus put a hand to his forehead. "I apologize, Mirri. I designed specifically the hall to the prison ward to keep prisoners out. We made the effects to be frightening and suffocating."

Mirri stood with her hands on her knees. "Then why are you just fine?" she wheezed, looking around at the concrete room.

"Centaurs are not affected."

"Right." Mirri laughed shakily. "Of course." She straightened, giving a small smile to the centaur next to her, holding her up.

Kryptus stared at her, his eyebrows raised. "In truth, you did quite well. In tests, it was most common for prisoners to pull their hair out in fear."

Mirri stared at him, wondering if he was being truthful. Before she could ask, he turned abruptly and stepped to the wall across from them.

Mirri watched, trying to relax her breathing. What was this place? A plain, gray concrete room? After a trip down that hallway, she had expected something equally horrifying. And where was Lavinia?

The surrounding walls disappeared. Mirri jumped as the steel bars materialized in front of her. A prison cell had appeared out of nowhere, containing a cot, toilet, and small sink. A woman lounged on the small cot in the corner of the prison cell. Lavinia.

Mirri's eyes hardened as she stared at her. The woman's stringy hair hung over the bed, looking like it hadn't been washed for days. The prisoner ate a piece of fruit, loudly sucking the juices out of the food. One leg sat propped up on the other, bouncing lightly, as if she was enjoying a picnic on a summer day.

Lavinia paid them no mind but continued her scrumptious lunch. Licking her fingers loudly, she smiled and dropped the remains of her lunch on the concrete floor.

"Come to visit your auntie, dear?"

Her voice made Mirri cringe. A cold and sinister sound. Lavinia was playing with her, trying to anger her. Mirri's hands balled into fists at her sides. The nerve of this woman. After everything she had done.

Lavinia swung her legs off the bed and sat up. The smile on her face matched the calculating look in her cold stare. It was impressive—with her stringy, disheveled hair pale and sunken-in face, the woman could still evoke fear with her dark eyes.

"I knew you would be here soon, my dear niece. What shall we talk about?"

Mirri stood fuming, all words forgotten. She wanted to scream, to anger this woman, but her mind went blank. Instead, she stood, clenching her fists until they hurt.

Kryptus stepped forward. "We have come to talk about a night in Holmforth. The night Gwenna attacked you."

Lavinia's eyes rolled back in her head as she laughed and fell back on her cot. "So, it would seem you need a favor, hmm? Oh, Kryptus, I absolutely *relish* in you needing things of me." She hung her head off the side of the bed so it hung upside down, her dirty hair brushing the concrete floor.

Mirri wanted to smack that smile off her face. But she refused to play this game with Lavinia. She took a deep breath. "What happened that night? Why did my mother attack you?"

"Ohh, dear sweet Gwenna. It would seem she is in a bit of a bind, wouldn't you say? A small, twisted sort of homlock?" She laughed at her private joke.

Kryptus narrowed his eyes. He abruptly turned and spoke to the guard. "Open the entrance. We're leaving." Kryptus took Mirri by the arm.

"I remember it so clearly . . . Everything fell into place so nicely."

Mirri pulled her arm from Kryptus's grasp and stepped toward the steel bars. "What did you do to her? What did you do to my mother?"

"Oh my dear, it wasn't anything *I* did. It was more what I *knew*."

Lavinia sat up and strode to the bars of her cell, gripping them and sticking her face against the steel. "Gwenna has more than a few secrets, you know," she whispered.

"What secrets?" Mirri demanded before she could stop herself.

Lavinia's eyes gleamed. "Perhaps you should ask Theodisis . . . I'm sure he would be more than happy to answer that question for you."

"What about Theodisis? What happened with Theodisis?"

"Mirri . . . do not let her deceive you," Kryptus warned.

Mirri ignored him. "Tell me about Theodisis."

"Oh dear, that is the question, isn't it? The truth is just *buried*, isn't it?" Lavinia smiled, showing off her stained and yellow teeth.

Mirri clenched her jaw. Lavinia was playing with her. Did she expect that this horrible woman would just give away information?

"We are leaving. Now," Kryptus boomed. He grabbed Mirri's arm again, and this time she followed.

"Good luck, Mirri! I do hope you find the *matsala* you are looking for! If you need a hand, don't hesitate to ask!" She laughed again wildly, nearly falling off her thin bunk.

Mirri turned to glare at her as walls appeared all around her, blocking her view of the prison cells. As soon as the three of them stood in the concrete room alone, Mirri turned to Kryptus.

"What was she talking about?" Mirri demanded. It came out harsher than she intended.

Kryptus shook his head. "I am unsure." His brow creased, and his normally placid face looked troubled. "We need to remember who we are talking to, Mirri. She could easily be lying."

Mirri shook her head. "She was hinting at something. I know it. What does 'matsala' mean? And homlock?"

Kryptus opened his mouth to reply, but the guard standing against the wall interrupted him. "Kryptus! The Voktare needs you right away! There is an emergency!"

Kryptus sighed and rubbed his forehead.

Mirri put her hands on her hips. "What? Don't believe him or something?" She had an edge to her voice. Now, she understood what Smidge had been talking about. Kryptus didn't treat him with the respect he deserved.

Kryptus's eyes snapped toward Mirri. "No," he said. "I simply think that *sometimes*—"

"The Voktare says an enemy approaches the Imperium!" the guard yelled.

Kryptus stepped to the stone wall at once. They entered the dark hallway as soon as the door opened and ran through the din, Mirri trying her best to avoid the crawling of her skin and her stunted breath. She ran as fast as she could, but not as fast as the centaurs. The walls began to close in on her as Mirri slapped herself in the face. *It's not real,* she thought to herself. *It's not real!* She gasped for air and forced her eyes straight ahead, avoiding the red eyes of the menacing creatures ready to pounce on her. She tripped and fell to the floor, yelping as she felt the oily fur of the monster statue. He turned his head and growled, baring his teeth at Mirri. She pulled her hand back and gasped, confusion taking over.

"Mirri!" Kryptus yelled from the end of the hallway. He and the other centaur stood waiting at the doorway to the Imperium.

"Go!" Mirri choked out. "Hurry!" They had to get to Smidge. The village was being attacked. "Go!" Mirri demanded in a stronger voice. "I'll be fine!"

Kryptus nodded, and he and the guard opened the door to run out. Mirri got to her feet shakily, wincing and holding her head. If she could only get out of here . . . Sweat was dripping into her eyes, blinding her. She hobbled toward the door, reaching out. It was so close, she could make it—just a little further . . . The hall began tightening around her, suffocating her as she stumbled forward, her hand outstretched.

She gasped as she fell against the door. Or what she thought was the door. She pounded on the stone wall. This had to be the door. She had reached the end of the hall. The insects were back, all over her body, crawling slowly at first, then faster. Then the laughter. Lavina's cold giggle filled her mind and clogged her brain. She slumped against the wall, holding her head in her hands.

"Please," she whimpered. "Please let me out."

The statues broke from their places along the walls. They began creeping toward Mirri, slinking toward her, ready to pounce. Mirri cried out, slapping at the wall behind her, feeling the insects under her skin now, working their way toward her head. "No," she moaned as the creatures neared her, licking their lips in a kind of evil hunger.

Mirri put her head down and hugged her legs to her body. She squeezed her eyes shut and put her hands over her ears, praying someone would find her before she tore her hair out.

Chapter Seventeen

A blood-curdling scream made Mirri jump. Her head snapped up, the sounds of chaos filling her ears. Instead of a dark hallway, she was sitting on a grassy knoll, leaning against a large tree. Instead of creeping statues with gleaming eyes advancing on her, Kolts ran past her, white hair flying in all directions.

Looking around with wide eyes, she zeroed in on the building behind her, the tall roof covered in flames, with a gaping hole in the orange stone wall. Another crash sounded behind her, and Mirri instinctively threw her arms over her head. Wait—she peeked out, remembering. She could not feel pain here. She had to know what was happening.

All around her, people were screaming, dragging children, running in their nightclothes. What in the world was happening? Flashes of light, trees falling over—was Koltaria being attacked? She ran toward the concrete building, not sure why she felt the need to go there, but knowing she must.

Panting, she looked through the wall that was now crumpled on the dirt ground, seeing papers and books scattered throughout, blankets torn to shreds, and a small table lying on its side. Mirri swallowed thickly and took a small step in, ducking under the smoldering wall. She made her way around a desk to a curtain, reaching out to move it back. Her hand breezed through the thin cloth, and Mirri grimaced, remembering she could simply walk through objects. She bit her lip and took a large step forward, stepping through the fabric.

Mirri took only a second to recover. Smoke seeped out of the wall a few feet down, and Mirri automatically stepped toward the cloud of black smog. At the same time, a young girl with red hair fell out of the smoke, coughing, her face stained with glistening tears. She landed against the opposite wall, wiping her face with her hand, leaving a black streak running up her face.

Mirri froze as she watched Gwenna stand, give one last look into the room, and run straight at Mirri's invisible form. Time seemed to slow as Gwenna neared Mirri, a gold necklace with a ruby bouncing off her chest. Mirri felt the girl run through her body, the tears that became her own. And, for a moment, she felt something else. A stab of pain deep within her soul, a darkness that clouded her vision. Mirri put a hand to her chest, suddenly feeling exhausted when—

Mirri gasped and opened her eyes. She cried out in pain as her back scraped against the concrete floor of the hallway, still dazed from her latest memory.

"Mirri! Are you all right?" Kane stood above her, lines of worry disrupting his handsome face.

Mirri turned and looked around wildly. "No, no—I have to go back! Kane, please—"

"We have to go! Hurry!" Kane picked Mirri up easily and stood her on the floor. "Can you walk?"

"Yes, but I have to—"

Instead of letting her finish, Kane pulled her by the hand, running through the well-lit, pleasant hallway of the Imperium. They skidded to a halt at the end of the hallway, and Kane put an arm around Mirri.

She squeezed her eyes shut as the familiar feeling of swirling came over her body. She bit back the nausea as she opened her eyes.

"Mirri!" Smidge was running toward her as fast as elf legs could go. "You're all right! Kryptus sent me to get you, he was so worried, I'm sorry, I—"

"I'm okay, Smidge," Mirri said, giving her harried-looking friend a quick squeeze. "What is going on?" She peered over his shoulder, looking down the long hallway to the front entrance.

Smidge's voice dropped an octave. "It is the Koltarians. They have demanded to speak with Kryptus."

"I thought you said the Imperium was under attack?"

Smidge's eyes narrowed. "I at first thought it was. A small army of warriors approached, weapons held high. They pushed villagers to the ground, they ignored my requests to halt, and did not stop until they were facing the Imperium."

"What about all the centaurs? The guards?"

"They continue the search of the woods! I did not know what to do Mirri. I was unable to stop them!" He looked at her with pleading eyes.

Mirri patted his shoulder. "You did the right thing, Smidge. Where is Jinx? And Rose?"

Smidge looked up guiltily. "They are trying to listen to the altercation. Jinx is outside, eavesdropping."

"Show me," Mirri said, straightening up.

The three of them ran down the hallway, skidding to a stop at the front entrance. Mirri peeked out the door, getting another view of the Koltarians.

Sure enough, she immediately recognized the men with the long white braids. They wore suits of armor and held gigantic swords. Mirri swallowed, wondering if these men also carried a blade in their belt, as

Cormac had. The warriors stood encircling the Imperium. Kryptus was standing nose-to-nose with a man, a fellow centaur standing behind him, poised with his halberd.

Onlookers of the village were standing in a hushed group well off the road, huddled together for protection, fear written on their faces.

Silently, Mirri slid out the entrance and snaked her body out, much to the objection of Kane. She ignored his hiss at her to get back inside. She had to know what the Koltarian wanted.

"I demand you turn the prisoner over! She is responsible for crimes in Koltaria and deserves to be punished!" His beet-red face stood out against his white braid that draped over the front of his armor.

"What proof do you have that this prisoner committed these acts? It will take more than your word to convince me she is guilty of what you say," Kryptus said, holding his halberd to his side.

"Your prisoner has stolen a precious relic from my kingdom! I demand its return! My kingdom has suffered for 109 years because of this human!"

"If the prisoner is guilty of what you say, she will be justly punished. *Here.* In my kingdom."

"And what of my relic? Our Homlock? Are you saying it is simply a loss?" The man's voice shook with rage, and his hand lowered to his side, near his sword.

"We will recover this Homlock if this prisoner did what you say."

"I demand you allow me to speak to her! At once!"

Kryptus paused. Until now, Mirri thought he had done a satisfactory job of wasting time. It seemed the truth would have to come out eventually.

"I cannot allow that," Kryptus said.

"And why is that? Do you wish to start a war, or do you consent to let me speak to your prisoner?"

Kryptus squared his shoulders. "The prisoner has evaded us. At present, she is being searched for."

The Kolt stared at Kryptus a moment, then threw his head back and laughed. "You are telling me you lost this *human* for who you were responsible for? A prisoner has escaped your army of centaurs?"

"Yes, this same *human* that swindled your precious Homlock," Kryptus bit back.

The two leaders glared at each other. There was an unnatural hush throughout the onlookers. Mirri shrunk back against the wall.

The Kolt nodded slowly and looked at his sword. "We shall join this hunt for the prisoner."

"That is quite unnecessary," Kryptus said. "We will locate the prisoner and your relic and return it to you."

"No. This human has committed crimes in my kingdom. The treaty clearly states that we lay claim to the prisoner, as do you. Or do you wish to cancel this treaty of peace?"

Kryptus stared at the man, then spoke. "You may join this hunt, but rest assured, I am in charge. Your warriors will take orders from no one but me." Kryptus paused. "And also, my second in command."

"Your dear friend Theodisis, no doubt? The foolish centaur who has managed to lose his weapon?"

"No," Kryptus said, a ghost of his smile playing at his lips. "I have a new second in command. The Voktare who saved my village from the Panthera."

Mirri gaped at Kryptus. She looked down at Smidge, standing next to her, who looked positively horrified.

Kryptus drew his arm back toward Smidge. "May I introduce you to Humdinger Wishyswenson the Third. The Voktare."

Smidge stood with his mouth hanging open. Mirri nudged him with her knee just hard enough to shake him back into reality. He snapped his mouth shut and took a small step forward. Kryptus gave him a small nod, and he stepped to the centaur's side with his chin held high.

"Humdinger, this is Tolok. Leader of the Koltarian Kingdom. I trust you shall give his warriors the utmost leadership and skill."

Smidge nodded and pushed his shoulders back. He cleared his throat. "Of course, Kryptus."

Tolok looked at Smidge in outrage. "You expect my men to take orders from an undersized elf? You mock me, Kryptus," the Koltarian seethed.

"I assure you, Tolok, the Voktare has been leading my centaurs while I have been attending the other duties of my kingdom. If you have a problem with my ranks, you may leave now. As our treaty states, you are on Althord Loch land. And you will follow Althord Loch's rules of engagement."

Tolok narrowed his eyes at Smidge. "Fine. My Kolts will take orders from you or your *Humdinger*." He looked at Kryptus. "We will join the hunt immediately."

Mirri looked at Kane with wide eyes. The hunt? For her mother? Until now, she believed the centaurs would find her mother and return her peacefully. But these Kolts looked angry. Angry enough to exact revenge. And if given the chance, she had no doubt they would take it.

✦

"A Homlock. Lavinia said something about a Homlock, didn't she?" Mirri was shaking but didn't want Kryptus to notice. "What was

stolen?" She had a terrible feeling. An ancient relic. Perhaps a necklace
. . . with a ruby.

"He claims Gwenna stole this Homlock," Kryptus said, putting his
hand on his forehead. "It is a type of necklace, I am told."

"A gold necklace?" Mirri swallowed. " With a red stone in the
center?"

Things were beginning to unfold. Gwenna had taken the Homlock. Mirri knew, to the depths of her soul, that Gwenna had been
wearing the Homlock when she ran out of that burning room. But
why?

Kryptus narrowed his eyes. "What memory did you see? Did you
see Gwenna take this necklace?" he demanded, nearly stomping on
Mirri's foot.

"No, I—I saw her running out of a burning building wearing it,"
Mirri said, slumping on a chair. "Surrounded by Koltarians. Something horrible was going on—a hell storm, or the end of the world
or something—it was awful." Mirri chewed a fingernail madly. "Why
would she steal that necklace?"

Kryptus stood still, examining his halberd. "There are many
anganos about this necklace. Many stories, I am told. Perhaps your
mother believed them."

"Maybe when she was a teenager! But she is a grown woman now!
What if—what if she's trying to return the necklace?" Mirri turned to
face Kryptus. " She's trying to get to Koltaria. Maybe wants to undo
what she did so long ago!" She grabbed Kryptus's arm. "That's what
she's doing. I know it!"

Kryptus stared at Mirri for a moment. "I suppose it is feasible. At
this point, I highly doubt she is still in Althord. And I do not believe
she is running to escape the charges against her. She has a destination
in mind."

Mirri paced across the room. "She is going to Koltaria. I saw it, Kryptus, I saw Koltaria." She turned to face him, her arms still tightly crossed. "I need to get there."

Kryptus shook his head. "It is far too dangerous, Mirri. The Kolts are a crude race. Warriors. I do not know how they would react to a human entering their land."

"We have no choice! We have to find her before the Kolts do! What if they find her and take her back to some horrible dungeon or something? Or hang her from her ankles and torture her or something?" Mirri ran her hands through her hair. Horrible thoughts flashed through her mind when she realized she may not be far from the truth. The Kolts were furious with Gwenna. Mirri had to find her first.

Kryptus was staring at her with his mouth set in a grimace. He was hearing her thoughts, listening to Mirri's worst fears. And he must have believed them.

He turned and strode to the entrance. The wall faded away, revealing a centaur standing at attention. "Get me the Voktare," he barked. "And find Kane."

The centaur nodded and marched off.

Kryptus turned back to Mirri. "You will take Kane and the Voktare. Pattick can get you as far as Waylor Ravine. It should set you near the Koltarian border. I will remain and distract the Kolts."

Mirri nodded. "Yes, yes, okay. We will go now."

"I must see Kryptus! It is a matter of life!" The high-pitched, breathless voice of Arlo rang out down the hallway.

"What is it now?" Kryptus walked to the wall as it evaporated. "Let him in," he called to the two centaurs at the front entrance.

Arlo came dashing down the hallway, skidding to a stop in front of Kryptus. "I need to see Mirri!" he said. "Where is she? Please, I need to see her now!"

Kryptus put his hands on the Leet's shoulders. "Arlo, calm down. She is standing right there."

"What? What's wrong?" Mirri asked, running across the room. The look on his face made her insides twist.

Arlo took a deep breath and stepped to the table. He laid a large book down on the table, loose pages spilling everywhere.

"The insects, Mirri. The ones you said attacked you. You said their eyes glowed."

"Uh, yeah." Mirri looked at Arlo. "Do you know what kind of bug they are?"

Arlo shook his head. "They were not insects, Mirri." He looked at Kryptus and swallowed thickly. "I believe they were the Manna Kai."

CHAPTER EIGHTEEN

"The what?" Kryptus asked, sighing loudly.

"The Manna Kai. I believe Mirri has witnessed a Manna Kai."

Mirri stared at Arlo. Then at Kryptus. Kryptus was doing his best to hold his temper in check.

"Arlo, I appreciate your research, but I believe we have bigger things—"

"No, Kryptus, you do not understand! A Manna Kai is a blessing of the most significance!" Arlo dropped the book and put his hands to his head, striding about the room. "Imagine seeing a Manna Kai, being in the exact right place at the exact correct time, seeing oneself for its true form, truly learning what you had always—"

"Arlo!" In one large stride, Kryptus had the Leet by the shoulders, up off the ground. "Calm yourself!"

Arlo snapped his mouth shut and nodded with wide eyes.

Kryptus set him down gently. "Now explain the Manna Kai."

Arlo nodded again and flipped open the enormous book he had brought in with him. He turned pages rapidly, muttering to himself. "Here!" he announced.

Mirri and Kryptus leaned over the table, looking at the faded page. A woman with glowing eyes hovered in the air, arms spread wide, a young being at her feet.

Arlo read slowly. "The Manna Kai was a blessing from the gods. A blessing said to show you what you yearned for most in life. It could solve the thing your heart yearned for most. It gave you power, knowledge, whatever your heart needed to complete your mission in life." Arlo's voice lowered. "But it will come at a high price. The information you receive will not come free. Your soul will be challenged."

"Challenged how?"

Arlo shook his head. "That is the most frightening part. We do not know. It will put her through a trial of her own inner strength. Testing herself to the limits. Only if you pass this test will you find what you search for."

"And you are sure this is a Manna Kai?"

Arlo nodded. "Yes. That is the angano."

"An angano? This is all based on a silly angano?" Kryptus slammed the book shut in front of Arlo. "Out!"

"No, no, Kryptus, you must believe me! This research is pure; the writing is legitimate! Mirri must prepare herself for the trial of her soul! I beg you, please!"

"Guard!" Kryptus yelled.

"Understand, Kryptus, all anganos are based in fact! It is true! We must document the significance of these findings! As soon as Mirri discovers the answers to her puzzle, she will—"

"GUARD!"

"Mirri!" Arlo turned to her, desperation written all over his face. "Your puzzle is unfolding, Mirri. It will come together—you must be prepared for the journey!"

A centaur appeared at the door with Smidge at his side, Jinx fluttering behind him. "Kryptus?" the guard asked.

"Escort Arlo home." Kryptus turned to Arlo, who was practically shaking. "Thank you for your assistance, Arlo. We will take it from here."

The guard stepped into the room and put his hand on Arlo's shoulder, leading him out of the room. "You must believe, Kryptus! You must! Mirri! The truth will come, but at a great cost!"

Mirri listened, wide-eyed, hearing Arlo's shrieking all the way down the hall. She looked up at Kryptus, her hands trembling.

Smidge stepped into the room, looking confused. "What was that all about?"

"Nothing. Nothing at all." Kryptus shoved the book to the end of the table and turned to Smidge.

"But—but Kryptus," Mirri asked, rubbing her forehead. "What if he's right? Is it possible that those things were the Man—Manna thing?" Arlo's words echoed in her mind. A test of her soul . . . what could that possibly mean?

"Did you say the Manna Kai?" Smidge squeaked.

"Anganos," Kryptus said, turning to face her and ignoring Smidge, "are tales told to amuse children. Silly stories with no basis in fact. I suggest you forget his words."

"But what if he is right?"

"Whether or not you believe in silly children's tales is beyond the point. We have more important things to deal with," Kryptus said, staring Mirri down. She swallowed and nodded. That signified the end of the conversation.

Mirri nodded and looked down, biting her lip. She would follow Kryptus's advice to the ends of the earth, forever. She nodded to herself and cleared her throat. Always.

Smidge's wide eyes as he stepped away from Arlo's thick book didn't even bother her. Neither did the tremble in his lower lip as looked up at her with the fear locked in his stare. Not one bit.

◆

Mirri, Kane, and Smidge strode down the path with Jinx perched on Mirri's shoulder. Smidge kept glancing up at Mirri with a creased brow. Jinx stayed stationary on Mirri's shoulder the entire walk, using a furry paw to pat Mirri gently from time to time. Mirri couldn't stop hearing Arlo's warning in her mind. A trial of her inner strength. Testing her inner soul. What did that mean, exactly?

Part of her had wanted to run straight to Arlo's front door and have him describe to her this angano. Kryptus had brushed it off as nothing, a silly story and a waste of his time. But what if this was all true? The bugs . . . The glowing eyes . . . Arlo had seemed so worried. Mirri could still hear the fear in his voice. But the other part of her brain pictured her mother bleeding, tied up, and in pain. She had to find her. Now.

By the time they reached Pattick's hut, the Manna Kai had been pushed from Mirri's mind. Mirri winced as Kane pounded on Pattick's front door, so hard that the slab of wood shook. The door cracked open, and the green rabbit peeked out.

"Kane? Mirri?" He opened the door. "What is going on?"

"Kryptus sent us. We are in need of another portal."

"Ah. Come in, come in. Let's see what I can do."

Pattick hobbled back to the desk as the group entered his hut. Mirri led Smidge and Jinx to the center of the hut where they stood, Mirri doing her best not to tap her foot. Smidge looked a little more at ease, still glancing up at Mirri from time to time. Mirri wondered if he had used this method of travel before. Or perhaps he was relieved to have gotten away from the leading the Kolts.

Jinx flew overhead, inspecting the wall of books. She had the look of an excited child as she floated around the room, inspecting the intricate carvings and books that lined the walls. Mirri reached up and grabbed a bit of her tummy fluff gently to tug her back to reality. Jinx's eyes were still wide and filled with wonder as Mirri perched her back on her shoulder.

Pattick dug in a drawer, muttering to himself. "Glasses, glasses, never can find those finoodling things . . ."

Mirri reached into a box near the desk. "Will these work?" she asked, forcing a smile. She held up the wooden frames that were sitting atop a pile of dusty books and clay dishes. These were carved from a different bark, much darker. Still beautiful. She wondered how many pairs of glasses this guy owned.

He took the glasses from her and perched them on top of his nose. "All right, where do you need to go?"

Kane stepped forward. "We need to get to the Koltarian Kingdom. As quickly as possible."

Pattick raised a bushy white eyebrow. "Kryptus is sending you to Koltaria? Whatever for?"

"There is no time for explanation, I'm afraid. Can you do it?"

Pattick licked his green finger and began turning crinkling pages. "I believe I have it in here somewhere," he muttered to himself.

They stepped to the napran and waited. And waited. Mirri's teeth were grinding, impatiently awaiting the slowest creature she had ever encountered. He flipped a page and picked up a pencil as Mirri's heart leaped. He slowly put the pencil behind his ear and kept turning the pages, humming quietly to himself.

Smidge stood next to Mirri, wringing his hands. Jinx fluttered up and down the shelves, looking as Mirri must have on the first day she arrived. Mirri kept reaching over to grab Jinx by a foot or ball of fluff and yanking her down back to her shoulder.

Mirri bit her bottom lip, deciding she would throttle this rabbit and find the address herself if she had to stand here one more minute.

"Here we are!" he announced, flipping open the suitcase that Mirri hadn't noticed and fiddling with dials and levers. Pattick leaned close to the small dials and knobs, his glasses falling off and landing on the desk. Reaching over slowly, he perched them back on the end of his nose and resumed his work.

Breathe, Mirri told herself. *Just breathe.* As much as she wanted to at the moment, she could not strangle the only creature who could get her to her mother.

Just as she opened her mouth to ask if he needed help, Pattick inserted the gold spiral on the end of the chain, flipped a switch, and yanked it back out.

"Kane!" Pattick tossed the necklace to him. As Kane put the chain over his neck, Mirri wondered if Pattick had been told they had lost the first necklace. Or maybe you needed a different one each time? She hoped it wasn't some precious stone that he only had a few of.

"Good luck, kids!"

The same spark, bang, and Pattick disappeared from view.

❖

Mirri lay there, waiting for her head to stop spinning. She put her hand to her head, willing the peach and pink sunset to stop spinning around her. She groaned—whatever she landed on was poking her in the back. And poking her in the head. Just her luck to land in an enormous pile of branches.

Mirri raised her head to look for the others, pulling at her cloak. She lifted her hand to wave, seeing them several yards in front of her, when she stopped. Smidge had his hand to his mouth, eyes wide with terror. Kane held his fists clenched, his mouth set in a grim stare.

Slowly, Mirri turned her head. In the distance, she could see the snow-capped mountains and dense forest. Taking a deep breath, she leaned over and looked down.

She stared, her head forgetting to tell her chest to breathe. Directly underneath her, the rushing water surged through the ravine—white, choppy waves hitting either side of the rock walls, sending water flying through the chasm.

Her eyes closed in on what sat in front of her, though it took her mind a moment to process. The enormous branch holding her above the ravine. Realization slowly seeping into her brain, Mirri breathed faster and faster, tears of fear welling in her eyes. She was sitting in a cozy nest at the end of the telephone pole-sized branch, some twenty feet from her friends, hanging over a rushing river. A human-sized nest, most likely for some enormous bird creature.

"What—what do I do?" Mirri called shakily to Smidge and Kane, suddenly afraid to raise her voice louder than necessary. She forced her eyes to remain trained on her friends' frightened faces.

"I will come to you," Kane called back. Mirri watched him say something to Smidge, who shook his head vehemently. Smidge pointed at himself directly in the chest. Kane shook his head back, pointing at Mirri.

Mirri watched their ill-timed argument from afar. Too scared to breathe, she tried to push herself into a sitting position. The branch cracked and shifted down. Mirri froze. She squeezed her eyes shut, waiting for the inevitable three-hundred-foot drop into the maniacal waves.

Nothing happened. Slowly, trying to ease the bile rising in her throat, Mirri reached forward. Inch by inch. She was sitting now, heart pounding in her chest, trying to decide what to do. Wincing, Mirri reached for a smaller branch sticking straight up toward the sky. She grasped it and gave it a small tug.

Mirri nodded to herself—nothing to it. *Easy as pie,* she told herself. Holding onto the small branch with one hand, she put her other hand down into the mess of branches.

Mirri gasped as her hand shot straight through the branches and into the air. She whipped her hand back and held it to her chest, squeezing her eyes shut just in time to hear the next cracking of the log.

She held her breath, frozen in place. She watched as Smidge turned toward Mirri, let his hands fall to his sides, and took a deep breath. He closed his eyes.

"No!" Mirri yelled, gasping as another cracking sound echoed all around them.

Smidge's eyes flew open as Mirri let out a breath of relief.

"Don't blossom, Smidge! It—it can't hold you!"

Kane yanked Smidge back by his collar, causing Smidge to stumble backward. Mirri watched, wincing, as Smidge stepped back up to the log and shoved Kane out of the way. Smidge was stepping onto the log, arms out to his sides. He set his mouth in a firm line, doing his best to act brave.

Mirri swallowed and tried to give him a comforting smile from her position of terror above a rushing river. She was doing her best not to scream at him to get a move on already. Closing her eyes, she forced herself to count to ten.

The log lurched to the side, and Mirri cried out and squeezed her arms to her chest. After a second, she forced herself to continue breathing. Smidge had reached down and grabbed the log for support. He looked near tears. But he got up slowly and began shuffling toward her again.

And where was Jinx? Smidge needed her. By the time Smidge tip-toed out here, she would be nothing more than bird droppings falling from the sky. Mirri forced the thought from her mind and concentrated on not moving. She watched Smidge work his way down the tilting, six-inch wide bridge. His chest was rising and falling rapidly, and Mirri could see his eyes watering. *You can do this,* Mirri thought. *You're so close.*

He took another small step. A small *'pop'* made him jump and lose his footing. His arms turned wildly in the air as he teetered back and forth on the narrow log.

"Smidge!" Mirri cried, reaching forward, though he was still well out of her reach.

At the same time, a green glow shot out of the forest. Jinx slid under Smidge's small body and held him in place, her wings beating so fast they were invisible.

Mirri let herself breathe a sigh of relief. Jinx helped Smidge stand upright, then continued to hover under his small arm. A bit of a guide on this ridiculous journey.

Mirri bit her bottom lip as they neared her. She reached toward them as much as she dared. *Just a little closer. Just a little closer . . .*

They were mere inches from Mirri's outstretched hand when they heard it. Another loud splitting noise, like a bolt of lightning just split a tree in half.

Things seemed to move in slow motion. Mirri's wide eyes connected with Smidge and Jinx's horrified stares just before the log gave one final jerk, leaving Mirri hanging onto her small branch with one hand.

And then she was falling.

CHAPTER NINETEEN

Mirri's body hit the water with a force she had never felt before. The pain radiated through every last bone in her body. The temperature of the water forced Mirri's mind to awaken. Holding her breath, she kicked. Pulled the water with her arms. Breathe! She had to breathe!

The rushing water pulled her along as she thrashed when, finally, her face broke the surface. Mirri gasped and took a large breath, only to have a wave of water thrown over the top of her again.

Even with her head underwater, Mirri kicked and pulled at the rushing waves. She felt the cold air on her face once again, determined to keep her head above water.

The raging current refused to slow, dragging Mirri through the winding river. Waves knocked her back and forth, slamming her into the rock wall. Mirri reached and grabbed with every ounce of her being every time the river flung her body against the stone. Coughing and sputtering, she grabbed at the side of the smooth ravine, only to be pulled back under.

The river laughed at her, mocking the young woman trying to stay afloat. Mirri's tiring body continued to be pulled down the roaring river, all of her energy spent on keeping her head above water.

Her feet dragged on something below. She felt the pebbles and rocks with her sneakers, and her clogged brain tried to make sense of the receding river. The ravine wall to the right was gone, giving way to something helpful—land. Mirri caught sight of the tall grass and dirt that ran along the river—nice, dry, flat land. If only she could—if only—Mirri grunted and pushed her body back under the waves.

There! Her tennis shoes dragged along the river floor, but the water was still moving too fast to stop. Using all of her might, Mirri pushed back off the river floor, trying to eject her body to the land on the other side. It was a pathetic attempt, Mirri forgetting just how heavy the water was.

A branch. Mirri felt a branch. She grabbed and held on for dear life. Her legs continued to be pulled in the water, but her body remained wrapped around the branch. Water flowed around her, pulling her body, dragging her under again.

It was too much, the branch too wet, she—she couldn't . . . Mirri tried to scream but only swallowed another mouth full of river water. At the same time Mirri let go of the branch, she felt powerful hands grab her shoulders. The freezing evening air felt blissful and still on her wet cheeks. Mirri coughed and sputtered as her limp body was dragged onto dry land. She lay on the rocks, too exhausted to thank whoever had just saved her life.

The hands that saved her picked her up under the waist and her legs and carried her like a rag doll. Mirri swayed back and forth as the large body hauled her away from the sounds of the rushing river, the sounds of her near-drowning. She leaned her head against the warm chest, not caring if this was friend or foe, and fell asleep.

Mirri turned, enjoying the sunlight on her cheeks and breathing in the pine trees all around her. Forest surrounded her on either side, though this forest seemed . . . different, somehow. The surrounding trees were tall, taller than any trees Mirri had ever seen in Althord. They weren't as dense as the trees Mirri was used to trekking around or climbing up, either. Odd. Was she still in Althord?

Mirri turned when she heard the '*oomph.*' She made her way through the trees toward the noise, remembering she didn't need to push these branches out of the way. The sharp edges didn't scratch her skin, and the leaves didn't brush against her face. Her sneakers scraping through the brush remained silent. The grunting became louder as Mirri stepped into a clearing.

Gwenna was there, her back to Mirri, digging in the ground with a stone on the other side of the clearing. Though this Gwenna seemed different from the Gwenna she had come across in these memories. Mirri recognized her mother's haircut, much shorter and more straight than the young Gwenna. She wore a dress that at one time must have been white but was now filled with streaks of dirt and rips at the seams.

Mirri stepped out of the trees to approach her as Gwenna pulled something out of the forest floor with a grunt. Gwenna held the trunk for a moment, wiping the loose soil from the top and sitting back on her heels. Mirri cocked her head, her curiosity growing, when Gwenna turned and dumped it on the ground. Wiping her brow with the back of her hand, Gwenna sorted through the pile of soil and pulled out a gold necklace, the sun shining off the red jewel in the fading sun. Gwenna paused for a moment, staring at the necklace in her hands.

She stood up and ran, stuffing the necklace in a satchel Mirri hadn't noticed hanging down by her side. Once Gwenna disappeared into the woods, the forest around Mirri became fuzzy, fading. Mirri turned her head in confusion.

Mirri jumped, her eyes still closed, very aware of lying on the ground instead of standing on it. The sounds of a crackling fire were near, and she could feel the pleasant warmth surrounding her body. She slowly opened her eyes and gazed at the dancing flames.

A man sat opposite her, poking at the fire with a stick. A piece of something green hung out of his mouth, and Mirri's eyes immediately went to the long white hair that hung in a mess around his shoulders. His ears stuck out from under his white hair, and his chin came to a fine point, just like the man she had seen in the memory.

Mirri swallowed thickly. A Kolt. Had he noticed she was awake yet? Could she slip away unnoticed? She decided to lie on the dirt floor and keep up the facade of unconsciousness. Closing her eyes, she listened to the crackling of the fire. Surely, he would have to get up at some point. Maybe to find more firewood. Or relieve himself.

"Finally awake, eh?" the man spoke. He continued poking at the fire.

Mirri glanced up. Her body remained rigid. Apparently, she hadn't fooled him.

"You must be hungry," he said. "It would be much easier just to sit up."

He looked at her. His blue eyes had a bit of a smile about them, a tiny little glint of humor.

Mirri relaxed. Slowly, she worked herself into a sitting position, never taking her eyes off the man in front of her. Off to the side, jeans and a cloak were hanging on a homemade clothes line, strung up over the fire.

She pulled the blanket around herself, staring at him warily. She sat, her eyes tracing the thick trees surrounding them, unsure of what to do. Mirri studied the man sitting in front of her, trying to gauge her danger situation. No white robe, she noted. But the face. He had the face of a Kolt, even if he didn't braid his long white hair.

The man reached into a pocket of his brown leather vest and pulled out a chunk of what looked like bread. He tossed it over to her, the bread landing on the ground in front of Mirri.

Her stomach growled as she looked at the food. Truthfully, she couldn't remember the last thing she had eaten since being in Althord. She had been too worried and too angry to care about food. But the bread lying in front of her looked positively scrumptious.

She reached her hand out of her blanket and snatched up the bread, bringing it to her mouth. Taking a small nibble, Mirri breathed in the heavenly scent of food. Forgetting her fear of this Koltarian, she gobbled up the rest of it, finishing it by licking her fingers. Oh, how she wished there was more.

Mirri swallowed the last of her bread crumbs. "Thank you," she muttered.

The man nodded. "Human, huh?" He chuckled. "My whole life, I been taught to be wary of you creatures, but darlin', I don't think you could hurt a jaymar."

Mirri stiffened. Although she was grateful for the food, she didn't appreciate his tone. And she had no idea what a jaymar was.

"Don't think so?" She glared at the man. "Guess you don't know who I've dealt with," she shot back. If only he knew.

The Kolt leaned his head back and laughed. "A tough human, huh? Well, I have to admit, I'm impressed you made it through the river still breathin'." He leaned forward and poked at the fire, tossing another twig into the flames.

Mirri bristled at his attitude. What a jerk. "Well, I've been told you Kolts are nothing but arrogant jerks who can't run an empire."

He chuckled as he poked at the fire. "Sounds 'bout right."

Mirri gritted her teeth and looked away. Apparently, this guy did not take offense easily. How annoying.

"So, how did you come to be nearly drowning in the Waylor River? Pretty far from Althord."

"What makes you think I'm from Althord?"

He raised his eyebrows. "Can't think of nowhere else you'd come from, darlin'. You aren't from Koltaria. No humans allowed there."

"Why not?" Mirri asked before she could stop herself.

"All humans do is cause a right bit of trouble. Jam things around. Destroy empires, that type of thing."

Mirri opened her mouth to laugh in his face. But she stopped. Was he talking about her mother? Was she the reason these warriors hated humans?

"What kind of trouble?" Mirri asked, avoiding his blue eyes.

The man leaned back against his tree and looked at her. She didn't fool him. He knew she was fishing for information.

"A bit strange, if you ask me," he said. He pulled another plant stalk from his pack and popped it into his mouth.

Mirri had to ask. "What is?"

"Oh, just the kingdom-wide search for that wretched human. Then I come upon another human, drowning in a river. How 'bout that, huh?"

Mirri shifted in her blanket. This guy was smarter than she thought. "So, why did you save me?"

He shrugged. "Couldn't very well leave a tiny little human to be killed, could I?"

Mirri fought down the glare that she wanted to unleash upon him. She shrugged back. "Guess not."

He stood and spit the plant into the fire. Then he stomped onto the fire with his brown boots. "Best time we get going, eh?"

"Going where?"

He scrutinized her. "You wanna stay in this part of the forest the rest of your life? Kolts hunting you down?"

Mirri looked up at him, surprised. His question sounded like he wanted to help her. "I guess not," she said.

He nodded over to the homemade clothes line. "You'll want to get those strange clothes back on. Pretty harsh weather around here." He bent over to collect his bag.

Mirri glanced back up at the clothes hanging over the fire. She gasped as she felt her bare legs. At least she still had her T-shirt on. "You took my clothes off?" she demanded, pulling the blanket tighter around her shoulders.

"Relax," he drawled. "They were soaking wet. You would have died of mandrane if you laid around in them things in this weather." He pulled her jeans off the clothesline and tossed them to her. "Strange things," he muttered. "Took forever to dry." He tossed her the cloak as well.

"I'll be right over here," he called over his shoulder as he walked into the trees.

Mirri hesitated. Then she grabbed her stiff jeans and pulled them under the blanket. She struggled into them quickly, still under the blanket. She stood and threw the cloak around her, shivering in the morning breeze. Looking behind her, she noticed a path leading into the woods. Should she run? But what if he took the same path? Maybe just yell a thank you and stroll away. But he seemed nice enough . . .

Before she could make up her mind, the Kolt stepped back into the clearing and picked up the blanket, rolling it into a tight roll. He attached a strap around it and threw the strap around his shoulder. "Let's get going." He bent over and picked a sword off the ground.

Mirri gasped and backed away. He ignored her and swung the sword over his shoulder, tucking it into a strap or sheath she could not see.

The white-haired man headed out of the clearing, pushing his way between the trees. Mirri stayed where she was, looking around, wondering if she should trust him. He had saved her life, after all. Twice, actually. He dragged her out of the river and then built a fire and wrapped her in a blanket. She gnawed on her fingernail. It's not like she had many options, she reasoned. He had plenty of time to kill her if he had wanted to.

Sighing, she stepped after him, pulling the cloak tighter around her. The Kolt didn't seem all that concerned with her presence. He certainly wasn't treating her as his prisoner. Maybe not all Kolts hated humans, she reasoned. Maybe Kryptus had been wrong to assume those things about all Kolts. Maybe. As soon as she knew where she was, she would take off on her own. For now, she needed his help.

"So, uh, what do I call you?" she called after him.

"Lonar."

"Loner?" Seemed appropriate.

"Lonar. For the third moon."

"Oh. Right."

Lonar glanced back at her with a grin.

Mirri couldn't quite figure this guy out. He had been told how dangerous humans were, yet he was here, walking around with one? Pulled one from a river instead of letting her drown? Was he not the slightest bit wary of Mirri?

They stepped out onto a well-worn path, and Lonar turned to the left. Mirri halted. Left didn't feel right . . . She looked to the right. Dense forest blocked the path. She followed him, though her stomach was turning in circles. Still in Koltarian land, she didn't feel as confident going off on her own. The next path, she decided. At the moment, her best option seemed to follow him.

"Where are we going?"

"Wherever I can get a decent night's rest."

Mirri relaxed. That didn't sound so bad. "So, uh, why aren't you with the rest of the Kolts?"

"They don't like me too much."

"Why not?" Mirri asked to his back.

He shrugged. "I steal stuff."

Mirri glanced around, her nerves jumping back into action. So he was one of those types. They trudged on in silence, Mirri keeping a close eye on the sword that hung from his back. After an hour or two, she relaxed. As soon as she figured out where she was, she would get away from him. Maybe a town? A little inn, perhaps?

Her attention turned to her trio of friends she had left behind at the ravine. It occurred to her that Smidge had been teetering off that log as well when she fell. What if he had fallen after her? No, she shook her head. He had Jinx. Jinx would never have let that happen. Mirri just had to find them. She would head to Koltaria. That was the original plan. And that's what she would do. They must be back in Althord by now, safe and sound. But what if they had tried to make it into Koltaria? What if someone found and interrogated them, or worse?

Of course not, she argued with herself. They aren't human. An elf, centaur, and Loofa wouldn't anger the Koltarians. Right? Her inner voice was beginning to waiver. The more she argued with herself, the less sure she felt. What if her friends were in danger at this very minute?

Not two minutes later, they came to a fork in the road. Lonar stopped, pulled a jug of water out of his pack, and offered her a drink.

She took it with a nod and took as big of a gulp as she thought polite. He popped the top back on and headed to the right. Mirri eyed him for a moment, then crept away in the opposite direction.

"I wouldn't if I were you," he called over his shoulder.

Mirri stopped in her tracks. Slowly, she turned to face him. "I, uh, need to go find my friends. Thanks for everything." She turned and began walking down the path at a fast pace.

She gasped when she felt her arm yanked backward. Confused, Mirri tugged at her right hand with her other. Something was . . . holding it. It felt as if a rope was bound around her wrist—a rope she could not see.

"What—what did you do to me?" She tugged at her arm again. "Let me go!"

"No point in fightin'," he said, sipping his water, watching her struggle. "Scabian bracelet. The only thing that can remove it is the key."

"When" —Mirri cried— "when did you do this?"

"Oh, you've had it on since I fished you out of the river." He pressed a button on his own wrist. A golden bracelet appeared. Mirri looked down at her own wrist, where she felt the pressure. An identical gold band had appeared, heavy and thick.

"Why?" Mirri gasped, trying to pry her hand out of the metal band.

"How else was I supposed to get you to Koltaria? Quite a price for you humans these days."

"Wh—what?"

"Don't worry, darlin'. Human sacrifices go quick." With that, he nodded and headed down the path. And no matter how hard she struggled, Mirri had no choice but to follow.

CHAPTER TWENTY

Mirri sat curled up on a tree stump, her eyes darting back and forth. She had pulled her cloak up over her nose to keep out the smell of Koltarian body odor. Her head developed a constant throb the longer she sat. Men yelling, strange animals honking, and a large white-haired woman singing in a horribly low voice at the front of the room. She was a scantily clad female, wearing something these hooligans must find attractive on an overly large woman. Buckets lined the floor, along with random tables and stumps lying all over the place. She tried not to stare at the feathered animals in the metal cages, hooting and cawing miserably.

Lonar sat across the small table, drinking something out of a dirty metal cup. He spoke to another Kolt in a low voice, keeping his mouth hidden behind the cup. He had gotten Mirri another piece of bread and one of those metal cups filled with water. At least, she thought it was water. She took one look into the cup and pushed it away. She would have to be dying of thirst to drink liquid with things floating in it.

Mirri picked up the hard bread and nibbled on a corner, forcing herself to swallow a bite. Across the room, a heavyset man with a long white beard stood around a large square fire pit. He wore what looked like a long leather skirt with no shirt. The skeleton tattoos printed all over his back gave Mirri chills. He had a roaring fire going, with pots hanging over on hooks and a large animal roasting in the center. *Might have been a pig,* she thought. By now, it was too black and charred to tell.

Mirri glanced at her wrist. Tapped the gold bracelet. She didn't know what this thing was, but she knew she did not like it. At first, Mirri had assumed it was a leash. Leading her along. But it was more than that. After Lonar had shown her the bracelet, and she could see it, Lonar could . . . kind of—control her. Back at the fork in the road, she tried to run, but she couldn't. Her legs wouldn't do what she wanted them to do. As they walked down the trail, Mirri noticed her stride matched his perfectly. If he stopped with a foot in the air, so did she.

At one point, she even tripped over a hole in the road. Lonar stumbled as well—just a bit. Mirri filed that piece of information in her memory for later. Might be useful to make her captor fall.

Mirri nearly fell off her seat when the shirtless man at the fire yelled, "Yemek!"

A stampede of enormous men with white braids ran toward the man at the fire pit. Men roared with laughter, punching each other in the face and dumping smelly drinks over each other's heads. Mirri edged closer toward Lonar, though she wasn't sure why. Maybe because he was one of the few Kolts in this place who seemed somewhat sober.

No one seemed to care that a brown-haired teenage girl sat in here with two Kolts. With the fuss that was made about humans, she expected more of a reaction, though she was grateful for the lack of attention. She assumed the alcohol helped distract these men. The way they slapped each other on the back and laughed together was not the story she pictured from the stories she had heard about Koltaria.

Lonar slammed his cup down on the table, sending drops of ale flying. He wiped his mouth with the back of his hand. "How do I know this thing's real?"

The Kolt raised his eyebrows. "A demonstration, perhaps?"

Mirri glanced between the two Kolts with wide eyes. She stiffened as the man reached under his white robe near his neck. Mirri winced, expecting a lethal dagger or weapon, when he threw a gold pocket watch on the table. At least, it looked like one. Mirri furrowed her brow, leaning over to see exactly what lay across the table.

Before she could get a glimpse, the Kolt slammed something down on the watch, nearly knocking over the stone table. Mirri yelped and jumped back, staying on her stump only because of Lonar's sudden grasp on the neck of her cloak. Breathing heavily, Mirri sat up, feeling the heat in her cheeks. She cleared her throat and pushed her hair behind her ear, focusing on the table in front of her and shrugging away from Lonar's grip.

Her eyes widened as the man picked up the gold chain, letting it dangle in the air. The watch. It was . . . gone. In the place where it had lain on the table was now a swirl of smoke, twirling up and away from the stone table.

He swung the empty chain in the air, tossing it at Lonar's chest. "Your demonstration." He nodded at Lonar.

Lonar held the empty chain up, studying it for a moment, and pursed his lips, nodding. "Done." Lonar reached into his bag on the floor and lifted out a small brown sack. The sound it made when he plopped it on the table was unmistakable. Coins.

The Kolt held up a small silver object between his fingers. Mirri leaned forward, eager to see what object could do such magic. He held the point between his fingers, almost like a knife, but more like a metal rod simply bent in the shape of one. The handle was carved to look like something, maybe a—

Before she could get a better look, Lonar snatched it out of his fingers and tucked it into the breast pocket of his vest.

Lonar stood. "Up." He nodded to Mirri as if she was nothing more than one of these poor animals trapped in cages.

She felt the tug on her wrist, and her legs automatically led her out of the bar, matching Lonar's long stride.

"Hey, what was that thing?" she called to Lonar, who ignored her. "Hey!"

Lonar kept walking, his tall legs walking at a pace somewhat uncomfortable for Mirri.

"Hey!" she yelled, turning a few Kolts' heads entering the bar.

Lonar spun to her with a glare. "Keep your durn voice down. You want every Kolt in this place to know a human is walking around?"

She shrugged. "Maybe. Might be better than getting hauled around by you."

He laughed out loud. "Darlin', a sober Kolt would do a lot worse than trade you for some coin."

"What was that thing?" When Lonar still said nothing, she tried again. "I'm just gonna keep asking, you know."

Lonar shrugged. "I don't mind conversation."

She gritted her teeth, her legs moving even faster, in a wider stride than before. Mirri wrapped the cloak around her and stomped after Lonar, wishing she could get closer, but the man seemed to be able to keep her at a distance with those bracelets. What were her friends doing right now? How long had she been missing?

Her mom. What was she doing right now? Mirri's irritation with Lonar turned into a pit of anger, sitting deep down inside her belly. In trying to save her mother, Mirri had gotten lost in the woods, almost gone crazy in Lavinia's prison chamber hallway, and she needed to prepare for the Manna-something curse to crush her soul. Now, she was about to be traded to the Kolts.

Mirri's breath started coming in ragged gasps as the path began up a steep hill. Though Mirri had always considered herself physically fit, it appeared Lonar was in much better shape. His long stride did not wane as they climbed, and the bracelet forced Mirri's legs to continue.

"Can we—can we stop for a . . . second?" Mirri gasped.

Lonar stopped mid-pace and looked down at her. He shrugged. "Guess it's about time for a rest, anyway." He leaned against a large tree to the side of them while Mirri collapsed on the dirt path. She lay there, breathing hard and hating the man called Lonar.

Mirri sat, wiping her brow, and looked up at the night sky.

"I don't get it," she said, when her breath had finally returned to normal.

"You don't, do you?" he asked, taking a swig from his water container. He handed it down to Mirri.

She greedily gulped down the water until Lonar's hand pulled it away, spilling the precious water down her chin. Mirri wiped at her face with the corner of the cloak.

"See? You give me water and food. You saved my life twice. I slept in your blanket; you turned your back while I dressed." Mirri ticked off the points on her fingers. "Why are you so nice if you're such a jerk?"

"Jerk? I can only assume what that means." He took another swig from his cannister, looking up at the silvery sky.

"Well? What's the deal? Are you a jerk or a nice guy?"

"Let's just say I know how to treat a lady. My father taught me that. But not much else."

"Your father?"

"Yes. Quite a jerk, as you would say, to the ladies. I never approved. Good ol' Cormac."

Mirri's head snapped up. "Cormac? Your father was Cormac?" Impossible.

"About time we were getting along, darlin'." He stowed his water and stood, forcing Mirri's legs to do the same.

"Wait!" Mirri's legs began walking. She grabbed at his cloak as they continued up the hill. "Did you say Cormac?"

"That I did. I take it you heard of him?"

Mirri's mind raced. Cormac. That night. He said he was going to sacrifice the baby. But what if he didn't? What if he kept his son? Mirri gave it one last shot.

"Was your mother named . . . Chloris?"

Lonar stopped dead in his tracks, so fast Mirri lost her balance and stumbled. Lonar's arm stopped her, shooting out to grab her bicep so tight it hurt.

"What do you know of Chloris?" Lonar brought his face to Mirri's, his bright blue eyes piercing hers.

Mirri shrunk back at his sudden change in demeanor. "I . . . I . . ." Should she tell him of her memory? That she watched Cormac murder his mother and leave her in a pool of blood?

Suddenly, Lonar's demeanor changed. He dropped her arm and straightened up, strolling back up the hill. Mirri strolled right along next to him, relieved that he had returned to his casual self. But she felt the tension in the air.

The baby. She had seen Lonar as a baby. If Arlo was right, that meant Lonar was a piece of her puzzle. The Manna Kai seemed in full swing. And she wasn't sure how much more testing her soul could take.

Chapter Twenty-One

Mirri stared up at the gates in front of them. She had never seen gates so tall, even in Althord. Even the gates at Avi's resting place didn't seem this tall. Two columns stood on either side, with horrible statues perched on top of each. Mirri gasped when one of the horned, winged statues turned to her and growled, its tongue flicking out as it did. She grabbed at Lonar's arm instinctively, but he continued walking, forcing Mirri toward the enormous entrance.

They climbed the cracking stairs, as much as Mirri tried to force her legs to stop. What would happen next? Would he toss her through the gate and leave her here? Would a Kolt with a sword kill her the second she entered the gate? Her heart was hammering in her chest, and the bracelet was heavy on her wrist. Despite the bone-chilling wind, Mirri felt beads of sweat gathering on her neckline.

Much too soon, Mirri's sneakers hit the last step, the trembling overwhelming Mirri's body. The gate had more of the horrible creatures carved into it—frightening creatures with horns and stakes. Each had curling fingers and wicked smiles on their pointed faces. Mirri sucked in a shaky breath as she looked all the way up the horrid gate.

She jumped again as Lonar pulled the sword from his back. Was he going to kill her right here?

An ear-splitting, creaking moan filled the air, making Mirri yelp and throw her hands over her head. After what felt like minutes of screeching, she felt herself being tugged along, her legs being pulled toward her expected doom. Her breath came in quick gasps, and she bit her upper lip to keep from crying.

As soon as they walked through the gate, Lonar stopped, forcing Mirri's feet to become planted on the cracked stone path.

"Welcome to the Koltarian Kingdom," Lonar said.

Mirri wrinkled her nose at the site in front of her. Holmforth may have been deserted, but this place reeked of misery. Buildings had gaping holes in the sides, and murky, foul-smelling water filled the ditches that lined the path. Black gnarled trees curled up over the buildings, as if the earth was trying to pull them down in its clutches. Everywhere Mirri looked, it was black or gray—the earth dead, destroyed. Even the sky above them had turned gray and miserable.

They walked past a wooden structure missing most of its front wall. Jagged boards lay scattered, littering the dirt in front of the hut. A Kolt lay inside on the rotting wooden floor, snoring loudly. Two Kolts ducked under the sheet and stood, arms crossed, staring at Lonar and Mirri as they passed. Mirri tried not to let her fear show, but the men with narrow eyes and thick bodies were a bit intimidating. She kept her head down and did her best to stay close to Lonar. The man who was taking her to be traded, she thought with a scowl.

Sheets hung from the roof of the next shack—a pathetic attempt to replace a wall. A loud argument was taking place behind the curtain, and Mirri jumped as a loud scream echoed through the area.

An old woman with a cane hobbled toward them, wearing a shredded cloak, mumbling to herself. Mirri winced as the woman stepped into a ditch of murky water and waded through, her long skirt dragging behind her.

"Quite the place, isn't it?" Lonar asked.

"What happened here?" Mirri asked, wrinkling her nose, her gaze spreading over the area. The scent of decayed sea food lingered in the air, increasing as they walked.

"The place went to Relnok after some human stole the Homlock. They all blamed one another. Killed and maimed each other. Easier to fight than to speak to one another, I suppose." He shrugged and veered around a large ditch in the road that had a greenish color about it.

"What about all those guys back at the bar? They seemed to love each other."

Lonar laughed. "As long as you stay outside the gates of Koltarian Kingdom and have a good amount of whiskey, it can almost seem peaceful. In here is where it's pathetic. Where I grew up."

"So why even stay?"

"Pride, I suppose. And I don't stay," he added.

She followed Lonar down the muddy path, pushing aside her disgust to concentrate on what lay ahead. Was this where her mother had stolen the necklace? Had she been standing in this very place in her memory? Mirri tried to remember the building she had entered. A pointed roof . . . An odd color . . . She looked around as they walked, stepping over potholes and dead animals. Nothing looked familiar. No shack or construction looked even close to what she had seen.

A wooden building sat in front of them, probably the only structure in the area that stood intact. It had several pointed roofs, one stacked on top of the other. Reminded Mirri of a Christmas tree past its prime. A large flag hung down from a pole that sat on the top roof, the white flag hanging limply.

She glanced at Lonar. "Is that where you are taking me?"

"Mm-hmm. Figure I can get a decent price for a human."

She glared at him. "That's it? Just leave me here in this place?"

He shrugged. "It's how life is, darlin'."

The area in front of the structure swam with brown, bubbling water. A few pieces of wood were laid over the ditch to make a sort of bridge. Mirri tried to pause, unsure the rotten boards would hold her, but her legs kept going just as fast as Lonar's. Gritting her teeth, she stepped into the slimy pit next to Lonar before actually reaching the wood pieces. The black water came up to Mirri's ankles, sliding under her jeans and into her sneakers. Her stomach turned as she felt the muck stick to her ankles, and she hoped she never found out why it made that wretched odor.

Lonar put his hand on the gold bracelet on his wrist when they reached the front door. Mirri looked down at her own bracelet and watched as it disappeared. Grabbing her arm before she could turn and hop back into the slime, he waited patiently. Mirri's heart beat frantically. There had to be a way out of this place. She twisted her arm, trying to pry herself out of his death grip, but Lonar stood calmly, letting her struggle without loosening his hold on her. A Kolt with a sour look opened the door, his sword held down at his side.

He grunted, and Lonar shoved Mirri toward the grumpy-looking man. She dug her feet down into the floor, cowering in front of the stranger.

"Please . . ." Mirri gasped. "Please don't . . ."

Lonar continued shoving her further into the wooden room, toward a Kolt sitting at a large table. Metal loops stuck out at various heights along the wooded walls, and splatters of dark red stained the floor underneath. Mirri couldn't keep the image of her being tied to one of these loops and tortured for her mother's crimes.

Tears of fright burned in her eyes as the Kolt stood, dusting off his white robe, and looked her up and down with bushy eyebrows raised.

He stepped to her and bent to look her in the eyes, white stray hairs brushing her face. He reeked of rancid meat, or maybe how her tennis shoe smelled at that very minute.

Even though the man turned her stomach, Mirri forced her face to remain forward. She learned a long time ago to hold her ground. Better to appear strong than afraid. Or weak. His dark face made his white hair even brighter, and his pointed nose practically touched Mirri's forehead. But she held her stare.

"Lonar. What have you brought me?" the man spoke directly in Mirri's face.

"I have brought you a human, Frile."

The man smiled and nodded to the Kolt at the door. "How very thoughtful of you, Lonar. How very thoughtful."

◆

Mirri glared across the jail cell at Lonar. "Comfy?" she asked him sarcastically.

He had his eyes closed, and his head leaning back against the metal bars. His lack of worry and agitation irritated her beyond belief.

He yawned, stretching out his arms and throwing his white hair behind his shoulders. "I've had worse."

"Guess it wasn't a great idea to kidnap someone with bracelets you had *stolen*."

He ignored her and kept his head against the bars, feigning sleep.

After being shoved through a door that Mirri had thought was a bookshelf, the Kolt had dragged her and Lonar down a twisting flight of stairs. Another Kolt stood there and opened the door into the lovely jail accommodations Mirri sat in now.

Mirri supposed she should be glad for the company. At least she wasn't sitting in the freezing dark alone. Another prisoner lay in the cell next to her, sprawled out on his back, a line of drool seeping down the side of his face. Hmm. She watched him for a moment, studying his chest for movement. Probably be better company in that cell, she thought with a sigh, wrapping her cloak tighter around her.

Mirri counted six cells. All laid out in this stone circular prison, not terribly different from the Imperium's dungeon. The rusted metal bars left a disgusting orange chalk all over a cloak, Mirri soon found out. So instead, she sat against the wall. Not a single window. Not that there would be much of a view, but maybe at least an attempt to get some fresh air. The smell hanging in the air was making her nauseous—like putrid, rotting fish. Mirri hated seafood. It seemed everywhere in Koltaria had a distinct scent of the same odor: fish.

Mirri scowled at Lonar, who sat perfectly at ease with the situation and the horrid smell, not to mention those rusty bars. "Don't you wanna get out of here?"

"And do what?"

"How about leave this disgusting place?"

"How do you suggest we do that, darlin'?"

Mirri glared at him again, crossing her arms over her chest and looking away. She had absolutely no idea how to break out of prison but figured there had to be a way.

"Tell me about Chloris." Mirri looked straight at Lonar, waiting for a reaction.

Lonar finally opened his eyes. "Why?"

"Because we have nothing better to do."

He stared at her for a long time, then turned his head. "Don't know if Chloris was my mother. But I take it she loved him. Not sure why anyone would feel that for Cormac, though." He closed his eyes.

"What happened to her?"

"Why do you want to know?" His eyes remained closed.

"Aren't you the least bit curious why I even know about her?" Her attempt at getting him worked up was failing fast.

"Not really."

Mirri gritted her teeth. "Your father killed her. I think you were supposed to be sacrificed, but he changed his mind. Is that anywhere close?"

"I don't know where you come up with these ideas, darlin', but they are quite lamarable."

Mirri twirled a piece of hair around her finger, picturing the woman's dark, curly hair. "She wasn't a Kolt, was she?"

Lonar tilted his head to the side. "Why wouldja—"

Mirri jumped as a loud thumping came from the other side of the metal door they had entered through. The door opened with a high-pitched creak, and a decrepit old Kolt hobbled in. He carried a wooden bucket and threw a wilted vegetable in each cell, not even caring that four stood empty. What looked like a moldy carrot landed on top of the unconscious Kolt in the cell next to Mirri and Lonar's. The man let out a snort and a snore and rolled to his side. So he was alive.

The old vegetable fell near Mirri's feet. She grimaced and scooted away from it. She wasn't hungry enough yet to eat moldy food. Maybe soon, though. After a moment, she picked it up and threw it at Lonar, hitting him straight in the face.

Lonar jumped awake. "Rahat lard, what was that for?" he growled, throwing it back at Mirri but missing and hitting the wall.

"Tell me about the Homlock. That the human stole. What happened?" Mirri demanded.

She finally got a glare from Lonar. "Just a stupid angano, nothing to throw a stinky dritt about."

"What was it?"

He leaned back. "Apparently, someone took the thing from the Temple of Mallah. It caused a plague across the kingdom. Plants failed to thrive, sickness, death, mah, mah, mah." He closed his eyes again. "All that over a Homlock."

"What does it look like?"

"Never seen the thing. Never really cared to find out."

Was her mother truly responsible for the downfall of this entire kingdom? Lavinia must have known about it. She must have known everything that happened, the way she spoke in that jail cell. But why would her mother do it? Just because she was a wild child, she thought it a good idea to steal some ancient relic?

Mirri chewed on her bottom lip. Her mother had been wearing the Homlock in the memory. She had hidden it before she left Althord, buried it in the box in the forest. When had she retrieved it? Mere hours ago?

And this still didn't tell her who had killed Avi. The reason they were all here. The reason she was in Althord to begin with. She squeezed her eyes shut, refusing to let tears of frustration fall. Especially not in front of *him*.

"Who are you?"

Mirri scoffed. "Oh? Want to know my name now?" She scowled at him. "You could have asked earlier. Then we wouldn't even be in this mess."

He rolled his eyes. "Oh, really? You someone important, I suppose?"

Before she could muster a reply, a loud, throaty giggle came from the other side of the metal door. Both of their eyes swung toward the exit of the jail.

"What was that?" she whispered.

Lonar said nothing but stood up, his interest piqued. Mirri followed suit and moved to the bars at the front of the cell.

Someone spoke, but quietly. Mirri's breath caught in her throat. Another laugh. Mirri looked at Lonar. They shared a silent moment of excitement. A loud crack, then a thump. Mirri gasped as the door flew open.

A woman burst into the room, breathless, pulling a dirty, white, low-cut peasant dress along with her. The long, white braided wig fell off the side of her head as she turned and stared into the jail cell.

"Mirri! What in God's name are you *doing* here?"

Chapter Twenty-Two

"Mom?"

Mirri stared at the woman standing before her, holding a metal pipe in her hand. Her red hair stuck out at various angles, and the sweat pouring down the sides of her face left streaks of dirt. She fussed with the white dress she wore, pulling up the front and straightening the black cloak hanging around her neck.

Memories of the first day she was in Althord came swirling all around her—her mother standing in front of her in a completely bizarre scenario. But this one topped them all.

"Mirri—what are you doing here?" her mother demanded, trying to straighten the white wig while still holding the pipe. She kept glancing over her shoulder at the door.

"Me? How did *you* end up here?" Mirri cried, her anger outweighing her surprise. "I have been searching for you and got myself kidnapped!"

"Oh, this wasn't supposed to happen like this." Mrs. Langley fiddled with the lock on the prison bar. "Ugh!" she screamed as she slammed the lock against the bars. "Okay, everybody stand back!"

Mirri and Lonar looked at each other. "Why?" they asked in unison.

"Get back!" she screeched.

Mirri and Lonar jumped backward, and just in time. Mirri's mother shot her hands forward, emitting some sort of firecracker-like sound that sent Mirri's hands straight to her ears. Mrs. Langley's face screwed up tight in concentration, staring at the bars with narrowed eyes. Mirri watched as her mother breathed in deeply and relaxed her shoulders, closing her eyes.

The white dress blew forward as her hands shot toward the jail cell again. Lonar grabbed Mirri and pulled her to him just as the cell gate screeched and began to vibrate. Mirri's hands went right back to her ears as the sound of twisting metal filled the room.

Mrs. Langley's face squeezed tight in concentration; her fingers stretched at an awkward angle. Slowly, the metal at the top of the gate stretched outward and down, the sound of bending metal downright horrific to any creature's ears. Mirri watched her mother work with her ears covered; her eyes wide in fascination.

After a few moments of hand work from Mrs. Langley, Mirri's mother dropped her hands, breathing hard, and ran her hands through her wig in frustration. She ran to the bars. "That's as good as it's going to get! C'mon, let's go!"

Mirri and Lonar looked at her stupidly, looking up at the metal bars that still held them captive. The bars had bent outward, just at the top, and only a small amount of space was open under the ceiling.

Mrs. Langley threw her hands in the air. "Can you at least try? Now? They'll be here any minute!"

"Here." Lonar bent at the waist and weaved his fingers together, giving Mirri a foothold. Mirri shook her head and stuck her foot in his laced hands as he heaved her up to the top of the bars. She grasped for the bars and grunted, grabbing the curved bars.

Swinging her leg over the top, she pulled her foot away from Lonar's hands. She laid flat over the bent bars and scooched her body through.

"Hurry!" Lonar urged her.

Mirri grunted in response and grabbed two of the bars tightly. She swung her legs over toward her mother.

"Just let go!" her mother whispered.

Mirri jumped, landing on all fours. Lonar jumped immediately after, landing on top of Mirri and smashing her face into the ground.

"Get . . . off . . ." she said into the ground.

Lonar rolled off her and stood. "How 'bout those guards upstairs?"

Gwenna nodded, reached down, and grabbed the white braided wig off the floor, adjusting it back on her head. "Should be taken care of by now. Let's go."

She flung the door open and stepped over the Kolt, who was lying face down on the floor. Mirri halted in front of him and opened her mouth, but her mother cut her off.

"Don't ask." She shook her head and grabbed Mirri's hand.

Mirri followed her mother in a daze, letting her lead her up the winding staircase. Who was this woman they called Gwenna?

Lonar stayed hot on their heels. "Just how do you plan to get out of here? The door opens into the main hall—guards are everywhere up there."

"It's taken care of," Gwenna called back over her shoulder.

"Wait—what? What are you talking about?" Mirri asked, still clinging to her mother's arm.

"Later," her mother hissed. She had stopped at the large door and put her ear to the wood, listening. "Should be good," she said, shoving open the heavy door with her shoulder.

Gwenna pulled Mirri into the main room. Mirri gasped once more, disbelief clouding her brain. Four Kolts were lying on the floor, face down, wrists bound. A centaur bent over one, binding the Kolt's wrists with rope. The centaur stood, and Mirri stared at the sight of the creature she knew and despised. Theodisis stood before her, panting, wiping his brow, a streak of blood mixing with the blonde hair hanging around his face. Before Mirri could think of a rude comment to shoot at the creature, he tossed a length of rope at Mirri's mother.

"He's the last one. More are coming." He tossed the rope to Gwenna, and she caught it with one hand.

"More of who?" Mirri asked.

Mirri stood dazed as her mother bent and grabbed the last Kolt by his wrists, putting her foot on his back. He grunted as she slammed his face into the ground and bound his wrists in a quick knot, pulling the two ends of the rope tight.

Lonar grabbed a sword from the back of a restrained Kolt and ran to the front window. "Time to go. More are coming."

Gwenna and Theodisis shared a look. Mirri's eyes widened as her mother reached down and drew a sword up. She had the stance of a warrior, shoulders back, and ready to fight.

"Give me the bag," Gwenna ordered Theodisis.

"Absolutely not. You can only use it once. We agreed we would only use it in an emergency—"

"And what would you call *this*?" Gwenna swooped her hands through the air, her sword barely missing a wooden wall.

"They're here," Lonar hissed, backing away from the window, holding the sword out in front of them.

A booming voice sounded from outside the building. "Invaders! You will exit the premises immediately!"

"Fine," Theodisis muttered. He reached into the haversack that hung around his shoulder and tossed a small, flat object to Gwenna.

"Everybody, hold on," she said.

Without being told, the four of them made a tight line in the middle of the room, facing the door. Mirri only wished she had her own sword. She was trying to hide her shaking hands, only to have the rest of her body trembling. Was it fear? Excitement? Mirri shook her head and copied her mother's earlier pose, squaring her shoulders, and bending at the knees.

"I demand you exit our headquarters!" the voice boomed again. He pounded on the door. "Prepare to be taken prisoner!"

Taking a deep breath, Gwenna held the bottom of the device and turned the top.

Mirri squeezed her eyes shut and gripped her mother's arm, waiting. And waited. After a moment, she peeked out.

"It didn't work," Theodisis hissed.

"Yes, thank you, Captain Centaur," her mother whispered back. "I can see that." Gwenna turned it, clicking it once, then again. "It malfunctioned. I—I don't know what's wrong."

"Possibly trading with a known tapir was your first mistake."

"If you have a better idea," Gwenna shot back through gritted teeth. "I would be delighted to hear it."

Lonar sneaked back to the front window amid Gwenna and Theodisis's argument.

"Perhaps if we had avoided the Main Hall in Koltaria, this would not have been a problem."

"You are suggesting I would leave my daughter in Koltaria to rot in prison? That I am that horrible of—"

Lonar interrupted, "They are incapacitated."

"What?" Gwenna and Theodisis replied together.

Lonar nodded out the window. "Look for yourself."

Mirri, Gwenna, and Theodisis stepped to the front of the building. Shoving Theodisis aside so she could see out, Mirri got a glimpse of the Kolts holding her prisoner.

Six Kolts were bent over, laughing, clapping each other on the backs. One raised his hand in the air, as if he had one of those metal cups of whiskey in his hand, proposing a toast. The other five men raised their invisible cups and yelled an incoherent toast along with him. They danced and spun merrily, all thoughts of capturing prisoners forgotten.

Mirri looked at her mother and then at the device in her hand. "What is that thing?"

"Apparently not what I paid for." She shrugged and grabbed Mirri by the arm. "Let's get out of here."

Gwenna opened the door, still pulling Mirri along, and took a cautious step outside. While the large men continued hollering and laughing, they crept away from the Kolt's headquarters. Mirri followed her mother around back, then the four of them broke into a sprint.

"This way!" Gwenna motioned for them to follow, away from the prison, down a dusty road.

"Where are we going?" Mirri asked, careful to keep her voice down. Darkness was setting in around them, but Gwenna seemed to know her way around Koltaria well.

"To a safe place," Gwenna said.

Yelling and footsteps sounded around the corner. Gwenna grabbed Mirri and pulled her off the road, behind a wooden building that reminded Mirri of an outhouse. Mirri wrinkled her nose. Smelled like one, too. Gwenna kept one arm around Mirri's shoulder the whole time, refusing to lighten her grip.

"Over here!" A deep voice called, mere feet from where they were hiding. Mirri jumped as a rumble of footsteps sounded on the path, and the area brightened with torches the Kolts must be carrying.

Mirri leaned against the building, grateful for the warmth of her mother, who stood strong and in control. They listened to the rumbling of Kolts die away, most likely back to the prison. Mirri wondered how long the effects of that tool would continue.

"Come on!" Gwenna whispered, grabbing Mirri's hand and dragging her toward the next rotting structure.

Getting dragged around in the dark was becoming difficult, and Mirri wished her mother would lighten her death grip. Boards, rocks, and other soft, smelly things Mirri did not want to identify littered the ground, and the running had now turned into climbing. Hopping over a ditch and veering around a pile of rotting wood with nails protruding, Mirri did her best to keep up with her mother. Gwenna flew gracefully over puddles and practically danced between fallen trees and collapsed structures. Mirri gritted her teeth, trying to ignore the stabbing pang of annoyance she got every time her mother turned back and told her to hurry.

They leaned against the back of what Mirri assumed had once been a fence until Gwenna gave the all-clear.

"Almost there. Go, go." She pushed Mirri in the back.

"Will you give me a minute?" Mirri hissed back.

"Get over here!" Theodisis called crossly.

Though Mirri could not see him, she could hear the annoyance in his voice. Just the sound of that centaur was enough to make her want to punch something.

She hurried toward his voice, her mother dragging her the entire way. Theodisis and Lonar were shoving open a large door, making an awful racket as they did. Mirri looked up at the building, thinking it looked like a sort of barn perhaps, though instead of a bright cheery red color it was black and crusty.

Mirri glanced over her shoulder, seeing the small light that was approaching on the dirt road. Distant voices and rumblings were approaching. "Hurry," she urged as the two males struggled with the large door.

As soon as it opened enough to fit the four of them in, Mirri stumbled in and collapsed, immediately regretting sitting down. Her leg sat in an unidentifiable goo, and she groaned as she climbed back to her feet. Theodisis and Lonar succeeded in closing the door, and they were rewarded with a pitch-black covering that smelled strongly of fish. What was it with this place and fish? Mirri thought as her stomach turned.

"Mom?" Mirri whispered into the dark.

She heard shuffling and groaning off to one side and walked with both hands in front of her, wondering if this was what it felt like to be blind. Tripping, she fell to her feet, finally resigning to stay still. Who knows what she might land in, step on, or run into?

A crack, a grunt, and then a small light stretched out from the floor. Mirri ran to the light and looked down, peering into what looked like an elf's hold.

"Hurry, go!" Gwenna urged her.

Mirri sat down and lowered herself into the cellar, falling farther than she thought. She landed hard on her rump, Lonar falling on top of her again. She shoved him off her and they scrambled out of the way as Theodisis's humongous form landed next to them.

"Mom? Are you coming?" Mirri craned her neck up, worried for one second that her mother was going to leave them down here and run. A moment later, a white dress and a mess of red hair swooped down next to her.

Theodisis shoved Mirri to the side as he and Gwenna grabbed a hanging rope and pulled it. The door over their heads thumped shut, leaving them in total darkness once again.

CHAPTER
TWENTY-THREE

"I guess you have a few questions." Gwenna leaned back next to Mirri, setting the white wig on the ground.

Mirri scoffed, pulling her knees into her body. "Yeah, just a few."

Lonar looked to be asleep while Theodisis paced back and forth around the small area. Gwenna lit several candles she had pulled out of a wooden box, giving them some well-needed light, and passed around some fruit she had stashed somewhere as well.

It seemed this was a frequent hiding spot, one her mother used recently, given the freshness of the fruit Mirri had consumed. The more Mirri sat and thought of their situation, of Smidge and Jinx, the more her anger built up. Yet, here she sat with her mother—this brave, strong, Indiana Jones woman who knocked large Kolts out cold and broke her out of prison, bending metal with her mind. And she felt a foolish type of . . . well, adoration, she supposed. But she was still angry. *Yes*, she assured herself. *Still angry.*

Mirri looked over to her mother, who sat with her knees in her chest, her red hair hanging down across her face. Instead of blue scrubs, she wore the white, old-fashioned dress that showed off her bosom nicely and framed her small body. Her face was soft in the candlelight, and her green eyes twinkled as she stared at the candle flickering in front of her.

Mirri had never known her mother to look so beautiful. So . . . alive. As much anger and resentment as she felt at the moment, she had to admit, she was more intrigued.

"So you grew up here?" Mirri finally asked.

"In Holmforth. With my father and sister. I believe you had the chance to get to know Lavinia." She rolled her eyes at the mention of her name. "Quite the drama queen, isn't she?"

"Who . . . who was your mother?" Mrs. Langley had always told Mirri that her parents died when she was young, and she cared for herself after she turned eighteen. Why hadn't Mirri asked anything else?

Her mother shook her head. "I never knew her. Father didn't speak of her often. Only when I asked. Her name was Leila."

"Your father was . . . Avi?" This still seemed too unreal. Too fresh. This man, this legend, she had trekked all of Althord in search for—the whole time, it had been her grandfather?

Mrs. Langley smiled. "Yes. He was a magnificent father." Her voice became small. "I wish I had told him that." She looked down at the ground and began tracing her finger in the dirt.

"You didn't get along with him?"

Gwenna gave a small laugh. "I gave him more than a few headaches, that's for sure." She sighed and leaned back against the dirt wall. "I made so many mistakes, Mirri. Took him for granted. He tried so hard to help me, to be there for me. And all I cared for was myself." She stared off, her eyes glistening. "But I think he knew."

"Knew what?"

She paused. "Knew that—well—they were just mistakes. That I was foolish and young. As much as we disagreed, he knew that deep down, I was not a terrible person. Deep down, I cared for others besides myself."

Theodisis snorted at that comment, still pacing the small room. Gwenna ignored him, so Mirri let that one go as well.

Mirri had one more question, one question she burned to know. As much as she didn't want to, she had to ask. "Did you do it? Did you do what they say? To Avi?" she whispered, looking her mother straight in the eyes.

Her mother looked back at her, lips pursed. "I didn't wrap the beads around his neck, Mirri. But it's my fault he is dead."

"But—"

"Let's get some rest, shall we?" With that, Gwenna pulled her daughter close and blew out the candles.

❖

"How . . . How far do we have to go like this?" Mirri complained, her back aching.

"Just a bit further," her mother panted. "We need to stay out of view."

They crawled along on their hands and knees through the tall grass that sat behind the village to escape the main road without being seen. When they peeked out of their hiding place that morning, the dirt road held a variety of beefy Kolts marching with their swords to little old women walking small lizards on leashes.

The four of them made it out of the large barn, which Gwenna had referred to as a "fish house". Now that it was light, and she wasn't running and stumbling in fear, she noticed the large ditch off to the right, on the other side of the fish house. Dried-up and crusty, she had to wonder where the fish smell actually came from.

And here they crawled through the obnoxiously extensive field, Theodisis grumbling even more than she was. Lonar remained silent, and Mirri wondered just how long he planned on sticking with them. They needed him. She wasn't sure why she knew this. But he would stay. She would make sure of that.

"Okay, this should be good. Stay low, and head for the tree cover," Gwenna instructed. "Theo, you need to stay down 'til we get there."

Mirri smiled as Theo glared in her mother's direction. Mirri smiled as she watched her mother boss Theodisis around. Though the thought of her mother teaming up with this arrogant jerk still baffled her.

Mirri and Lonar made it into the trees as Gwenna crawled along with Theo. She stood up when she reached them, swatting at her cloak, which was now covered in burrs and blades of grass. "God, I miss scrubs," she moaned as she loosened the cloak at her neck.

"Anybody have a plan?" Lonar drawled behind them, with a blade of grass hanging out of his mouth. "Or am I just traipsing through Koltaria with three fugitives for fun?"

Gwenna straightened up. "We need to return the Homlock. Then we will return to Althord."

Lonar, still leaning up against a tree, let out a lazy laugh. "Oh, right. Return the Homlock. Sure. Well, let's just walk on over there, hmm?"

Mirri sensed the sarcasm in his voice. "Uh, where exactly do we return it to?"

She watched her mother and Theodisis exchange a look. Her mother cleared her throat. "We, uh, don't exactly know where to return it."

"You don't know? How could you not know?"

"Nobody knows, darlin'," Lonar said from his seat against the tree.

"Where did you steal it from? You did steal it, right?" By now, that should be obvious, Mirri guessed. But she still needed her mother to say it. She needed to hear it.

"We borrowed it," Gwenna said, with emphasis. "We never meant to steal it."

Lonar laughed. "Quite the distinction, eh?"

"But why take it in the first place?" Mirri asked.

Gwenna seemed very interested in the overhanging tree all a sudden, while Theodisis glared at her, his arms crossed over his chest. She cleared her throat. "Uh, it's, uh, not important now. We need to find the location."

"Okay, how did you take it in the first place?" Mirri asked her mother, who was still examining a green leaf with feigned interest.

When her mother didn't answer, she looked at Theodisis. "Well? How did you take it?"

"She took it from the temple." Theodisis stood with his arms crossed, a scowl clearly imprinted on his face.

"Then why can't you return it to the temple?" This made no sense.

"The temple burned to the ground. Struck by lightning the minute Gwenna left the building."

The temple. The memory in Koltaria. Mirri had been there, in the temple that evening, with her mother. The same night Gwenna stole the Homlock. The chaos, crashes and booms. Was it all because she took the Homlock?

Mirri shifted her weight, suddenly uneasy about what had happened in the room Gwenna fell out of, tears down her face, and smoke billowing out around her. What had Gwenna done? Mirri swallowed. "How did you steal it? Mom?"

When Gwenna didn't answer, Mirri stepped to her and grabbed her shoulders. "Mom? How?" Mirri looked back and forth between her and Theodisis. They were having one of those silent conversations; she knew it, and it drove her insane.

Mirri grabbed her mother's chin, forcing Gwenna to look her in the eyes. "Mom, tell me. What happened when you took it?"

"Your mother here is quite good at taking advantage of people." Theodisis leaned against a tree, glaring at Gwenna. "Especially old Kaplans with a heart."

Gwenna shot him a murderous look back.

"And what is that supposed to mean?" Mirri asked. "Mom? What is a Kaplan?"

Gwenna pressed her lips together. "A . . . priest. He stood guard over the Homlock. Lived in the temple. He took me in. I . . . uh, told him I was a lost soul. Abandoned." She kicked at the ground as she spoke.

"Okay," Mirri said nervously. She had a feeling she knew how this story ended but said nothing.

Gwenna sighed. "I had planned to take the Homlock and leave in the middle of the night. Just take it and walk out. But something happened." She paused. "Something went wrong."

Theodisis scoffed. "You mean besides burning it to the ground?"

Mirri started to snap at the centaur but stopped. The look on her mother's face startled her—the trembling of her chin, the tears in her eyes. Mirri bit her lower lip and waited for her mother to continue.

"I didn't know it would happen. I never wanted him to get hurt," Gwenna spoke to the field in front of them, to the open air around her. She gazed at the outline of the desolate village they had just left, her voice filled with regret and sadness. "I waited until the middle of the night, after he said his prayers to the Homlock. I had him fooled. He thought I was a young, innocent girl that he was helping," she whispered with her back toward them.

Mirri stepped closer to her mother, hearing the pain in her mother's voice. Mirri longed to reach out, hold her mother, tell her it would all be all right—but she waited. Gwenna needed to tell the story. She needed the world to know what she had done.

Wiping her face, Gwenna wrapped her arms around herself, as if trying to hold her soul together. She continued in a whisper, "I sneaked into the room where the Homlock hung. It was on a hook on the wall. I grabbed the pendant, and—and" Gwenna let out a sudden sob, shaking her head. "He was there. In the doorway, watching me. He grabbed his chest and fell." Gwenna collapsed on the forest floor, sobbing, holding her knees, letting her hair cover her tears. "I never even knew his name."

"Oh, Mom," Mirri whispered. She kneeled down next to her and threw her arms around her. "You can't blame yourself like this. You don't know that's why he died."

Gwenna pulled back from her embrace. "No, no, you don't understand, Mirri. It was my fault. He was the Guardian over the Homlock, and I stole it. I opened the curse, I brought it to life, it—it was all my fault. Everything." She stared at the ground.

"I hate to interrupt this special moment, but can we get out of this place? If you three have forgotten, we are being hunted at this very moment," Lonar called from behind them.

Gwenna nodded and wiped her face. "Right."

Theodisis lent a hand and pulled Gwenna to her feet. Mirri stood, eyebrows raised as she glanced at Theodisis. Quite a change from the young Theodisis she had witnessed, who would push Gwenna into a bush of thorns and laugh.

"Enough of this. We need to finish the task we started. Somehow, we need to find where the dusk met the dagger."

"The dusk met the dagger!" Mirri exclaimed. "That is where you return it?"

"Uh, yes." Gwenna stopped and bit her lip. "Then we, uh, mix the blood of her brethren, to quiet the destruction of the curse."

"Whose brethren?"

"Uh, I would assume the Mother Kolt."

"How do you know all of that?" Mirri asked.

"The priest told me about the dagger." She pulled a small, worn book from her satchel. "And I, uh, read the rest in this book."

Gwenna ran her finger over the cover. It had been blue at one time, Mirri could tell.

Mirri glanced at her mother, closing her eyes and sighing. "Would that have been one of Arlo's books, by any chance?"

Her mother gave a sheepish smile and cleared her throat. "Uh, Theo found it for me."

They had broken into Arlo's shop. Of course. Theodisis and her mother. They had stolen and destroyed his hut, looking for information on the Homlock.

Mirri just shook her head. What next?

Chapter Twenty-Four

"You fell out of the room. Then you ran right through me. Wearing the Homlock."

Mirri watched Gwenna sneak a look at Theodisis. He rolled his eyes to answer her. Mirri felt her frustration growing.

"So, you have been having memories? That some bugs gave you?" her mother asked.

"Yes," Mirri said, glaring at Theodisis. As if he could doubt her when she described what a complete jerk he was in the other memory. No one could deny that.

"Hmm," her mother said. "Anything about a dusk or dagger?"

Mirri closed her eyes and gritted her teeth. "No." The looks between her mother and Theodisis were getting on her nerves.

"They've stopped. The memories," Mirri realized. "I haven't had one since I woke after the river. Arlo said it was some sort of blessing. A Manna Kay or something."

"The Manna Kai?" her mother asked quietly.

"Yeah, yeah, that was what he said. Kryptus said it was some silly ang—anga—"

"Angano?"

Theodisis snorted. "Ha! Arlo was the type to believe anything."

Mirri ignored him and looked at her mother. "Do you?"

Her mother paused. "Avi told us this story when we were children. I have never heard of this actually happening." She looked up at Mirri sharply. "Your soul will be tested. It . . . it would be a great test of your inner strength." She stood and stepped to Mirri, grabbing her upper arms. "If this is true, you need to be very careful, Mirri. I . . . I don't know what would happen if . . . "

Mirri yanked her arms away. "I'd say my soul has been tested a number of times in the last few days and I've gotten through just fine."

Lonar sat against a tree, his eyes closed, with his head tilted back. Without thinking, Mirri picked up a stick and hurled it at him. It hit him in the chin, leaving a red mark.

"Oi!" He batted at his chin as he sat up, glaring at her. "What was that for?"

"Do you have anything to add? You're the one who knows this place best. Where is this dagger?"

"Sorry, darlin', but I got no clue what you're talking about. Don't believe in that halafrinlo to begin with." He leaned back against the tree with his arms crossed, but at least he looked a bit sour this time.

Her anger was boiling over, and Lonar's attitude made her want to pull out her own hair. Did he care about anything? Mirri grabbed a handful of dirt this time and chucked it at him again. This time, it missed, flying past him wildly.

He looked at her with narrow eyes. "You going to throw something at me again? You better be prepared to defend yourself."

"What? Don't have your sparkly bracelets this time? Gonna lock me up?" Mirri screeched. She was losing control but didn't want to admit it. Her mother and Theodisis thought she was crazy, and Lonar just didn't care. These memories were of no help to her, and she had absolutely no idea how to get her mother out of this mess. Anything she had set out to do when she stepped into that painting in Rose's shop had failed miserably.

She felt a hand on her shoulder and spun away, stomping off, away from the crowd of non-supporters. Mirri swatted a tear away, hating herself for crying at a time like this. She fought her way through a grove of dead shrubs, yanking her cloak along with her.

After fighting her way through the crispy foliage, Mirri stood looking down at a large ditch, which she assumed had been a lake or river at one point. Now, it stood, cracked and alone, empty of anything that had once made it what it was. She knew how it felt. Alone and damaged. Mirri reached down and grabbed a rock, hurling it toward the dirt, for no other reason than she felt like throwing something. She hated it when she cried because she was angry. Tears made her feel weak.

"Mirri?"

Mirri ignored her mother and kicked the dirt in front of her.

"You remind me so much of him."

"Who? *Theo*? Your best bud over there?" She turned back to the ditch, throwing another rock at the cracked surface.

"No. Your father."

Mirri stiffened at the mention of her father. His death still felt fresh on her mind, something she thought about every day. Whenever she needed advice or support. She wished her father was standing right beside her. The guilt Mirri felt over his death had become manageable, but the wound still ached. It had been over a year now.

Gwenna stood next to Mirri, looking out over the dried-up lake. "He was always so hard on himself. Thought he should have all the answers. Carried such a heavy burden. Whenever you had a problem at school or you were truly upset about something, he blamed himself. Said he should have been there to stop whatever problem you had."

Mirri shook her head. "That's crazy. Like he could be there every second."

Gwenna nodded. "Remember when you didn't make the gymnastics team? How upset you got? He punched a door that day. Broke straight through it."

Mirri scrunched up her face. "He *what*?"

Gwenna laughed softly. "Don't you remember? We didn't have a bathroom door for a week."

Mirri looked at her, amazed. "Yeah, but you said the hinge broke."

Mirri remembered the day they did not accept her into The Landing Legends Gymnastics team. She had been ten-years old, and rejection of her Olympic dream was the worst possible pain she thought she would ever experience. The sobbing and tears, her father holding her and telling her she would make it next year. Until that day, her father promised they would practice and practice. Together.

Smiling, her mother looked down. "Your father thought it was his fault you didn't make it. He should have bought you the practice balance beam you wanted, and he should have practiced with you more. He shouldered your hurt and anger more than you could ever imagine, Mirri."

"That's ridiculous. Like it was his fault I had no coordination."

"Exactly." Her mother smiled. "You both take on the world, Mirri. Expect so much of yourself. I just wish every now and then you could remember you are a sixteen-year-old girl. And I wished your father could remember he was a father. That he couldn't be there to soften every blow. You had to live your own life, make mistakes. That's just what life is."

Mirri shrugged, kicking at the dirt. "Yeah, I guess."

Her mother put an arm around her shoulders. "This is my problem. My fight. I wish you had never been involved."

"No, I need to be here, Mom. I heard everything you said, but this is where I am meant to be." Mirri squeezed her hand.

Gwenna smiled as she ruffled her hair. "You know, it is said the Manna Kai can show us exactly what we are looking for. Maybe it led us to each other."

Mirri chewed on her bottom lip. "The memories have stopped . . . since you were here. Do . . . do you think that's why? Because we found each other?"

Her eyes glassed over as she nodded. "Yes, I think we definitely found each other. Finally." She pulled Mirri into a fierce hug and put a hand to the back of Mirri's brown hair, where they stood, holding tight to one another, swaying in the breeze.

Gwenna pulled back and smiled. "But! Let's not get sappy with each other, hmm?" She gave Mirri another one-armed hug and wiped at her eyes. "Let's go find this matsala together, right?"

Mirri's eyes widened as she pulled away from her mother slowly. "What did you just say?"

"A matsala. It's what the Kaplan called the safe place they kept the Homlock." She registered the look on Mirri's face. "Why?"

Mirri groaned. "Oh, no."

◈

"Absolutely not, Mirri. No. No," her mother repeated, hands on her hips.

"We have to, Mom. She knows. I know it. Lavinia knows where it is, and we need to talk to her."

They stood in the same clearing and fought for hours. The subject would die down when Gwenna and Theodisis would start arguing or giving snide comments about something that happened years ago. Mirri wished they would drop it for two minutes and get back to the problem at hand.

Theodisis stepped in. "We are fugitives. There is no way we can go back, strolling into Althord undetected."

"We have no choice!" Mirri yelled at him. "Lavinia knows, and we have to ask her. We have to go back there!"

Theodisis looked away, swatting at a low-hanging branch. Lonar was curled up on the dirt floor, snoring softly. Only that man could sleep through all this screaming.

Gwenna shook her head. "No. Lavinia would make things worse and would make us believe she was being truthful. She would love for me to show up, act a fool, then need her help. Absolutely not."

"We need to hear what she has to say! We don't have to *do* anything! But what if one of her stupid little clues tells you something important? She loves to drop little hints, like the matsala, I know she does! You have to talk to her, Mom!"

Gwenna stood, chewing madly on her bottom lip. "Lavinia knew. She knew everything about the Homlock. Remember?" She looked at Theodisis, then down at the ground, rubbing her face. "God, she just knew everything. That day" —Gwenna groaned with her face in her hands— "she made me so angry, I practically—I just—I lost it." She turned away, biting her lip. And if Mirri wasn't mistaken, those were tears of frustration shining in her mother's eyes.

Mirri let this sink in. The anger and frustration—Mirri knew this all too well. "That's why you two were fighting. In the middle of Holmforth. When Kryptus pulled you off her. She knew you had taken the Homlock..." Mirri murmured. "But how had she known?"

Gwenna stood, tugging on a piece of her red hair. "I don't know. She . . . threatened to tell everyone. Threatened to tell the Kolts what we had done. She even knew where we had hidden the Homlock. She called me weak and pathetic, and I just—lost control."

"It's a shame you hadn't succeeded," Theodisis grumbled.

"Wait a minute—you never told me why you took the Homlock." The one question her mother kept avoiding. She couldn't avoid it forever.

Gwenna shook her head. "It seems so silly now. I wanted to be free of my powers," she said, sighing. "My powers are incredibly hard to control, and I—I couldn't control them, couldn't master them. Lessons were useless. I was sick of trying, of failing. Father called them a gift. Maybe that's why I was so angry with him," she said, more to herself than anyone.

The gift. In the woods. She had been speaking to an elf about her powers; he had been training her to use her magic . . . Smidge's father.

"There was an—accident." Gwenna hung her head. "I almost killed your grandfather."

Images of Rose's beautiful script handwriting flashed before Mirri's eyes. The journal entry. She remembered. "The accidental reversal of magic. Lavinia saved his life, didn't she?" Mirri said, realization creeping into her brain. Things were beginning to come together.

Gwenna gave a slow nod, her chin trembling. She wrapped her arms around herself like she had been doing so often for the last few hours. "Yes. And after that, Father decided to train Lavinia to be the next ruler of Althord."

"But why did you need the Homlock?"

Gwenna took another heavy sigh. "I was so ashamed, Mirri. I almost killed him, my own father, because I lost control." Her voice had turned angry. "Because I was too weak and pathetic to control myself.

So, I went for the easy way out. It was said that the Homlock could take away a heavy burden. Free a person from their torment. I wanted . . . to be free of my power. Forever."

Mirri chewed on her lip. "But . . . you still have powers." She shuddered as she remembered the spine-chilling noise the bending metal made. "It didn't work?"

Finally, the truth was coming out.

"No," her mother whispered. "There was a part of the Homlock I didn't know. If unworthy hands took the Homlock, the blessing would become a curse. It wouldn't take away a burden, it would take away something dear." She stopped, turning away, as her voice went cold and flat. "Then my father was killed. And I put Koltaria to rubble."

Mirri stared after her mother. So that was why her mother blamed herself. That was why she believed she deserved punishment. Why she wouldn't defend herself against cries of murder. Gwenna shouldered the guilt of her father's death all these years, even if she hadn't wrapped those beads around his neck.

If only she had talked to her mother . . . when her own father had died so suddenly. If only she had told her mother the truth . . . to carry the burden of one's father's death. To think, if only Mirri and her mother had spoken more about things, tried a little harder to hold a meaningful conversation. Let each other in. Maybe they would have known each other's darkest secret.

Gwenna's shoulders sagged as she looked Mirri in the eyes. "Everything was my fault, Mirri. If I had never lost control, Father would have never trained Lavinia, I wouldn't have stolen the Homlock, and none of it would have happened. Father wouldn't be dead." A single tear ran down her face, one solemn tear that Mirri knew had been waiting to fall.

For a moment, no one spoke. The only sound in the forest was the rustling of brown leaves in the gentle breeze. Mirri stared at her mother, wondering just how many secrets they had kept from each other.

"Well, as lovely as this little family moment is, I think I'm going to take my exit," Lonar announced, getting to his feet. "It's been a real treat getting to know you three fugitives." He nodded at them and turned down the forest trail.

"Wait!" Mirri yelled after him.

Theodisis reached out and grabbed him by the collar, lifting him off his feet. He swung Lonar around so he was facing Mirri.

"You can't leave," she said. "You have to come with us."

"And why is that?" Lonar asked, dangling in the air with his arms crossed.

Mirri paused. "I don't know yet. But you do."

Theodisis dropped him, and Mirri watched him fall on his rear end with a grunt. She and Theodisis smiled at each other for just a moment, and then both quickly turned away. She had almost forgotten she hated the centaur.

Gwenna stood, her hair smoothed back into place, a look of determination on her face. "I think Mirri is right," she announced. "We need to speak to Lavinia. I don't know why or how she knows what she does about the Homlock, but it makes sense. She knows where the location is."

"And you just expect her to tell us?" Theodisis asked with eyebrows raised.

Her mother stopped and put a hand to her chin. "Good point."

Mirri put her hands up. "Wait a minute, aren't we forgetting the most obvious problem? How do we even *get* back to Althord? Don't we need a portal or something?"

"A portal." Gwenna's eyes suddenly widened. "Or a Maylark."

Theodisis groaned. "Not again, Gwenna."

"Again? What? How do we get a Maylark all the way over here?" Mirri asked. "Grab him," she added, pointing to Lonar, who was attempting to crawl through a clump of brown bushes.

Theodisis reached his front hoof out and stamped on Lonar's hand, making him cry out and fall back. Mirri fought the urge to grin again and instead looked at her mother. "How do we contact a Maylark?"

Her mother smiled. "Well, it's a bit of a long story. But the best part . . ." She leaned in toward Mirri with wide eyes.

"What? What is the best part?"

Her mother's eyes glowed with excitement. "Is how much Theo *hates* flying on them."

Chapter Twenty-Five

"How does she do that?" Mirri asked in amazement.

Her mother perched herself high in a tree, her cloak swept to the side and dress bunched up in one hand. Gwenna had swung up on a branch easily and climbed the tallest tree in range in what seemed like seconds. Now, she made a strange cooing sound, calling into the setting sun toward Althord.

"Your mother has a strange connection with the Maylarks," Theodisis said. "Always has. Can cure them, too. No one really knows why."

Mirri looked up at him curiously. His usually sour face had a soft smile on it, staring up at his partner in crime. He sensed Mirri's stare and cleared his throat, turning to tend to their prisoner, Lonar.

Mirri shook her head, still amazed. So Theo had a soft side. The longer she spent around these two, the more she could tell they had been through quite a journey together. And they cared a great deal for each other, even if they would never admit it.

She looked into the pine tree in time to see the enormous flapping wings reach her mother, the same wings that had saved her and Kane on that cliff. At the thought of Kane, Mirri felt a pang of guilt. Her friends. She hadn't given a thought to Jinx, Smidge, and Kane since landing in a Kolt prison. Did they think she was dead? Were they still searching for her?

Before she could think further, the Maylark landed in front of her, her mother hopping off the back shell of the gigantic creature. Two legs popped out of the bottom of the humongous turtle-like animal, and the Maylark her mother had been riding bowed his long neck to Mirri.

"Keeper," he said lightly.

"Mirri, I believe you know Cam," her mother said, her hand still resting on the Maylark's back.

"Hi again, Cam." Mirri smiled at the Maylark and at the way her mother stood next to the creature. They looked very . . . complete together.

"Cam and I have been through a lot," her mother said with a smile.

"For Gwenna, I would do anything," the Maylark said. "She saved my life. And the life of my friends." He nuzzled her cheek with his beak. "Gwenna is a woman with genuine spirit."

Gwenna smiled. "Oh, Cam, you hush."

To Mirri's surprise, her mother reached to the side of Cam's shell and lifted it, revealing a large, empty area. Mirri's face wrinkled as Gwenna bent over the shell, digging around in what Mirri had thought was the Maylark's body. She pulled out a long piece of cloth and dumped it on the forest floor.

"Thanks for bringing it, Cam."

"Of course, Gwenna."

Gwenna bent over and began digging through the cloth, looking for the end. She tied a large knot in the cloth and situated it over the center of Cam's tortoise shell.

"What are you doing?" Mirri asked as Cam stood, and Gwenna tugged on the loop hanging to the ground.

"Making Theo's transport." She grinned. "He and Lonar will hang from Cam while we fly, sort of like sitting in a swing."

"And, uh, we will sit on top?" Mirri asked, running a hand through her hair.

"Yup."

Oh, dear. Theodisis backed away from the Maylark and stood with his arms crossed, gazing around at the sky. Mirri noticed the sweat glistening on his upper arms and forehead.

"What do you think? He look nervous?" Gwenna chuckled. "Poor Theo."

She went back to work tightening the knot, leaning over the Maylark.

"Hey, Mom?"

"Hmm?"

"How did you and Theodisis become . . . you know, friends? I thought you hated him."

Gwenna straightened and looked over at Theodisis, who was growling instructions at Lonar. Mirri couldn't hear what he was saying, but Lonar rolled his eyes, as usual.

"Well, I did hate him. More than you know. That memory you told us about? When we were headed to see the Maylark? I saved his life that day. A vicious hell storm swept the village, and he was near death. I dragged him over a mile back to the village. Nearly killed me in the process." She pulled an end of the cloth through a loop she had made on the other end. "Anyway, centaurs take life debts very seriously. He was in my debt when I asked him to help me retrieve the Homlock all those years ago. So when I asked him to accompany me, he had no choice but to come along." She sighed and leaned against Cam, who was sitting and munching on something crawling along the dirt. "And when I asked him again a few days ago, he agreed again. Took some persuasion. But we both wanted to be free of the Homlock. We messed up. And this was our chance to fix it."

Gwenna straightened up and tied her red hair back in a knot. "Are you ready for this?" Her eyes were shining. "There's nothing like flying on a Maylark. Just ask Theo."

Mirri smiled and shook her head as her mother called out, "Oh, bo-oys! It's time to go!"

✦

Mirri wasn't sure what she expected flying on the back of a Maylark to feel like. Being above the clouds, feeling the wind whipping her in the face, seeing the stars so much clearer than she had ever imagined—it was exhilarating. Terrifying, but truly exhilarating.

She held tight to the back of her mother, who laughed and steered Cam higher, higher, until Mirri was sure she could reach out and touch a twinkling star if she wanted to. Then, her mother would take them into a dive, speeding toward the tops of trees and tips of mountains, letting out a whoop of excitement. The freezing wind cut across her face as they flew, stinging her eyes and cheekbones, but Mirri couldn't bring herself to care. She ignored her freezing limbs and instead gazed at the stars as they flew, resting her chin between her mother's shoulder blades. Mirri could hear Theodisis screaming at Gwenna from below them, and though she couldn't make out his words, she was pretty sure she knew what he was saying.

Since centaurs couldn't ride on the back of a Maylark comfortably, Gwenna and Theodisis had rigged the system years ago to let a centaur hang *below* the Maylark in flight. With his horse's body resting in the cloth strap like a swing and his four legs dangling in the sky, his hands no doubt clenching the strap for dear life. Mirri couldn't see him from her position atop Cam but was fairly certain he looked ridiculous. Lonar rode on Theodisis, adding extra weight to the strap, but Cam didn't seem to mind his two extra passengers.

Mirri listened to her mother shouting down at Theodisis, telling him to hold on tight, and couldn't help but laugh with her. The way these two bickered one minute, then helped each other up the next. Were they in love? Maybe not in love . . . But maybe how you would feel about an older brother or sister. Theodisis was growing on her, as much as she hated to admit it.

The crazy ride turned into a calm flight the closer they got to the Imperium. Mirri could see lights around the Imperium now, the tallest building in Hadleigh Village. It was late. Mirri had no idea exactly how late, but it appeared most of the population was at home, snuggled in their beds, asleep.

Gwenna steered them over the Imperium, high enough to avoid being seen by the centaur guard standing at the front door. They lowered at the edge of the forest, where the tree line met the field behind the Imperium.

Theodisis hit the ground with a *thud* and another thump as Lonar toppled off the centaur's back. She and her mother slid off Cam's back as he stepped to the ground, no doubt exhausted from the long journey.

Her mother's face and bare arms were bright red. Gwenna shivered and rubbed her arms roughly, pulling her cloak tighter around her. Mirri wrapped her arms around herself as well, trying to work some feeling back into her freezing limbs.

Theodisis picked Lonar up from the ground roughly and dragged him to where Mirri and her mother stood. They peered at the Imperium through the trees, the tall building standing quietly.

"All right, we need to make this quick. Sunrise will be in about an hour. Theo, Cam, where do the Maylarks check in?"

"There," he said, pointing to a lit window with an illuminated balcony.

Mirri was shocked to realize it was the same balcony she jumped to last year after climbing down from the roof. Lavinia's old bedroom, the room that Kryptus now called Command. Mirri nodded to herself, remembering the Maylark that had appeared at the window and spoken to the centaur standing ready. Yes, this plan might work.

"Okay. Cam will take me up there, and I will get down to speak to Lavinia. You all will wait here until I give a sign."

Mirri shook her head. "No. No way. You are not going in there by yourself."

Gwenna grabbed Mirri's shoulders. "No, stay here. I can't risk you getting hurt. If you really did witness a Manna Kai, a test of your soul could be at any minute."

"Why would they hurt me? I'm the Keeper, remember? You're the one they are after."

Theo stepped to Gwenna. "And just how are you expecting to get through the centaur at Command?"

She threw her hair over her shoulder haughtily. "I'll think of something. I always do."

Theo grabbed her arm. "These are not ignorant Kolt warriors. These are centaurs, and you know as well as I do, they are more dependable. I will go first and take care of the centaur guard. Then I will take you to Lavinia."

Mirri stepped up beside Theo. "No, I'll go first. They all know me; I'm the Keeper. I'll make something up, then they'll leave—"

"And just how do you expect to get past the guard at Lavinia's holding cell?" Theo hissed. "I will take Gwenna in, and I will get her to Lavinia. You two will wait here," he said, motioning at Mirri and Lonar.

"No!" Gwenna practically stomped her foot. "This is my foul-up, my sister, my problem. You all will wait here, and I will get to Lavinia."

The three of them stood staring at each other, breathing hard, each one knowing that each plan was doomed to fail. Kryptus was not a stupid centaur, and he had trained his forces well.

"Seems to me like you three need a plan that will actually work," Lonar spoke from the darkness.

They all turned in unison, having forgotten he was even there.

"Oh, yeah?" Mirri called to him. "So what's your brilliant plan, then?"

He shrugged. "Why don't we all go?"

Chapter Twenty-Six

Trying to be as quiet as possible, Mirri slid off Cam's back and stepped onto the balcony, followed by her mother. Cam lifted himself high in the air to allow Theodisis and Lonar to step off with a bit of grace this time, and they stood, pressing themselves to the railing, out of sight. Cam landed in front of the door to Command, giving a loud coo noise and knocking with his beak.

The door slid open, and they exchanged quiet words. Mirri strained to hear what they said, but it mattered little. Theodisis stepped forward and knocked the centaur in the head, stunning the great creature just enough for the others to jump into action. Gwenna and Lonar grabbed the cloth Theodisis had ridden on and bound the centaur awkwardly, pushing him back into Command against the far wall. Gwenna wrapped the last of the cloth into his mouth so he could not scream. Mirri winced as she watched the centaur struggle, one she recognized as Willec.

"Hurry," Theodisis instructed. He placed his palm against the wall, and the door vanished, allowing them into the hall. He stood, waiting for the others to crowd around him. Mirri took one last glance at poor Willec, bound and gagged inside the most important room of the Imperium. Then she grabbed her mother and held on for dear life.

The toilet lift wasn't as bad this time. Mirri learned she would much rather be flushed down the Imperium than up. Much easier on her stomach.

The Imperium was quiet this time of morning. According to Theo, patrols stood at the front entrance and walked the corridors every half hour. They tiptoed behind him, stopping when he stopped, flattening themselves against walls when he held his hand up.

One problem still existed in Mirri's mind. To make it to the doorway that led to Lavinia's special prison ward, they had to pass in front of the entrance to the Imperium. As they neared the front entrance, Mirri chewed the inside of her cheek until she tasted blood. Theodisis paused at the last corner, peering around the corner to where a guard should have been standing at his post. He brought his head back around quickly. Apparently, the guard was standing on duty, doing his job, making their task so much more difficult.

They stood silently for a moment, when it occurred to Mirri that any second now, the guard may turn and walk the corridors, tripping over the four intruders. She stood wedged in between Lonar and her mother, her mother gripping her upper arm tight enough to leave a bruise. Sweat ran down Theodisis's brow as Gwenna nudged him, and he shook his head, grimacing down at her. Mirri watched as they had a silent argument, Gwenna motioning to the front while Theodisis shook his head and gritted his teeth at her.

Just as Mirri was about to tug them back down the hall, away from the guard, a large whoosh sounded from the front and an unmistakable cooing noise. Mirri heard the front door slide open, the hooves of the centaur walking outside and away. Cam. He had landed outside the Imperium, calling the attention of the guard elsewhere. Gwenna turned and nodded at her with a smile.

Mirri supposed her mother had summoned the Maylark silently somehow when Lonar shoved her from behind, almost knocking her over. She didn't have time to turn and glare at him. Instead, she hurried across the entryway behind her mother to another toilet lift. She glanced out the door as she passed. Though it was still dark, she could see the large outline of Cam, who was doing a most excellent job of keeping the centaur guard occupied.

They crept to the lift, flattened themselves against the wall, and the lift dropped them to a darker level of the Imperium. They stepped off the lift quickly, then stopped as Theodisis reached back to Gwenna. She dug in her sack and pulled out her white wig that she had worn to fool the Kolts. While still in the forest, she had cut it to be a bit more centaur-like, but as Theodisis placed it on his head, Mirri had to suppress a giggle. He looked ridiculous.

He walked to the stone door Mirri had walked in only a few days ago with Kryptus. The others hurried past the door, doing their best to make themselves invisible, hoping that the centaur wouldn't think to look in this direction. Theodisis banged on the door loudly, and the door creaked open.

"There is a problem. They need you in the Red Room."

"The Red Room?" the guard asked. "The Red Room is off-limits. Kryptus's orders."

Theodisis hesitated. "Well, his orders were for you to move upstairs. Immediately. He needs more guards at the front, *near* the Red Room."

Silence. Mirri closed her eyes. Theodisis was right. It wasn't easy to fool a centaur guard.

"Where is your weapon?" the centaur asked. Mirri could practically hear the guard's eyes narrowing at the strange, white-haired centaur.

"Are you going to ignore your orders?" Theodisis brushed off the question. "Or should I send for the Voktare now?" His voice rose to a yell.

"These are the Voktare's orders?" The guard sighed. "Fine."

Mirri breathed a quiet sigh of relief. She had to applaud Theodisis on his quick thinking. Kryptus would never give an order that made little sense. Smidge, however, just might.

They held their breath as the guard exited the door and turned left, not noticing the three beings smashed against the wall. Mirri swore her heart stopped beating as she watched him stop at the lift. *Please don't turn around*, she silently begged him. *Please don't turn around.*

The centaur walked up to the wall, turned, and yawned, waiting for the lift to take him upstairs. Mirri felt her mother tense as she too watched the centaur staring directly at them, holding his halberd in the right hand as he rubbed his face. Mirri scrunched up her face as she waited for his accusatory scream, the thundering of his hooves toward them. But instead, he yawned and stretched, and disappeared upward in a whirl of color.

Mirri sagged against the wall for a moment, finally allowing breath to return to her lungs.

Gwenna marched to the door, holding the strap of her bag firmly. "Okay. Let's do this."

Lonar stepped in line behind her, Mirri bringing up the rear. She frowned as Lonar stepped into the hallway, directly on Gwenna's heels. He seemed a bit too eager to be sneaking into the prison ward to speak to an evil woman he had never met.

But all thoughts of Lonar escaped her mind as the stone door shut behind her, filling the hallway with darkness. Instead, a different unease filled Mirri's mind, making her head whip behind her.

Theodisis led them down the hall at his usual fast pace while the three visitors crept down the dark corridor, gaping at the frightening stone beasts who were crouched in an attack position. Mirri forced her eyes forward, trying to remind herself of what Kryptus had said. It was an illusion. Just an illusion. The hallway was not closing in on her. The statues were not staring them down, preparing to pounce.

Mirri ran into the back of Lonar, who had frozen, staring at the red-eyed beast. She gave him a shove. "It's not real. Just keep going." She tried to keep her voice steady, but it came out shaking.

Gwenna came to an abrupt stop ahead of Lonar, causing the three of them to gasp in unison. Gwenna reached out and grabbed Mirri's hand so tight it made Mirri cry out. The surrounding walls were tightening, the torches lining the dark hall getting closer and closer.

"It's . . ." Mirri panted. "It's—it's not real, Mom. Go, go!" Mirri shrieked, desperate to escape this horrible place. She shoved her mother, who was turning in confused, shaking circles, and grabbed Lonar with her other hand, getting ahold of his vest. Squeezing her eyes shut, she pushed her mother ahead of them and pulled Lonar behind her, forcing them toward the light at the end of the corridor.

Gwenna stopped, scratching at her legs, gasping as the invisible bugs started up her legs. Lonar started spinning in circles, batting at his own head. Mirri felt the crawling up her legs, underneath her jeans, but fought the urge to scream and scathe herself.

"Go, go!" Mirri cried again, doing her best to ignore the insects attacking her body, reaching up for her face. "GO!" She shoved her mother forward and gripped Lonar's sweaty wrist, digging her toes into the stone floor.

The three of them fell into the bright room, out of the suffocating nightmare they had just ran through, splaying themselves out on the floor. Theodisis turned and run his hand through his blonde hair.

"Sorry about that," he muttered. He leaned to help Gwenna, picking her up under the arms, ignoring the other two, who climbed to their knees. She stood shakily, and Mirri watched as Theodisis wrapped her in a hug.

"It wasn't real," he murmured in her ear.

Gwenna nodded and pulled back, smiling weakly up at him. Lonar stood quickly, dusting himself off, keeping his eyes on the ground. *Finally*, Mirri thought, as she took a deep breath and stood. He did have a shred of humanity in him.

They all turned toward the concrete wall as it slowly faded away. Mirri held her breath as the steel bars came into view, and the prisoner behind them came into focus.

Gwenna, standing beside Mirri, straightened her shoulders and took a deep breath.

Lavinia stood in the middle of the cell, gazing at them, her dark eyes blazing. It was as if she had been waiting for them, somehow knew they were on their way to her. A hint of a smile played on her thin lips and her pale face looked even whiter against her dark eyes, giving her the appearance of a frail, sick human with an evil purpose.

"Gwenna."

"Lavinia." Her mother's voice came out low and hateful, a voice Mirri had never heard her mother use.

Lavinia smiled and laughed. "Oh, you arrived much sooner than I expected, dear sister! So, tell me, what is it that you *need* from me?"

Mirri narrowed her eyes at the spiteful woman standing behind the bars.

Her mother gave a sweet smile. "I simply had to see you imprisoned, Lavinia. My daughter has been telling me all about the joy of conquering you."

Lavinia cocked her head as her smile faded. "Yes, it was simply delightful getting to know my niece. Her love of elves is simply deplorable." She grabbed the bars in front of her. "Theo. How are you, my dear centaur?"

Mirri glanced back at Theodisis, who had not said a word since his embrace of Gwenna. He stood at attention behind Gwenna and remained silent. He had to remember Lavinia well. Centaurs used to be Lavinia's personal guards before Smidge exposed her as a fraud and an ordinary human being.

Lavinia smiled darkly. "So, Theo—just like old times, no?"

Mirri looked from Lavinia to Theodisis, but he remained quiet. He could not keep the heat from creeping into his cheeks. She was toying with him; that much was clear. Lavinia knew something. Something that Theodisis did not want the others to know.

Gwenna stepped in. "So, how has prison been treating you, Lavinia? Enjoying your three meals a day?"

Lavinia didn't answer but looked thoughtfully at Lonar.

"A Kolt, hmm? Quite the image of Cormac, that's for sure," Lavinia said, giving a sly smile.

Lonar looked up in surprise, then looked at me, bewildered. How would Lavinia know Cormac?

"Enough playing, Lavinia. We need the location of the Mother Kolt," Gwenna demanded.

Lavinia threw her head back and laughed. "Oh, Gwenna, I admire your naivety! You actually think I am going to give you the location of the Mother Kolt!"

"I know you will, Lavinia." Gwenna stepped toward the cell, almost close enough to reach out and touch her.

Lavinia's gaze hardened. "And why is that?"

"Because I know your secret, sister. And I will have no problem telling everyone in this kingdom the truth."

Lavinia rolled her eyes. *"My* secret? You'll have to be a bit clearer, I'm afraid. I have a few of them." She tossed her hair and flounced down on her bed, appearing bored.

"I know his name, Lavinia. I know the name of the one you think no one else knows. He was quite . . . important to you, was he not?"

Lavinia glared at her sister. It was silent for several moments as Mirri looked back and forth between the sisters. What name? What secret? Gwenna stood with a quiet smile while Lavinia sat, studying her.

"You have no proof. No one that would even care, sister."

Gwenna nodded, putting her fingers to her chin in deep thought. "True, true." Gwenna shrugged and turned, throwing her hands up. "So I might as well tell them. Tell them all. Let us leave this dim place!" she announced to the rest of them as they turned toward the exit. She put her arm around Mirri. "There is something you need to know about Lavinia, Mirri. She was in love."

"Stop."

Her mother smiled sideways at Mirri, giving her a wink.

Gwenna turned, a broad smile on her face. "Yes?"

Lavinia's head cocked to one side, her chin lifted. "I will tell you the location. On one condition."

This time, it was Gwenna's turn to laugh. "One condition? It doesn't seem you are in a bargaining position."

"I want to see the Homlock."

"You want to see the Homlock?"

"Yes."

"Why?"

Lavinia paused. "I want proof you have what you say."

No one spoke. Mirri swore she could hear her mother's beating heart and wondered if her mother could hear hers. Theodisis still stood with his arms crossed, his muscles tensed.

This did not feel right. Something about this felt too . . . easy.

Mirri opened her mouth to tell her mother to stop, to not reveal the necklace. But why? She swallowed, breathing fast, deciding to trust her mother's judgment. They needed that location, she reminded herself.

Gwenna reached into the bag she wore around her body and withdrew the necklace. Mirri watched as she slowly pulled the gold chain up to reveal the pendant. It swung in the air gently as Gwenna held it up for Lavinia to see for the first time.

Once Gwenna held the necklace in the air, time seemed to slow. The red stone dangled in midair, swaying gently on the end of the chain. Gwenna stood several feet away from the bars that held Lavinia prisoner, greedily watching the Homlock swinging back and forth. The woman's dark eyes became alight, and she reached through the bars, her long and unkempt fingernails stretching for the pendant.

At the same time, Gwenna realized her mistake, and the pendant flew from her mother's hand into Lavinia's.

All Mirri could hear was her own scream. "No!"

But by then, it was too late.

Chapter Twenty-Seven

Mirri opened her eyes, taking in a gasp of cold air, and immediately coughing it back out. Something foul—like expired, chunked-up milk—filled her nostrils, making her cover her nose with her hand. She rolled over on her side, trying not to gag, coming face to face with something hard. Using her hands in the darkness, she felt the object in front of her, running her hands up the smooth, uneven, hard surface. She sat, running her hand as high as she could reach up on the slick surface. Looking up, she could see nothing but darkness. Mirri stood, leaning against the wall, hand still holding the polished surface.

Mirri turned, staring into the sea of darkness. The stillness around her felt unnatural, as if someone should be talking, or something was right in front of her face, invisible to her own eyes. Goosebumps broke out over her flesh as she felt it. Someone was here with her. Someone she did not want to be with her. For a moment, she flattened herself against the cool wall, afraid to speak, afraid to breathe.

Then, it all came rushing back to her. Her mother. Lavinia's prison cell. The Homlock. How long had she been down here?

"Mom?" Mirri whispered into the sea of darkness around her. Her voice came out shaking, but could not match the insurmountable fear that she felt at this moment. She was not alone in this place. Lavinia was here, with her. She could feel her eyes watching Mirri, those dark, evil eyes.

"Mom?" she tried again.

"M—Mirri . . ."

"Mom! Where are you?" Mirri whispered, still afraid to leave the safety of her rock wall. She reached out into the cold air. "Mom?"

"Mirri . . ."

Mirri dropped to her knees, crawling along the dirt and pebble floor, holding one hand out in front of her. The whisper of her mother was faint, barely there. She was in pain, maybe near death. Had Lavinia done this to her? Had Lavinia attempted to kill her mother?

Mirri stopped when her hand connected with something warm and sticky. She swallowed, holding down the wave of nausea that crept into her stomach.

Her fingers were soaked in the blood. She could smell it. Feel the thickness of it. Now, both her hands were sitting in the thick puddle.

"Mom!" Mirri cried out, reaching, searching, running her hands along the uneven, bloodied floor. "Mom!"

Mirri cried out as someone grabbed her wrist.

"Mirri."

"Mom!" Mirri dragged herself through the blood and felt the woman lying on the ground. Used her fingers to work her touch over her soaked dress and to the base of her neck.

"Are you all right?" It was a stupid question, really. Her mother lie in a dark pit, soaked in blood. But at the moment, in the sheer joy of finding her, the words tumbled out of her mouth.

"I'm fine, Mirri." Her voice was a little more than a whisper, and Mirri could hear her labored breathing.

"Oh, Mom." Mirri found her mother's hand and squeezed, ignoring the slippery substance that covered it. "Mom?" Mirri whispered, trying to hold back tears. "What happened? How long have we been in this place?"

"I . . . don't know. But I'm glad you're safe." Gwenna coughed and gasped, as if the coughing caused her inextricable pain.

Mirri felt drops of blood hit her on the face but kept her position over her mother.

"I landed on something sharp, I think. I was lying on it when I came to—it must have been a stone, or . . ." Her mother's voice faded away as if just the act of talking exhausted her.

Mirri fought with the cloak she had been wearing for days. She tore it off, making sure one hand was always in her mother's bloody, limp grip, and bundled the worn fabric up. Mirri pressed it gently to her mother's chest. When Mrs. Langley did not respond, Mirri moved the shirt closer to her abdomen, which caused her to cry out in pain.

There. Mirri held the cloak in place, trying to fold it like a person was supposed to if their mother was bleeding out on a rock floor.

"Where is Lavinia?" she whispered, close to her mother's ear. Her mother shook her head slightly, possibly because talking caused her too much pain.

A loud sigh caused Mirri to jump back, knocking her head into something hard. She pressed one of her bloody palms over her chest, maybe to hold her heart in place. It was ramming into her rib cage so hard it hurt.

"Lavinia?" Mirri called out, her shaky voice echoing. She turned her head, looking for any sign of the woman. But the darkness was thick and held her prisoner more than these walls ever could.

"Yes, my dear niece, it is me," her bored voice called from somewhere above Mirri.

Mirri took a deep breath and lowered herself back to where her mother lay. *You have defeated this woman once*, she reminded herself. *Do not be afraid.*

She kneeled back and found her mother's hand. She stayed quiet, though Mirri could feel her mother grip her hand back.

"Where are we?" Mirri called out. "Where did you bring us?"

Lavinia sighed again. "That is the question, isn't it? I'm afraid I'm not sure where the Homlock has brought us, child. I'm a little rusty, apparently."

Mirri glanced up and thought she saw movement above her, almost as if Lavinia were sitting on something, swinging her legs back and forth.

"What did you do to my mother?" Mirri glared up into the darkness.

"Oh, child, I have not done a thing to your mother. It brought her here exactly as she is now."

"What did? The Homlock?"

"Either that, or I took a wrong turn somewhere." She giggled at her own joke, her laugh reverberating off the walls that surrounded them.

"Where are Theodisis and Lonar?"

"I expect your mother's love centaur is still lying on the floor of my prison cell. Along with that handsome Kolt," she said dryly.

"Why did it bring us here?" Mirri demanded.

"Well, if I knew that, I wouldn't be sitting here with you, waiting for my sister to take her last breath."

Mirri bristled at the darkness, wishing Lavinia could see the dirty look she was giving her. Instead, she sat down on the rock and put a hand on the fabric she held against her mother's body.

She gripped her hand tightly. "You'll be okay, Mom. I'll get us out of here," she whispered. "Please, just hold on a little longer."

Her mother gave her hand a reassuring squeeze and Mirri leaned her head down to meet her mother's. "Please hold on."

Gwenna didn't answer, but Mirri felt the grip on her hand give a light squeeze. Or perhaps she imagined it. She bit her bottom lip as the tears fell, gently dripping on her mother's face. "Please hold on."

❖

Mirri kept one arm wrapped around her bare arms, rubbing them to build some warmth. She kept the other hand on her mother. At times, her mother's grasp on her hand would lighten, and Mirri's heart would stop. She would hold her breath until she felt her mother's chest rise, or the grip on her hand move. Then Mirri would allow herself to breathe again. She sat on the hard floor, up near her mother's head, tight up against her for warmth. Occasionally, she would lean forward, checking her mother's ill-placed bandages.

The top of the bloody cloak felt crusty and stiff, and Mirri would bite her bottom lip to keep from moaning. She was no nurse, but it seemed the bleeding had stopped. That was a good thing, right? The blood had clotted, or whatever blood does? Her mother still drew breath, uneven and painful breaths, but she was still alive. Mirri could hear her soft moans of pain every so often, and gritted her teeth, telling herself moans of pain were a good thing. Mirri dreaded the silence between them.

Her tears had long since dried. A sorrow, a heaviness in her heart had replaced them, a heaviness that filled her with her own form of pain and torture: her guilt. Her mother was dying while she sat here, stuck here in some pit of darkness with her evil, murderous aunt. And she couldn't do a thing about it. If there was, she would have saved her mother's life hours ago.

The thought of her friends made her heart ache more. Smidge and Jinx. Kryptus, Kane, and Theodisis. What were they doing now? Searching for them? Mirri let herself give a tiny smile as she imagined Jinx fluttering madly, losing control, screaming her high-pitched scream. What she would give to see one of them again. If she ever did.

Lavinia remained silent from her perch above. Mirri's hatred for the woman had boiled red-hot for the first few hours but had dwindled. It was difficult to feel much of anything but despair at the moment. Complete and utter failure. She had failed her friends, her mother, and could not complete the one task she had been called for.

Mirri scoffed to herself. A testament of her soul. It appeared Mirri had failed the Manna Kai, or whatever it was. She was not worthy of being the Keeper of Althord. Things had only become worse since she had become involved.

"Mirri?"

Mirri jumped, grabbing her mother's hand with both of hers. "Mom, I'm here. I'm here," she repeated, soothing hair back from her mother's eyes.

"I need to tell you something. Before . . . before it's too late."

Mirri halted the hair rubbing. "No, no Mom, you're just fine. Please don't say that." The tears welled in her eyes again, filling and spilling over before she could stop them.

"Please listen, Mirri." Her mother took a deep breath in the darkness. "It's my fault Avi is dead. I didn't wrap the beads around his neck, but he is gone because of me."

"You don't know that, Mom. The curse could've meant any-thing—"

"Not just the curse, Mirri. There's more."

Mirri forced herself to stay silent next to her mother, letting the tears stream down her face.

"The night he died, I came back through the portal. He gave me something to take back, and I left. I . . . I ran into Kryptus outside of my father's home. Demanded he take me back to the portal. He didn't want to. He was standing watch over my father like he was supposed to . . ." Her words trailed off, as if she was replaying them in her mind. "I begged him, pleaded with him to take me back through the forest. I thought if I had one last chance with him . . ." She coughed, grabbing her stomach as she did. Her head bounced off the rock floor, and the pain in her voice made Mirri cringe.

"He took me into the forest after I made a scene, begging him to come with me. I loved him, Mirri. I was so enamored with him that I thought I could convince him to come back with me. Stay with me." Gwenna sniffed, and Mirri could picture the tears running down her face as well. "It was while he was in the forest with me that Father was attacked. If he had been there, been where he was supposed to be, Father would still be here." Gwenna began sobbing quietly as Mirri ran her hand over her mother's hair.

Instead of insisting she was wrong, telling her it wasn't her fault, Mirri had something else to say. Something she had never told her mother, something that weighed on her heart every day. Though she came to live with her secret and to accept that her father's death was not her fault, it was still fresh on her mind.

"Dad was there, waiting for me, Mom. Where he was supposed to be. The day he died. I missed his text because a cute boy asked me to go get a smoothie with him. He left the library when I didn't answer and was killed by the drunk driver pulling out of the parking lot." Mirri pulled her knees up to her chest and rested her head on them. There. She told her. "I'm sorry I never told you," she whispered.

"Oh, Mirri," her mother whispered, clutching her hand. "I don't blame you for your father. Never. I blame the drunk driver." She squeezed her hand again. "Why do we keep these secrets from one another?"

Mirri shook her head. "I don't know, Mom."

"Let's not keep anything else important from each other, okay?"

Mirri nodded. "Okay."

They were silent a moment, gripping each other's hands, feeling the heaviness lighten, if only a bit. It felt good to tell her mother. Mirri hoped her mother felt the same.

Mirri smiled into the darkness, leaning her head back against the smooth rock wall. "You know, Mom, someone once told me that things happen exactly as they are supposed to. That we have to forgive ourselves. It's the only way to get home."

"Who told you that?"

Mirri patted her mother's hand. "Your dad did."

Chapter Twenty-Eight

I t was Gwenna's turn to be silent, though Mirri could sense her smile in the darkness. "Yes, that sounds like something he would say. I love you, Mirri."

"I love you too, Mom."

"If you two are finished?" Lavinia's sour voice came from above. "The display of love and tenderness is enough to make me gag."

Mirri felt her mother's grip tighten. "Sorry, Vinnie."

Mirri giggled, despite herself. "Vinnie?"

"Yup. Ol' Vinnie and I had a few pet names for each other."

Lavinia scoffed but stayed quiet.

Mirri leaned over and kissed her mother on the forehead. Light was filtering into their prison, and Mirri stood to look around. They were in a circular, deep pit, the rock walls around them shiny. Mirri stepped closer to examine the walls, running her hand along the smooth surface. Large camouflaged gouges, or divots, ran along and up the walls. Up even higher, a rock formation stuck out toward the other wall, almost bridging the gap to the other side. More protruding rocks stuck out here and there, all the way up the rock wall. Hmm.

Mirri looked up again, judging the distance to the top. It was fairly high. There's no way she could make it on her own. If only her mother could climb . . . She turned to her mother and kneeled down next to her, taking advantage of the rays of light filling the cavern.

Her face looked ghastly white, but she looked better than Mirri expected. She took a deep breath and removed her crusty cloak from on top of her mother. Biting back the bile rising in her throat, she inspected the gouge in her mother's stomach. The good news was the bleeding had stopped. The bad news was it was quite large. But maybe not too deep, Mirri thought, forcing herself to look at the dried blood and ripped skin.

Her mother's hand on hers calmed her immediately. "Mirri. You must get out of here. You can make it up these walls. I know you can."

Mirri shook her head. "Not by myself."

Gwenna glanced up at Lavinia, who had her arms crossed and eyes closed, leaning back against the wall. She was sitting on one of those large pieces of rock that stuck out awkwardly from the wall.

Mirri glanced back down at her mother with raised eyebrows. Her mother sighed and winced as she shifted her body. "There may be no other choice."

Mirri agreed. She might get up the wall a few feet, but without a second hand and someone to steady her, she wouldn't make it to the top.

Sighing, Mirri stood. "Hey, Vinnie?" she called.

Lavinia didn't answer.

Mirri tried again. "I was thinking about getting out of this place. Care to join me?"

Lavinia turned to give Mirri a look of utter disinterest, then rolled her eyes. "And I suppose you want your dear auntie to join you?" She gave a giggle.

"It's going to take two of us to get out of here. Unless you'd rather just sit here the rest of your life."

Lavinia rolled onto her back on her rock ledge so her matted hair was hanging off and she was staring at Mirri upside down. The Homlock dangled innocently from her neck.

"Ah. So, you need my help, dear?" She smiled and cocked her head, which was still hanging upside down. "I say, it is a mere *wonder* what you two would do without me these days." She laughed as Mirri clenched her jaw.

Mirri put her hands on her hips. "You know, *Auntie*, you never did tell us where the Mother Kolt was. I'd say we fulfilled our part of the bargain. Now, you need to tell us what you promised us."

"Oh, that's right, the Homlock." She sat straight up, throwing her legs back over the side to face Mirri. She leaned forward, her eyes wide. "Do you want to know? Do you?"

Mirri crossed her arms over her chest. "Where is it?" Lavinia was turning this into a ridiculous game and thought she held all the cards.

Lavinia put a finger to her lips as if telling Mirri to be quiet. She looked from side to side with her wide eyes and beckoned Mirri closer. Mirri held her position, far away from the ridiculous woman.

Lavinia's voice dropped to a whisper. "The answer is . . ." She paused. "I don't know!" She threw up her hands and laughed again, throwing her body back against the rock wall.

Mirri glared at her, unimpressed. "Very funny. Now tell us."

Lavinia sat up straight. Silent. "Why would I tell you?" she asked with a devilish grin.

"Because if you don't, your sister here will tell the entire world your little secret."

Lavinia rolled her eyes and put an arm over her forehead dramatically. "Oh no. Heavens, what would little old me do if everyone knew another one of my secrets?" She leaned forward. "Guess what, Mirri? I don't care!"

While Lavinia howled with laughter above her, Mirri's heart sank, far, far down. Lavinia didn't know where to take the Homlock. Even if she did, she didn't plan on telling them. She didn't care if everyone knew her secret, but it gave her the chance she needed to see the Homlock . . .

"You don't know? That's impossible! Why did we come all the way back, if only to wind up here?" Tears of anger stung at the corners of her eyes. She threw her hands in the air and turned, furious, pursing her lips tightly. "But you knew! You knew the words . . ."

Mirri trailed off, staring at the woman who laughed so hard tears slipped down her face. Mirri put her face in her hands, rubbing it until it hurt. She glanced down at her mother, lying there helpless with a bloody shirt holding her midsection together. She didn't want to meet her mother's eyes. Gwenna had been right. They never should have gone back to the Imperium. Once again, Mirri had screwed up. She had almost cost her mother her life. In trying to be a hero, she had gotten them stuck in a place where they would rot away until the end of time, listening to this lunatic.

"Mirri."

Mirri stepped toward her mother on the ground but could not meet her eyes. She wasn't sure if she was more angry at Lavinia or herself. Why, in all the world, did they think they could trust this evil woman? Why did Mirri beg her mother to bring her back, to break into the Imperium, and drag themselves through that torturous hallway?

And her friends. Smidge, and Jinx, and Kane. What if they were still out there, looking for her? They could be in danger for *her*. What of Kryptus and Rose? Did they run down to the prison cells and see the worst prisoner in Althord history gone? Because of Mirri? He had warned Mirri. Told her not to trust Lavinia. But she hadn't listened.

"Mirri."

Mirri kneeled down next to her mother, the hot tears leaving fresh tracks on her cheeks. She stared at the ground, at the little puddles they made in the dirt. "I'm sorry," she whispered. "For everything. You were right. I never should have brought us back."

Gwenna did not speak for a moment but let Mirri wallow in her self-pity. She stayed quiet long enough that Mirri finally looked up at her, waiting.

"When I was six years old, I found a baby Maylark. I had no idea where its parents were, but I knew it was alone and had been for a long time. It was so thin and weak." She sighed, picturing the small bird in her mind. "I brought it back home and fed it, bathed it. I even made a bed right next to my own. But I remember I was too afraid to sleep. What if it needed me and I was asleep, or what if something went wrong in the middle of the night? So I stayed awake. For two whole days. The Maylark had stopped eating, moving, anything. Couldn't even lift its own head. It died on the third day. I was absolutely beside myself with grief. I wouldn't get out of bed; I wouldn't eat *anything*. Your grandfather told me something very important that night. He said I didn't fail the Maylark; I learned from it. He said the failure was not the end, but the beginning of something great. And since that day, I have served and helped Maylarks to my greatest ability."

Mirri sniffed and nodded, still looking down. Her mother grasped her hand.

"If there is one thing I have learned from living in this world, it's that failure is necessary. Think of all you learned the last time you were here. This is not the end, Mirri. It is only the beginning." Her eyes shined at Mirri, then glanced upward toward Lavinia.

Mirri pursed her lips. *Failure is necessary,* she repeated to herself. Time to get back to her friends. It was time to do her job as the Keeper of Althord Loch. *I can fight this,* she thought. *I will fight this.* For Smidge and Jinx and Kryptus. For Gwenna. Mirri refused to let her mother die here, in a pit with only her daughter and sister to witness.

She followed her mother's gaze upward. Inwardly, she sighed as she watched Lavinia, lying on the ledge, swinging the Homlock back and forth.

She just wished she had someone else to help her.

◆

"No, just right there. Just put your hands down like this." Mirri held her hands to show Lavinia how to weave her fingers together. "Right there."

Lavinia held her hand up to her face, wiggling her fingers in front of her face. Mirri sighed, rubbing her forehead. She couldn't believe she was willing to trust this woman to get out of this place. But her mother was right. They had no other choice.

Mirri had tried. She had jumped, reached, and jumped again. But she could not reach a ledge or foothold on her own. There was only one option. Lavinia would have to help.

It took some convincing and quite a headache, but she finally convinced Lavinia they would have to work together or die in this pit. Mirri counted to ten silently, trying not to show her annoyance. But mostly because she figured out Lavinia loved it when she got angry. And that made Mirri angry. Boiling, red-hot angry, but she couldn't show it. And that also made her angry.

For strength, she looked at her mother. She gave Mirri encouraging nods, even though her cheekbones were sinking in and her face was turning a frightening shade of pale. Her nods turned to a faint smile, as if forcing her head up and down required too much energy. Mirri's nerves were on end, her anger ready to explode, and her desperation peaking at a new level. She needed to get her mother out of here. She had to find help.

Mirri turned her attention back to Lavinia. She stood leaning against the wall, studying her fingers intently as if fascinated by the way they moved in front of her. Mirri closed her eyes and took a deep breath.

"Come on. Let's go." Mirri faced the wall and waited, silently counting to ten.

Lavinia gave her a sly smile and leaned down to weave her fingers together for Mirri to step on. Mirri swallowed, aware that her aunt was enjoying this. She refused to let Lavinia get to her. *Keep it cool,* Mirri thought to herself as she screwed up her courage and put a foot in Lavinia's hands.

Grunting, Lavinia pushed her upward as Mirri reached for the ledge sticking out from the stone wall. Mirri bit her lip as the edge of the stone cut into her palm as she pulled her body onto the ledge. She sat on her knees, facing the wall, breathing hard. *Okay. That wasn't so bad,* she said to the wall. Now, she just had to stand. Legs shaking, Mirri pulled one foot to the ledge, and slowly stood, hugging the stone in front of her. Mirri silently thanked her track coach for the workout routine they did every day before practice. She may not be able to do a pull-up, but her leg muscle made up for it.

Mirri made it to a standing position and peered down. Lavinia stood, looking bored. Mirri took a deep breath. The ledge wasn't deep—it didn't stick out from the wall more than a few inches. But it was wide. Wide enough for two people? Mirri wasn't sure but was about to find out. She scooted to the right, as far as she could go, and swallowed thickly.

"Okay," she called down to Lavinia. "Ready?"

Lavinia nodded without looking at Mirri, but studying her nails. Mirri rolled her eyes to herself and bent at the waist.

"Come on," she said, fighting to keep her temper in check.

Lavinia looked up at her and reached a hand up. She rested her foot against the uneven wall a few feet up and grabbed Mirri's outstretched hand. Struggling, Mirri pulled Lavinia up just far enough for her to grasp the ledge. Mirri let go of her hand and teetered on the ledge, grabbing the wall in front of her. She scooted as far as she could to allow room for Lavinia and waited, the icy wall feeling calming against her tense body.

Copying Mirri's stance against the wall, Lavinia made it to her feet, holding tight to the stone. Mirri noticed with satisfaction the fear in Lavinia's eyes and her trembling hands against the stone. Lavinia's fright gave Mirri the lift she needed, and she reached for the ledge resting a foot or two above her head.

Pulling herself up on her elbows, she wiggled her lower body up onto her stomach. Luckily, this ledge stuck out almost to the other side of the stone pit. Mirri looked up, holding one hand to the wall. One more ledge and she would be free. Out of this place. She bit the inside of her cheek as Lavinia wriggled herself onto the ledge next to her. Before she could actually stand, Mirri pulled herself up to the next awkwardly shaped ledge. She wasn't too eager to be up this high off the ground with her murderous aunt next to her.

This one seemed higher. Mirri struggled, her foot catching Lavinia's shoulder. She scrambled up onto her butt and sat, wiping the hair out of her eyes. She could almost reach the top now. Be free of this place. Mirri swallowed. Hesitantly, she reached her hand over the edge and waited, grabbing at Lavinia's sweaty palm. Mirri pulled her up next to where she sat, leaning against the stone. Mirri watched Lavinia glance up, just as she had done, realizing how close she sat to the top.

They glanced at each other, daring the other to stand first. Before Mirri could think, her hand reached out and grabbed the pendant around Lavinia's neck, snapping the clasp. For a split second, they both stared at the gold necklace, the golden chain hanging over Mirri's palm. Then Lavinia jumped, surprisingly limber all of a sudden, and dashed away out of the cave.

Chapter Twenty-Nine

Mirri struggled to lift herself out of the cave while clutching the Homlock. She grunted and wriggled her body back and forth, finally collapsing on her back on the cool floor, staring up at the ceiling.

The ceiling. Wait—she looked around, confused. Mirri had thought they had been outside. Directly above them, an enormous gap appeared in the ceiling that she had been looking through, giving off the illusion of being outdoors. Half of the ceiling must have been missing. Mirri looked back up again, studying the blue sky and clouds. She stood, studying her surroundings, knowing she should race after the murderous prisoner escaping, but stood in shock.

The columns. The floor, these windows. She had been here before. She was in the castle, the one she had seen in the memory. Her heart began hammering at the thought of Chloris falling on the floor in a heap with a dagger sticking out of her chest. For a brief second, she scanned the floor, fearing she would trip over a murdered body. *Insane*, she told herself. It was a memory. It would have been years ago. Right?

She shook her head and tucked the necklace in her pocket. She had to find a way out; she had to get help. Concentrate.

Up ahead, a massive flight of stairs led down amid rubble and cracked columns. This was the same castle, she was sure of it, but it appeared much more damaged and abandoned than she remembered, like so many other places she had seen in this world.

Running, she hurried around boulders of stone and veered away from columns with jagged edges. What had happened to this beautiful place?

She ran toward the wall, planning on looking out the arched window that came almost all the way to the ground. There had to be some sort of landmark, something that told her where she even was in this world. Was it Koltaria? Althord Loch? Hopefully, the Maylarks were searching by now, Mirri assured herself. Yes, the Maylarks. They would fly directly to—

Mirri's thoughts were interrupted when her foot caught something large. She fell forward, on top of something, landing with a cry of pain. Except the cry was not hers.

"Lonar!" Mirri had never been so excited to see the Kolt and gave him an awkward hug as he lay on the ground. "What are you doing here?"

"I'd say I'm lying here dying, darlin'."

Mirri sat up on her knees, wincing at the fresh blood staining her hands. Lonar lay soaked in blood, his eyes squeezed shut in pain.

"Where are you hurt?" Mirri asked matter-of-factly, as if it would help. She had nothing to stanch the fresh blood flow, no way to help the man. As if she was a world-class nurse now, anyway.

"Can't tell. Hurts all over."

Mirri wiped her wet hands on her already bloodied jeans and inspected his front. The blood was bright and wet and looked like it was oozing from several parts of his body.

"What happened?" Mirri asked, as she studied the large stain that was growing on his thigh.

"Woke up under those rocks over there. Guess this was your dear aunt's doing." Even in this state, the man could sound sarcastic and indifferent. He took a large gasp and wheezed, wincing.

Mirri sat back and looked around. "But why here?" she said to herself.

"I'd have to guess it's that Homlock y'all keep going on about," he muttered with his eyes closed.

"But why?"

He winced. "I'm just dyin', sweetheart. Don't really care. But if you have an extra second—"

"Just shut up for a second, okay? I need to think." Even dying, the man could still irritate her.

The memory. Chloris. Her child. Cormac. Mirri closed her eyes, replaying the scene the best she could. She could see the dagger Cormac produced. The dagger. Where the dagger met the dusk . . . But it didn't make any sense. It had not been dusk in the memory. She could remember the sunlight shining in through the hole in the ceiling, making beautiful light designs on the floor. And why would that matter? They needed the Mother Kolt, not some dark-haired woman.

Mirri sat back, running both hands through her hair. "Why would the Homlock bring us here? Where I saw Cormac? I . . . don't . . . understand." Mirri gritted her teeth so the tears would not start again. "The Mother Kolt wasn't here. It wasn't dusk. Just some dark-haired woman stabbed with a dagger!"

"She was stabbed?" Lonar coughed, blood dripping down his cheek. "You never . . . told me that." He coughed again, this time gasping and holding his side.

"You never asked!"

"Twilight. That—that is how . . . how she signed her letters—Your Twilight," Lonar wheezed.

"What?" Mirri sat upright. Dusk. Twilight. Could they be one and the same?

"I read her letters . . . " Lonar drifted off, closing his eyes.

"No, no, don't you dare die on me now!" Mirri grabbed his chin. "Lonar!" When he did not wake, she slapped his cheek. "Are you telling me the dusk is Chloris? She is Twilight? They are the same woman?" When he did not respond, she slapped him again. "Lonar!"

He nodded, his eyes still closed. "The letters."

"What about the Mother Kolt?" Mirri grasped his chin. "What did she look like? Lonar!"

"Beautiful . . . Dark, curling hair . . . Dark hair . . ." Lonar drifted off again.

Mirri stared at the man in front of her. Was it possible? Had she seen the Mother Kolt murdered with a dagger? Was she the woman that fell begging for her child to be saved?

Mirri licked her dry lips. She had one last chance to fix this. She grabbed Lonar under the shoulders and pulled. He made no sound, no cry of pain, as Mirri dragged his lifeless body over crumbling rocks and bits of glass. Could it be possible? Chloris was the Mother Kolt? At this point, there weren't many options. She would soon find out if she had witnessed this blessed woman murdered before her very eyes.

Gasping, she pulled the man's weight toward the stairs. Could those be the very stairs Cormac had walked down when Chloris had paddled up the river? Mirri went from dragging his shoulders to dragging his arm, then pulling and tugging his wrist toward the staircase. She tried to ignore the red streaks that followed his body, glistening on the white marble floor.

"Lonar!" She gasped as she tugged at his arm. "You have to wake up!"

They reached the top of the staircase, and Mirri fell to her knees to catch her breath. There. She looked down. In the place of a river lay a dry bed of leaves, sticks, and dirt. It was there, in front of the river, at the base of the stairs. Where Mirri had watched Chloris hand Cormac the child. She had to get him there.

Forcing herself to stand, Mirri tugged at Lonar's forearm, grunting as he only seemed to become heavier. His head fell down on the first step and Mirri winced at the *thud* of his skull when it connected with the floor. Biting her lip, she continued the arduous process of dragging the near-dead man down, one stair at a time.

Thud. Pause. *Thud*. Pause. Mirri reached the landing, putting her hands on her knees. Almost there, she told herself, pushing the sweat from her eyes. She grabbed his arm again and yanked harder than she must have thought, as Lonar's body began to tumble down the stairs, taking her with it.

Mirri cried out as her back met the cruel edges of the hard stairs and gasped when her head banged on the floor at the bottom. Lonar's body lay in a heap next to hers. Though the large room around her spun, she grasped Lonar's hand and crawled along the floor, stopping every few feet to tug at his wrist.

She collapsed on her stomach on the cool floor, letting her cheek rest on the spot. The spot Chloris had fallen. She was sure of it. She knew it. The river that Chloris had boated down was right in front of her, now a long, dry ditch.

Turning over on her back, she reached into her pocket, producing the Homlock. For a moment, she lay there, gasping for breath, the Homlock in her hand, resting against the cool floor.

What now? Mirri thought. Her brain was fuzzy, her vision still spinning. Forcing herself to sit, she reached over and laid the Homlock in a smear of blood Lonar had left on the floor next to her. She closed her eyes and waited. After a moment, she opened her eyes. Lonar lay there, not moving, not breathing, peaceful. Gone. Never again to make a sarcastic comment, never again to act like he did not care.

Mirri put a hand to her head as she stood, trying to keep her vision steady. The Homlock dangled in her hand, Lonar's blood dripping steadily on the tiled floor. Nothing happened; no miracles were taking place. Still alone in this dank place, with only a dead man for company. Her mother lay alone and dying in a pit somewhere. Mirri's shoulders sagged as she looked around. Any hope she had of solving her mother's curse drained away, dripping on the floor as steady as Lonar's blood fell from the Homlock. She wanted to crumple into a little ball and sob, yet she felt too exhausted for tears to fall.

The roar echoed through the castle a second before Mirri hit the ground, face first. Lavinia shoved Mirri's body into the floor with a growl as the Homlock slid away, gliding across the blood-stained floor. Mirri cried out and swung her arm back, feeling a strand of greasy hair connect with her fingertips as Lavinia grabbed Mirri by the back of the neck. Mirri grabbed at Lavinia's hand, trying to pry the fingernails from her skin. The horrible woman laughed and shoved Mirri's face harder into the cool stone.

Gritting her teeth, Mirri slipped her own knee under herself and flipped her body over, Lavinia cursing as she toppled off Mirri. Lavinia still had a grip on her hair, yanking and twisting Mirri's long brown hair. Mirri threw her arm backward, desperately trying to free herself from Lavinia's tightening grasp. For a moment, they were a tangled mess of females on the tiled floor, biting, smacking and kicking, Mirri finally ripping her hair free.

Lavinia sat on the floor, panting, staring at the brown hairs sticking to her palm. Mirri struggled to stand without turning away, crying out as the back of her head collided with a cement column. She fell to her rear, holding her pounding head. Wincing, Mirri put her head down, knowing she was losing the battle. Tears streamed down her face—or possibly blood—and she leaned back against the column, dizzy, in pain, and defeated.

Then she felt it.

Her fingers landed on the gold pendant, her brain snapping into action. Before she could get to her feet, Lavinia dove. Mirri whipped the necklace in her face, making contact with her nose.

Lavinia stumbled back, holding her face, eyes alight with rage. She dove at Mirri again, flattening Mirri against the column and holding her neck against the concrete surface. Mirri's eyes watered at the sudden pain, and Lavinia kneeled on her legs, pinning Mirri in place. She put her forearm across Mirri's throat, causing Mirri to choke and sputter, the Homlock still dangling between her fingers.

"Why can't you . . . just . . . die?" Lavinia rasped in her face, pushing her neck tighter against the wall. Blood dripped down the woman's face and onto Mirri's hands as she clawed at Lavinia's powerful grasp.

Mirri's mouth opened and closed, seeking the air it required. She reached for Lavinia's hair, pulling and scratching at the woman, but she refused to budge. The hatred in her eyes penetrated Mirri's, alight with the joy of watching Mirri suffocate to death.

Mirri held Lavinia's chin in her hand, trying to squeeze, wanting to cause her pain, but the exertion was too great. Little flecks of light appeared in front of her vision, her eyes blurring as the fight faded from her body. It was over. Her hands fell to her sides, her eyes slowly closing . . . forever.

And then there was air. Mirri fell to the side, hacking and coughing, greedily taking mouthfuls of air, trying to bring the vision back to her eyes. She rolled to the side, falling to the cool floor, sucking in great gasps of air to fill the void in her lungs. She lay there a moment, waiting for the dizziness to pass, then forced her eyes open.

Lonar stood over her, a smirk on his face and a bloodied piece of rock in his hand. "About time, darlin'. You gonna lay there forever?"

Mirri stared up at him, unable to speak, unable to think. "You were . . . dead," she choked out.

"Was I now?" Lonar studied the front of his clothing, the dried blood now making his shirt and pants stiff and crusty. "Looks about right."

It wasn't until that moment she remembered the Homlock. It was lying next to her on the marble floor, blood speckling its beautiful pattern. Mirri remembered swatting it at Lavinia's face, seeing the blood fly through the air . . . Lavinia's blood. The brethren of the Mother Kolt.

"It wasn't your blood it needed," Mirri murmured. "It was Lavinia's. Lavinia was a Kolt?" At that thought, she sat straight up, wincing at the pain in her head. "Where is she? Where is Lavinia?'

"Don't worry, darlin'. She won't be going anywhere for a while."

Mirri turned and breathed a sigh of relief as Lavinia struggled against a column, her hands held securely in place with the leather belt Lonar had wrapped around her wrists.

He gave her a smile. An actual, genuine smile. "Maybe I'm starting to believe in all this halafrinlo, after all."

CHAPTER THIRTY

irri, Smidge, and Jinx sat outside the Imperium. Mirri was tapping her foot, eager to get things started, but still dreading the next few hours. Her mother's trial would start any minute.

By the time Mirri and Lonar had made it back to Gwenna, she was already halfway out of the pit Mirri and Lavinia had climbed out of. Healed, limber, and in the best mood Mirri had ever seen her. She had swept Mirri off her feet, literally, and they had laughed together, enjoying the freedom from the curse of the Homlock.

It wasn't until about two hours later that Cam and the Maylarks showed up, Theodisis in tow, along with Kryptus, Smidge, and Jinx. Kryptus had disliked riding a Maylark almost as much as Theodisis had but held his head high all the same.

Mirri had spent the last two days explaining what had taken place in Koltaria with Lonar and then in the castle where the Mother Kolt was killed all those years ago. How Lavinia was actually the daughter of the Mother Kolt and Cormac, hence the dark hair of both women. But how had Lavinia ended up the daughter of Avi, when the Mother Kolt had given birth to her? No one was quite sure what had happened or why Cormac had changed his mind about sacrificing the child. It remained a mystery, one that Mirri had no desire to pursue. Lavinia was gone, the Kolts taking possession of the prisoner, since it had been decided she was, in fact, a Koltarian. Hopefully, she would rot away in a Kolt prison, far away from Althord Loch. Telling the story, then retelling it again, then again, exhausted Mirri to a new extent. Finally, the Koltarians were appeased and seemed content with Mirri's recollection of how the Mother Kolt died, and how Mirri quieted the curse of the Homlock.

"Mirri? We're ready," Rose called to her from the entrance of the Imperium. Kryptus stood next to her, his hand in hers. Though they looked so happy together, the air around the Imperium held a tension—a silent, uncomfortable feeling weighing on her brain.

Mirri smiled at Rose despite the butterflies in her stomach. This was how she had imagined the two lovebirds. Even though the day did not call for celebration, it still made her happy to see the two of them together.

They all entered the Imperium, and headed straight for the Room of Ruling, as it had come to be known. Rose had been busy setting up and preparing the rest of the citizens for the trial. Mirri had no idea what to expect. For now, they decided this trial would be to hear and decide the charges against Gwenna for crimes against Koltaria. The Kolt leader agreed to the trial being held in Althord, and Mirri had a sneaking suspicion she knew why. Koltaria was a bit of an embarrassment at the moment, even though the lakes were now filled with water and the landscape was bright and green. They still had a long way to go to rebuilding the entire empire.

At the moment, charges against Gwenna for the murder of Avi had been put on hold. After hours of deliberation, the elders agreed more investigating should be done, and more than a length of beads was needed to send someone to the mines for the rest of their lives. Gwenna said she would be happy to return if needed when they were ready to hold a full ruling. For now, the murder of Avi remained a mystery, but one Kryptus assured all would continue to be investigated.

As the wall in front of Mirri disappeared, she blinked, looking from side to side. "Wow."

Rose had been busy. A heavy silence filled the large room, so quiet Mirri winced as her wooden chair scratched against the floor. In place of the long wooden table she had sat at the first day, an elegant marble slab now stretched from one end of the room to the other. At one end of the table, a small set of curving stairs led up to a wooden podium, where Mirri guessed the judge, Kryptus, would stand.

She swung her vision to the other side of the room, to a similar setup, but a table with two chairs instead of the podium. The elders and other key participants sat at the table, all sitting with their heads held high. Mirri wondered what they thought of this new room and partaking in such a different way of deciding someone's guilt or innocence.

Mirri took her seat, Jinx remaining on her shoulder. Various citizens filed in, taking their own seats, along with several Koltarians. All the same elders of Althord Loch were present, seated near the head of the table.

She smiled at Kane, who seated himself across the table from Mirri. Pattick, Meleara, and Uma sat near the head of the table, near the stairs leading up to Kryptus's chair. The citizens had voted, and decided that the elders, Smidge, Kryptus, along with six of the Kolts, would act as the jury.

Smidge gave Mirri a small wave and smoothed down his curly hair. He sat in the first seat at the table on the opposite side of Mirri. She hid her smile as she realized his chair was at least a foot taller than others. His arms rested comfortably on the table in front of him. He returned to his composure of Voktare, pushing his shoulders back and holding his head high.

Mirri nodded and gave Arlo, who was also across the table from her, a smile. *All of these creatures,* Mirri thought, as she looked around. It was truly amazing. Mirri wondered if relations with the Koltarians would improve now that the Homlock had been recovered. Theodisis was also present, but had resumed the look of a tough and grumpy centaur. Lonar, whom Kryptus had insisted attend, sat next to him and leaned back in his chair, his eyes closed. Mirri shook her head and rolled her eyes.

A loud gong sounded, making Mirri jump in her hard wooden seat. Mirri blinked, surprised to see Kryptus standing at the podium, his halberd in his hand as always, ready for action.

"Will everyone rise?" Kryptus announced.

There was more screeching as wooden chairs were pushed back against the floor as the participants of The Ruling stood, some on two feet, some on four. Another gong sounded, and everyone's heads swooped in the other direction.

Mirri followed their gaze, and of course, her mother and Rose sat at the small table, as if they had been there the whole time.

Rose gave Mirri a tight-lipped nod, and Gwenna forced a small smile. Surprisingly, Rose and her mother's attitude toward each other had turned cordial since they returned, and at times even friendly. To Mirri's even greater shock, Rose had offered to act as Gwenna's council for The Ruling. What happened between them, Mirri was not sure, but it was quite a relief that they could now sit at the same table.

"Gwenna of Holmforth. You have been accused of stealing the Homlock of Koltaria. How do you plead?" Kryptus announced loudly across the room.

Gwenna squared her shoulders and swallowed. "Guilty."

Kryptus gave his curt nod. "Please be seated," he said, looking around the table.

Rose remained standing and waited patiently for Pattick to tug his ear from underneath his chair leg. "Gwenna of Holmforth did, in fact, steal the Homlock," Rose started. "I ask her to stand now and tell us all the circumstances in which she came to Koltaria to take the pendant."

Rose took her seat as Gwenna stood, her shoulders straight and her head held high. "I possess powers I could not control. I was desperate for a way to rid myself of these powers. I" —she paused— "I sought the Homlock because I knew it could remove a heavy burden."

Gwenna continued the long story of finding the priest in the temple, and how she fooled him into believing she was a lost soul. She stared at the table in front of her as she recounted the night she took the Homlock from its place on the wall.

"He told me of the curse as he lay on the floor," she said as her voice shook. She cleared her throat and paused, glancing at Mirri before she continued. "I opened the curse to Koltaria and deserve to be punished. I regret my actions and can only say I took every chance to right my wrongs when I returned several days ago. It was difficult, but the curse of the Homlock has been closed, thanks to the Keeper of Althord Loch." She gave Mirri a tearful smile. "I am terribly sorry for my misdoings and ask your forgiveness."

Mirri held her breath as she stared at the Koltarians. There were four seated at the table, and the looks on their pointed faces were unreadable. Mirri bit her bottom lip as she looked back at her mother.

Rose stood. "I now ask Theodisis to stand and corroborate these events."

She fell silent. All heads swung toward Theodisis as he stood. "I corroborate."

Mirri closed her eyes. That was it? Her head snapped back to her mother, who had a smile on her face as if Theo had done some great deed for her. Or maybe she expected exactly what she had gotten.

Rose stood. "Thank you, Theodisis. Be seated."

Kryptus stood. "I now open the floor for questions."

Uma raised her hand. "Why did your father need you to come back to Althord all those years ago, Gwenna?"

All eyes swung toward Gwenna.

"He . . . had something to give me. Something to take out of Althord." She looked down at her hands. "And due to the advice of my council, I shall say no more about that."

The whispers began, and Uma spoke over the hushed noise. "And why is that?"

A pause, and Rose spoke out over the hushed voices. "Because of the sensitive nature of this item, it has been agreed upon by Kryptus and myself that we cannot reveal the item in question. Next question?"

Uma raised her hand again. "You'll have to forgive me if I don't agree. What if this object has something to do with Avi's death?"

"Kryptus and I have ordered Gwenna to remain silent. I have to assume that all in this room trust Kryptus and myself?" She looked around with narrow eyes, making everyone in the room shrink in their seats. "This object is of a highly sensitive nature and was something Avi said was never to be mentioned again. We will continue to respect Avi's wishes."

But Uma could not be quieted. "If that is true—"

"Next question!" Rose barked. "I remind all of those present. This is not the trial of Avi's death. It is the trial of the Homlock."

The room fell quiet. Mirri looked to the Kolts expectantly. Where were the questions, demands of imprisonment, and reminders of how they suffered? The four large men in white robes remained silent, their hands folded on the table in front of them.

Mirri raised her hand timidly. "Can I ask the status of Koltaria now? Now that we have quieted the curse?"

Eager eyes landed on the lead Koltarian, the one wearing the shiny helmet. He shifted in his seat. "Koltaria has been restored. Our crops have returned, and our wells are now filled with water." He glanced at Kryptus. "Though our village is still quite decrepit." His glance turned to a hardened glare at the centaur.

Mirri sneaked a peek at Kryptus. His face remained impassive, almost pleasant, and Mirri had to wonder what silent conversation they were having behind everyone else's ears.

Rose stood. "Are there any more questions?"

Mirri held her breath.

Rose nodded, and the gong that sounded behind her made her jump again.

"The trial is complete," Kryptus announced from the head of the table.

Chapter Thirty-One

"**Y**ou never told me what happened with you and Kryptus, you know."

Rose and Mirri sat on the same bench outside the Imperium she and Jinx had sat on Mirri's first day back in Althord. Mirri couldn't believe how many days had passed. Though on the one hand, it seemed like a lifetime ago.

Rose smiled. "Oh, I finally forgave him. He was right, I suppose."

"About what?"

Rose sighed. "I was so angry at him for summoning you back here. I couldn't believe he would do something like that without informing me first. When your friend there came through the portal" —she nodded at Jinx— "she told me what had happened. How Kryptus sent her to retrieve you. I came through the portal. Kryptus and I had words. I left and came back to my antique shop, only to find out you had already portaled through." She shrugged. "I . . . May have been a bit harsh with the Loofa, I suppose." She put her hand over Mirri's. "I was desperate to keep you away from harm. My plan was to get your mother, sneak her back, and disable the other portal."

Mirri looked at her, surprised. "You would have brought her back? Even then? I thought you hated her?"

Rose shook her head quickly, pursing her lips. "Oh, Mirri, I never hated her—I just—well, resented her, I suppose. But I made a promise to your grandfather long ago. To keep Gwenna safe. Forever. And I would never break a promise to Avi." She paused, looking off into the distance. "I see him in you. More than you know."

Mirri smiled and put her hand on top of Rose's. Together, they sat, watching the centaurs form a straight line, towering in front of Smidge. Even Theodisis stood among them, though he was the only one without a halberd. He had a bit of a sour look on his face, but Mirri was proud of how well he was holding in his anger.

"Wouldja look at that? Centaurs, taking orders from an elf?"

She turned her head to see Lonar, hands in his pockets. He was shaking his head, a smirk on his face.

Mirri stood and faced him. "Are you leaving?"

"Yeah, think I'll head back to my side of the woods," he said, gazing down the path. "That big centaur of yours said I could portal to Waylor Ravine."

Mirri nodded. She still wasn't sure how she felt about this man. He had saved her. Helped save her mother. She supposed he deserved her forgiveness.

"Thank you," she finally said.

Her tipped his head to the side. "Anytime, darlin'." He raised a piece of white fruit to his lips and took a bite as Rose excused herself and headed back into the Imperium. "You know, all that ruling and stuff didn't accomplish much, did it?"

Mirri scoffed. "Of course it did."

He looked at her with smiling eyes. "Oh, really? What?"

Mirri started to say something but stopped. She glared at him instead. "None of your business." It actually proved her mother guilty, but she didn't want to say that out loud.

He laughed, taking a juicy bite of his fruit. "Guess there are bigger things to worry about. Like who stole a Mahara Deity."

"A what?"

Lonar slurped up some dripping juice from his hand. "That Mahara thing your whole village is all worked up over. I gather that's what these centaurs here are still looking for."

The Mahara Deity—Mirri had forgotten all about it. It had been mentioned the first day they were here, but not since.

"What is the Mahara Deity?" Mirri stood and faced Lonar.

"Don't know, don't care, darlin'. Guess that will be the next trial, hmm?" He tossed the fruit core to the ground, wiping his hands on his pants. "Well, I'm gonna take my leave." He threw his pack over his shoulder and sauntered down the road, leaving Mirri standing with a frown on her face.

"The Mahara Deity." She remembered asking Kryptus at some point, but couldn't remember if she had gotten an answer. She'd had much bigger problems at the moment. Wait—Kane had mentioned it as well. What had he said about it? One of her fingernails worked its way to her mouth, where she chewed madly. Probably nothing important, she tried to convince herself.

Mirri glanced back at the Imperium. She wasn't sure how long the jury would deliberate in Althord's new form of trial. She looked down the road, then back to the Imperium. *I'll hurry,* she promised herself. *Be back before anyone knows I was gone.*

She took off down the road, racking her brain to remember the location of his hut. They had blossomed there the first time . . . she tried to picture the route Kryptus had taken her, weaving in and out of little shops and homes.

Luckily, that bright blue figure stuck out well, especially against the dirt road. He was dragging a large bag across the road as Mirri called his name.

"Arlo!"

He dropped the bag he had been holding, crumpled paper and other trash spilling out over the road. "Mirri! Is there news? What is to happen to Gwenna?" He ran to her and grabbed her hands.

"No, not that—I mean, we don't know yet—but I need help with something else. Can you tell me what a Mahara is?"

Arlo looked at her quizzically. "The Mahara Deity, you mean? Whatever for?"

"I just need to know," she replied breathlessly. "Can you show me what it looks like?"

"Of course, of course, dear, come with me." He led her back into the hut, Mirri practically pushing him from behind. She wasn't sure why, but she needed to know what this thing was. Now.

He leaped down the entryway to land directly in front of his desk. Mirri hurried down the stairs to join him, watching Arlo flip through pages of a notebook he pulled from under his desk.

"Luckily, the robbery did not include my family's notes," Arlo murmured. "I keep them locked in a drawer, for good reason, apparently. I believe my mother made a drawing of the Deity that hung right over Avi's fire."

That's right. The thing that had hung over Avi's mantle. The empty spot. But what did it have to do with anything?

"The Deity is a religious piece, the last one known in existence. It's quite a crime to take a religious piece such as that. I do hope they find it soon," Arlo muttered, flipping pages.

Mirri was losing her patience. "Can you just describe it to me?"

Arlo looked up and shrugged. "Well, it was a large piece with the expression one would use when they found their true purpose. The five marks of a creature's soul are mercy, truth, generosity, bravery, and unikilarity. Which is what the five points stand for the Deity wears."

Mirri frowned. That made absolutely no sense to her. A large piece with an expression? Wearing something?

"Wait—are you talking about a mask? Something someone puts up to their face?"

"A mask?" Arlo scratched his blue chin. "I do not know what that is, but yes, you could put the Deity to your face."

"And the five points?" Mirri pressed.

"They were placed here." Arlo pointed to his forehead. " A stone unlike any other, I am told."

Five points, Mirri thought. *Like a star, perhaps.* A star.

"Wait a minute," she said, digging in her jeans pocket. It must still be there. She hadn't seen it since that first day in Althord Loch. She dug into her pocket until she felt it—the pointed rock.

The star stone. It laid in her palm, a soft coral color with flecks of red. She moved her hand as she stared, watching it turn purple with the light. The stone that Pattick had given her.

Arlo gasped. "Where—where did you find that? The—Deity stone—where did you find that?"

"This is the stone? That goes in the mask?"

"But where is the Deity?" Arlo demanded. "It must be near for you to have found the stone! Where?"

"I found the stone in Pattick's hut, but I don't think he knew . . ." Her words trailed off. She remembered what happened next. The tunnel. Climbing under Pattick's hut through the darkness. The smooth piece, the piece that had the indentations. She was so concerned she had cracked it. . . could that have been a mask?

Mirri chewed on her lip, thoughts clouding her brain. "I—I should get back. Thanks for your help."

Arlo patted her on the shoulder in response, and Mirri climbed up the stairs slowly.

She stepped out onto the main road, hugging herself for warmth. Or was she trembling for a different reason? She picked up her pace, desperate to get back to the Imperium. She needed Kryptus. Now.

Mirri broke into a run, the cloak flapping behind her in the wind. It was getting dark now, the sun barely sticking out of the trees, and only a few of the village's residents were out. Many were probably still gathered at the Imperium, waiting for the ruling of the case against Gwenna.

"Mirri!" a small, croaking voice called out to her.

She stopped at once, knowing that voice. Mirri turned toward Pattick, her heart skipping a beat. He hobbled toward her, his long ears pulling up a cloud of dust as he moved.

"I'm so glad I found you." He leaned down on his cane to take gasping breaths. "Everyone has been searching for you! It's your mother—something has gone wrong!"

All hesitancy and uneasiness flew from Mirri's mind. "What happened?" she said, running to his side.

"I am unsure, but hurry, we can portal directly to the Imperium!"

Without thinking, Mirri nodded eagerly. Pattick held the silver ball on a string hanging from his neck and stood close. Mirri waited, holding her breath, when she felt a sharp pinch on the back of her neck. She gasped as her hand flew to her neck. the pain running down into her body. Staggering forward, she searched for someone, anyone. But the images in front of her became hazy, and colors mixed. No, no, she had to get to her mother . . . Her mother . . . Kryptus. Mirri tried to run but fell to her knees. She crawled a few feet, but the dizzying world around her forced her to stop and close her eyes. *I'll just stay here for a moment*, she thought. *Just for a moment . . .*

Chapter Thirty-Two

Mirri struggled at the cords wrapped around her wrist. She winced as they cut into her skin but refused to stop. She glared at the hairless rabbit, who had his back to her, humming while he worked at the table. He stepped to the enormous metal box in the corner Mirri at first had assumed was a furnace or something you would find in a basement back home. Knobs, dials, and oddly shaped levers stuck out of the three sides she could see, with a large wheel on the front.

Mirri's eyes narrowed as Pattick fiddled with the dials running up and down the sides. She did not like the look of this thing, nor the look of pure glee on the rabbit's face as he stood on his tiptoes to reach the top dial. Surely, Kryptus had noticed she was missing by now. Hopefully.

Whatever Pattick had stabbed her in the neck with worked well, and though she remembered the feel of his clammy hands on her bare wrists, she could not make them move. The room he held her captive in had only recently come into focus, and Mirri could finally force her body to struggle against her restraints. The best she could tell, she was in Pattick's basement, or, as villagers called it, a 'hold.' Dirt covered the floor, so packed that the long eras dragging back and forth didn't bring up any dust. The smell of a basement lingered in the air—musty and dank, like a place that hadn't been used in a long time.

"Almost ready, dear!" Pattick said, wiping his hands on his hairless legs.

"Ready for what?" Mirri asked, glaring as hard as she possibly could.

"For a miracle," he said, staring at the machine. He shook his head, as if he could not believe his own brilliance.

Pattick turned to her, wiping his hands together, leaning on his cane. "Never thought I'd see this place again, Mirri," he said, speaking as if they were old friends. He gazed around, his eyes landing on the framed picture of another bald green rabbit wearing a kind, proud smile hanging near the door. His voice turned quiet. "Father spent years down here, working. Perfecting things for *him*."

Mirri saw the opportunity. "For Avi?"

Pattick's eyes narrowed. "He did everything for that man. Anything he needed. That staff, that magical staff, anything. It disgusted me."

"Your father made the staff?" Mirri continued to work at the binds on her wrists and ankles while talking. The longer she could keep him on a trip down memory lane, the better.

"It should have been my father's." His large lips pursed together. "He should have been the leader of Althord Loch. Think of all he could have stopped." He hobbled toward the door, his voice barely above a whisper.

Mirri grimaced as she twisted her wrist under the cord. "So . . . you wanted Avi's staff? Is that why you killed him?"

Pattick laughed. "No, no dear. I wanted the Cristalli."

"The Cristalli?" Mirri's wrist stopped twisting for a moment, remembering the green stone that sat on top of Avi's staff. "You wanted the stone? Why?"

Pattick opened his mouth to speak, then stopped. He cleared his throat and pulled his glasses down over his eyes. "Enough of this. I see what you're doing. It won't work." He leaned into her face, so close she could smell his breath. Reminded her of how the kitchen smelled when her mother tried to season dinner with garlic. "Nice try." He shuffled back to his desk, leaning heavily on the cane for support.

"But why do you need *me*?" Mirri asked, her voice shrill and shaking. This was not working.

"You, dear, are the solution to my problems," he said as he looked through a lens attached to a wooden arm hanging off the wall. He shuffled through a pile of papers, discarding several on the dirt floor.

"How could I be the solution?" Sweat was building up along Mirri's forehead. Who would find her down here in this foul place? What if no one was even looking for her?

"Aha! Here it is!" he said, holding the paper up above his head. He turned again, his weathered face suddenly looking bright and youthful. "The Manna Kai!"

"The Manna Kai?" What could the Manna Kai have to do with anything? How did he even know? Mirri shook her head while biting her lower lip. Tears of frustration were threatening to fall. "I—I don't get it."

Pattick gave her a sympathetic smile. "Ah, but you will, in time." He scratched his head. "Or in time, I suppose you wouldn't." He gave a giggle. He stepped back to Mirri, heaved himself onto a tall stump that sat next to her, and patted her knee. "It's not your fault, Mirri. In another time, you and I might have grown to like each other. But I'm afraid you showed up at the wrong time. Well, wrong for you. Right for me." He smiled at Mirri and adjusted his glasses. "All I need from you is your blood."

Mirri stared at him. "You're going to kill me, aren't you?"

He shook his head. "No, don't need to. If everything works as Father intended it to, you won't be around to care."

"What?"

Pattick chuckled as he pushed his wooden glasses back up on the top of his head, sticking them over his white fluff of hair. "It couldn't have worked out better if I tried. Your blood contains the Manna Kai venom. To show you what you truly desire." His head swung toward Mirri. "And I desire to change the past." He grunted off his log and headed back to the table. "So, if you'll excuse me."

"Wait—I don't get it! How can you change the past?" Mirri demanded, trying to get the rabbit to turn back.

"Oh, I can, dear." He kept his back to her, speaking over his shoulder. "At first, when I was young, I thought the only thing that could do it was the Cristalli. I had the device ready to go, all set up, but it was too late. That wretched man had already sent the Cristalli away with *her.*"

"Gwenna—she took the Cristalli," Mirri said, thinking back to the memory. Her mother running through the forest in her nightgown, carrying the balled-up white cloth. "Avi knew, didn't he? He sent the Cristalli away with Gwenna! Then you killed him for it?"

Pattick paused, with his hands still in the air, resting on the large vial hanging on a hook attached to the wall. "Yes, I killed him for it." His voice filled with sorrow, and for a moment, Mirri wondered if he was changing his mind, if he regretted his actions.

"To think, if I had only been seconds earlier. Gwenna would have never left, we would be happy together, and Althord Loch would be a much happier place." He turned his head, clearing his throat. But not before Mirri saw the color rise to his cheeks.

"You were in love with my mother?" She was seeing where he was going with this, and dread filled her stomach, turning her fear into a sort of sickening nausea. "You want to go back to the past to be with my mother? You want to go back in time?"

He turned to her with a glare. "I will be the ruler of Althord Loch. I will stop the Panthera, the Koltarians, everything. Althord will be a better place because I will rule it." He paused. "And I believe Gwenna would make an excellent spouse, so yes, it is possible we would rule together." He picked up a large object that had a clamp on one side and what looked like a screwdriver sticking out of the other end. "And it will all be because of you, Mirri."

Mirri shook her head, her whole body, so hard the chair rocked back and forth. "The centaurs will never follow you. Kryptus will know! He'll tell all the centaurs, everyone!" Her words weren't making sense, but she had to waste time. She had to do something.

"Ah, the centaurs. Kryptus will follow me, Mirri. I have much experience in manipulating centaurs." He smiled widely, showing Mirri the missing tooth on the side of his smile.

Mirri paused, her heart skipping a beat. "You manipulate centaurs?" What was that supposed to mean?

He smiled and nodded. "Hmm. Your friend Kane was the easiest to control. He was more than willing to destroy the portal that was supposed to bring you here. But! I digress."

He walked toward her slowly with the object, grinning widely. "I only need sixteen vilos of your blood. Just enough to take possession of the Manna Kai virus."

"Wait! Kane—he destroyed the portal? Why would he do that?" Mirri shook her head, sure that the evil rabbit was lying, filling her head with tales to confuse her. Kane would never do that. Would he?

"Didn't you ever wonder, Mirri? Why the portal malfunctioned in the antique shop? Why Kane lost the return portal from Holmforth? Why he made sure you got lost in the forest?"

Mirri breathed faster, refusing to believe Kane would do that. Mirri's mind flashed back to that day in the forest. He said he hadn't been paying attention . . . Since when do centaurs not pay attention?

"Why would he do that?" she whispered.

"Stealing his uncle's halberd was the first mistake. Hiding it where a rabbit like myself could find it was the next mistake." Pattick studied the tool in his hand. "Worked out quite well, actually. Could have never accomplished so much without those strong shoulders."

Kane stole Theodisis's halberd. Kane destroyed the portal. The whole time . . . he had been working with this horrible creature?

She swallowed as Pattick shuffled closer, holding the wicked-looking object in his green hand.

"I will use the Manna Kai to find the truth. I will use the Manna Kai to change everything," he whispered with glowing eyes.

"No," Mirri shook her head, struggling in her chair. "If you change the past, I will never exist! My mother will never leave, never meet my father! How could you do that?"

Pattick stopped in front of Mirri. "For once, I deserve to be treated with respect. They will admire me. I refuse to live the life of my father in this pathetic hold."

He grabbed Mirri's wrist roughly and steadied the enormous tool.

"But—but what if you are wrong?" Mirri cried desperately. "What if you change everything, and it makes everything worse? The Manna Kai has to test your soul!"

He stopped and his eyes hardened. "Nothing could be worse than the life I've endured. Nothing could be worse than the pain of watching my true love fall for another. Of finding out he sent her away."

Mirri gasped as he jabbed the gigantic tool on top of her hand and watched his eyes fill with glee. The pain that radiated through her body stunned her, and made her double over. Mirri cried out as a bright light filled the room, momentarily blinding her, coming from her own hand. Gwenna. Throwing her hair back at a young Theodisis. A younger Kryptus, pushing her mother away. They were there, swirling around in front of her like wisps of light, like memories . . . But they were fading.

"No," Mirri whispered, trying to hold her head up. Her body felt so heavy. So heavy. "Please . . . help me . . ."

And then Avi was there. In her mind, or directly in front of her, it didn't matter. "Everything happens as it should, Mirri." He reached out and put a hand on her shoulder. "You should get back now, Mirri. Kryptus will be getting worried."

The pain in her hand faded as she fought to keep his warm touch on her shoulder.

"Don't leave me," she whispered.

"Help is on the way, Mirri. Help is on the way."

Pattick pulled the tool out of her hand, and the light was sucked back into her skin. Mirri panted, her head hanging on her chest, her hand throbbing. Oh, no. It was too late.

"Finally. I have it . . ." He held the device close to his body, her own blood filling the tool, his eyes closed.

Mirri struggled to sit upright in the chair. She did not know what he had to do to finish his time travel project, but she had to stop him. Her head spun in front of her, or maybe she was looking behind herself . . . No. She fought to focus on the green maniacal rabbit standing in front of her.

"You can't—"

A loud crack, then a crunch, and then Mirri screamed as a creature fell through the wooden ceiling directly on top of Pattick. The tool that held her blood scattered across the floor, toward the metal furnace-time machine-whatever it was, and disappeared from her view.

"Lonar!" Mirri cried. She had never been so happy to see the man who had tried to trade her for money.

He sat up slowly, blowing the white hair out of his face, looking around with wide eyes. "What in the block narl is this place?" His eyes landed on Mirri, and he jumped. "What are you doing here?"

"Just get me out of this thing," Mirri gasped. "Hurry!"

Pattick curled up on the ground, moaning, his glasses smashed to pieces. He held a wrinkled hand to his forehead, where a green liquid oozed between his fingers.

Lonar crawled to Mirri's chair and inspected the ties that held her together. He tugged on the cord for a moment, then the restraints at her feet, and finally stood up.

"Turn your head," he instructed her.

Mirri turned and winced, waiting for pain or flying objects. She felt the chair jolt to the left, nearly knocking it to its side. Then again. And again. Finally, the arm of the chair broke, freeing Mirri's right arm from the clutches of the wooden seat.

"The other side, hurry!"

Lonar began his kicking maneuver on the other side of the chair, shoving Mirri up against a table. The arm split, Mirri tugging desperately at the cord when Lonar's feet fell out from under him.

"Ha! Now stay there," Pattick said from the other side of the room, dropping the weapon he shot at Lonar's legs. Falling to his knees, he began searching the floor for his precious Manna Kai potion.

Lonar struggled to stand, but his legs had been stuck together by some sort of white wrap that wound its way slowly up his legs and continued up his stomach. He gasped, clawing at the white rope, writhing on the floor.

Mirri looked around desperately for something, anything, to get to Pattick. She clawed at the cording, pulled and stretched her own arm. Gritting her teeth, she began throwing her weight in the chair, rocking it violently. Anything. Anything to get out of this stupid chair. Grunting, Mirri gave one last thrash of her shoulders, and for a second, the chair paused, balancing on one leg. It tumbled down with a crash, smacking her head on the dirt floor and finally, falling into a pile of wooden slats.

She had to stop him from finding her blood. Tugging a piece of the chair through the cording, she freed her legs, still wearing cord bracelets around her wrists and ankles.

Struggling to her feet, she dashed toward Pattick, whose hands wrapped around the tool containing her blood. His green hands ran all over his machine, surely looking for where to insert the precious blood. Mirri tackled the small, frail bunny, slamming him up against the wall. He bit her on the arm, then slid out from under her grasp as she yelped.

Pattick slammed the tool with the blood into the machine, and Mirri fell back against the table as his contraption jerked to life. Mirri reached for Pattick at the same time he threw open the large door to the machine. The corner of the heavy metal caught Mirri on the cheek, causing her to stumble back and put a hand to her face.

"Finally!" Pattick yelled, jumping into the machine.

"No!" Mirri grabbed for the door, but it slammed shut, shaking the very floor she was standing on.

Mirri clawed desperately at the wheel he was turning, pulled, tugged, and screamed in frustration, but it was too late. The machine whirred and lit up, the dials turning frantically, and the bulbs turning so bright it hurt to look at them.

"No!" she yelled again, tears streaming down her face. "Please stop!" She pounded on the vibrating metal door. It was too late.

She slumped down against the machine, hanging her head, wondering how long it would take before she was gone. Just gone.

The room became quiet. Still. Is this what it was like to not exist anymore? Was she in some empty void of the universe, some hollowed-out place that had no tomorrow? She wiped at her cheeks with her head still between her knees.

Wait a minute.

Mirri scrambled to her feet, turning to the humming machine. She dove to Lonar, the man still clawing at the white foam moving up his body. Reaching into his breast pocket, she pulled out the silver tool, knocking him in the chin with the point of the small instrument. Without a second thought, she ran back to the machine and jammed the silver object into the center of the large wheel on the front.

A spark. A thunk. Mirri threw herself on the ground with her hands over her head, waiting for—something. Anything.

Breathing heavily, Mirri squeezed her eyes shut, expecting some sort of shock wave, or to wake up in a pit of blackness, or—or . . .

"Think you could get me off the floor anytime soon?" Lonar groaned.

Mirri lowered her hands off her head to glance around the room. Lonar still lay on the dirt floor, still covered in that strange white strap, all the way up to his neck. The room was still there, the table, all of Pattick's strange tools, and even the picture of his father still hung on the wall.

"What happened?" Mirri asked, refusing to believe it was that easy.

"I'd reason you got rid of that green rabbit. And that metal box he climbed in as well."

Mirri spun around, her hands flying to her mouth. In the place where Pattick's time machine stood, there was now only a faint square outline on the floor, a nice clean patch where his "brilliance" had sat for so long, unused. The silver tool lay on the floor, as if it were something that had been dropped and simply never picked up. Completely harmless. She reached down and picked up the instrument, laying it in the palm of her hand.

"It's gone," Mirri whispered. She looked down at herself, feeling along her T-shirt. "I'm still here! Are you still here?" She spun back to Lonar.

Lonar groaned. "Yes, I'm still tied up on this here floor. How 'bout hurrying it up?"

Mirri laughed and stood over him with her hand on her hip. "You know, I might like you better like this."

Chapter Thirty-Three

Lonar lifted the Maylark's shell and tossed his bag in. He lowered it and patted the Maylark named Saul on the back.

"I bet it will be a much more fun to ride on the top of one of these things," he said, raising an eyebrow.

"Ha!" Mirri had to laugh. The image of him and Theo on Gwenna's contraption had to be a sight. She was only sorry she didn't get a better look that night.

"So, where are you headed this time?"

Lonar shrugged. "Wherever the wind takes me, I suppose."

Kryptus had offered him a ride on a Maylark for his assistance in stopping Pattick. Kryptus's only other requirement was for Lonar to stay out of Althord. New portals were out of the question at the moment—Arlo and a few others were trying to master the art before Kryptus would allow anyone to travel through a new one. Luckily, there were still a few old ones still in use. The one Gwenna had used over a hundred years ago still worked, and would deposit them directly into Evermore Antiques.

Lonar hopped on the Maylark with ease, though his eyes widened just a touch. "Hope not to be running into you again, human!" he said with a wink, and Saul took off, Lonar grabbing him around the neck as the Maylark flew.

Mirri stood watching him until she could no longer see the enormous flying animal, wondering just what trouble Lonar would get into next.

◆

"You all ready?" Mrs. Langley asked Mirri. She sat down beside Mirri, Smidge, and Jinx on the bench outside the Imperium. Mirri smiled and shook her head—her mother was dressed in her dirty and wrinkled scrubs, large stains splotching her blue shirt. But she had never looked so happy.

They had voted for Gwenna to be free of charges from the Homlock. Part of Mirri had been surprised—the anger the Kolts had for the thief and crimes against their country—but the other part of her had wondered if Kryptus had something to do with it. His demeanor toward the Kolts led Mirri to believe he had intervened somehow. Perhaps he knew something about the Kolt leader that the other Kolts did not know? Whatever the reason, Mirri was beyond relieved. And it probably helped that Kryptus dispatched the entire force of Maylarks to help rebuild the village of Koltaria. The Maylarks were more than happy to assist, especially if it meant Gwenna would go free.

Mirri stood up with Jinx on her shoulder, setting her fluffy friend down on her mother's lap. "Be back in a minute."

Mirri had one more stop to make that morning, a stop she had been dreading all morning. She was going to visit Kane.

The centaur guard had argued, said it wasn't allowed for the Keeper to be in Holding alone. After some argument, Mirri consented to the guard accompanying her down to Holding. She walked in with her arms crossed in front of her, shoulders held high. She needed to hear it for herself.

"I didn't know what else to do," Kane said, staring down at the floor of his cell. "It was only supposed to be a prank. But Theo's halberd washed away in the river."

"How did Pattick know?"

He shook his head, holding the bars of his cell. "I don't know. I didn't want to do those things, Mirri, I swear. You mean so much to me. I—I care for you deeply. I never wanted to hurt you."

Mirri let her shoulders drop and looked away. She had cared for him, too. Instead of answering him, she turned and left, knowing she would never see him again.

She used the toilet lift to exit the prison cell, stepping gracefully into the hallway toward Command. The toilet lifts had become quite simple to use once Theo had taught her the trick: don't close your eyes. Easy as pie.

Mirri stepped to the wall in Command and waited for the door to disappear. She stepped in, exchanging nods with the centaur who stood guard and walked to the three-dimensional map where Kryptus stood, studying his table.

"Something is troubling you," he said absentmindedly, reaching out to the table and straightening a mountain range.

There was no point in trying to hide something from Kryptus.

"What will happen to Kane?" Mirri kept her eyes downward, focusing her attention on the miniature trees blowing in the wind.

Kryptus sighed and lowered his hands to the table. "If found guilty, I can assume he will be sent to the mines. He committed some serious offenses, Mirri. His trial starts in three days."

Mirri looked up. "He's having a trial?"

"Of course. Did you think The Ruling Room was solely for Gwenna? It is new law in Althord Loch."

Mirri didn't know if she was relieved or not. Yes, Kane would get a trial. Kane was guilty. He had admitted it freely. But still . . . Mirri sighed and ran her hand through her hair. She suddenly realized how exhausted she felt. She missed her home and her bed, and though she would miss her friends here terribly, she missed just lying around doing nothing.

"Rose is looking for you," he muttered absentmindedly as he picked up a small mountain and examined the bottom. "Says it's time to go."

"You coming to see us off?"

He looked up from the map that had been consuming him for the last week. "That," he said with a smile, "I would not miss for the world."

◆

Mirri smiled as she listened to Jinx's sobs, holding her furry body tightly. Jinx pulled away, hiccupping, and gave Mirri a teary smile. Mirri turned to Theodisis, waiting for him to finish the warm embrace he shared with her mother.

He ruffled Mirri's hair. "Try not to land in any more prisons or stone pits. We could use some normal days around here."

Mirri laughed and punched him jokingly on the shoulder. "I'll do my best."

She turned to Kryptus and wrapped her arms around his midsection. He put an arm around her and took her chin in his hand.

"Without you, Keeper, things would have worked out much differently. Once again, I thank you. Remember—things always work out how they are supposed to."

Mirri's eyes watered at the thought. The same thing Avi had told her. She nodded. "Thank you."

Kryptus stepped back and rested his arm on Rose's shoulders. Rose looked up at him. "Again, my love. I shall see you again."

Kryptus took her face in both of her hands. "I know, my love. I know."

They shared a kiss that made Mirri turn away in embarrassment. Smidge stood with Jinx on his shoulder, patiently awaiting his good-bye.

Mirri kneeled down and opened her arms. In the hug, Mirri tried to express all the feelings she could not say. She pulled back with wet eyes. "I guess you're eager to get back to work. Huh, Humdinger?"

Smidge smiled and looked down at the ground. Kryptus had named him First Captain in charge of the protection of Althord Loch. "I think I will go back to using my short name again."

"Good." Mirri smiled. "I will miss you," she added, squeezing his small hand.

He nodded and looked at her with teary eyes. "I will miss you also, Mirri."

Mirri smiled and wiped her eyes again, standing next to her mother. Her mother bent down to give Smidge a squeeze and murmured something in his ear that made Smidge go pink in the cheeks.

Rose, Mirri, and Mrs. Langley stepped toward the tree with the curved, low-hanging branch that made a near circle. The same portal her mother had used so many years ago. Rose stepped in easily, tossing her blond hair behind her as she did, blowing a kiss to the crowd.

Gwenna turned toward Kryptus, pushing a lock of hair behind her ear. They simply stared at each other, Kryptus finishing their silent goodbye with a simple nod. Gwenna nodded back, turning and striding through the portal. Mirri looked to Kryptus with a sad smile.

He smiled back. "Good luck, Mirri."

Mirri looked at her friends and pressed her lips together tightly. She swallowed thickly and walked into the portal, hoping this would not be the last time.

❖

Mrs. Langley shook her head. "Absolutely untrue. Never."

Mirri put her menu down with a laugh. "Oh, come on, Mom. He was so in love with you. Even your fake sister knew that."

Mrs. Langley pretended to study the laminated menu in front of her. "I have no idea what you are talking about."

Rose raised her eyebrows. "Really?" She picked up her iced tea and took a sip. "I recall a sunny afternoon when you were around thirteen. Something to do with a poem and your favorite color?"

Mrs. Langley shot her a dirty look. "That was *not* Theodisis."

Rose gave a hearty laugh. "I beg to differ, dear. The poem was his through and through. Even your father agreed."

"A poem? He wrote you a *poem*?" Mirri asked.

"Not just a poem. It was also a bit of a love song—"

"Anyway!" Mrs. Langley interrupted. She looked grumpily at the two of them across the table. "I know plenty of embarrassing facts about the both of you; don't forget."

Rose gave Mirri a sly smile. She leaned over to whisper something in Mirri's ear as Mrs. Langley's eyes narrowed.

Mirri nearly choked on her Dr Pepper. "She did not!" Mirri cried. "No way!"

Mrs. Langley cocked her head across the table, swirling her straw in her water. "I bet it isn't near as interesting as what happened at the Maylofest when I was sixteen. Rose could get a little cheeky after having a glass of Chesapile Ale," she said loftily, gazing at Rose over her cup. "Skinny-dipping doesn't only happen here on Earth, Mirri."

Rose cleared her throat and glared back, her cheeks turning just a bit pink.

Mirri just laughed, not sure she wanted to hear the rest of the story anyway. She wiped her mouth on the back of her hand, shaking her head. "So, what did you end up doing anyway, Mom? After you broke the Cristalli?"

The ease and laughter at the table stilled instantly.

Mrs. Langley glanced up at Mirri with wide eyes.

"When you were with Kryptus? In the forest? You were young, and . . ." Mirri's voice faded away when she saw the look on Rose's face.

Rose turned to Mirri's mother. "You did what?" Rose asked slowly.

It was like someone had blown out a flame of good cheer. Mrs. Langley looked down at her plate, pressed her lips together, and picked up her fork. She took a large bite of cold chicken and sipped her water, keeping her eyes trained on the plate in front of her.

Rose lowered her cup slowly and set it down on the table with a *thunk*, making Mirri jump in her seat. Bits of tea splashed out over the table, soaking the surface next to a discarded cloth napkin, yet no one made a move to wipe up the spill.

Rose stood, pulling her purse from the back of her chair. "It's getting late. I better be getting home," she said in a low voice.

She put a hand on Mirri's shoulder and then walked away without another word.

Mrs. Langley set her fork down and sighed.

Mirri's shoulders slumped forward as she put a hand to her forehead. What had she just done?

About the Author

Michelle Massie is a Texas mom looking to go full-time author! By day, she enjoys campfires, Jeeps, and playing floor-is-lava with her daughter and husband. With a love for all things magical, Michelle also enjoys any kind of crafting out there—from quilts to wood carving to leather work. You'll notice a lot of outdoor adventure in Michelle's stories, because, well, is there any place better? Keep an eye out for more of Michelle's stories—the adventure is just beginning!

COMING SOON...

<u>Book 3 in The Mirri Langley Series</u>

Learn more about Gwenna and Rose's first trip through the portal . . . and how they almost ruined things for good.